Kinman offered hi[s] [...]
make a move to shake it.

———————◆———————

"Come on, now," Kinman said. "After all the fun we had in Rock Springs, you can't trust me enough to shake my hand?"

"That was before you shot at me."

"That was before you were told what I do for a living."

"I knew about that back in Wyoming," Nick said. "I wouldn't have made it this long if I couldn't pick out a bounty hunter on sight."

"All right," Kinman replied, his hand still extended. "But shake it anyway."

Nick stepped forward so that his right hand could reach out and grasp Kinman's, as his left hand stayed within a few inches of his pistol. When he shook Kinman's hand, Nick kept his eyes locked on the bounty hunter.

"You're not planning on double-crossing me now, are you?" Kinman asked.

Nick shrugged and stepped back. "I don't know," he said. "What are you planning?"

Both men glared at each other uneasily, but neither gave an answer. Both of them already had all the answers they needed.

By Marcus Galloway

REAPER'S FEE
NO ANGELS FOR OUTLAWS
DEAD MAN'S PROMISE
BURYING THE PAST
THE MAN FROM BOOT HILL

THE MAN FROM BOOT HILL
REAPER'S FEE

MARCUS GALLOWAY

HARPER

An Imprint of HarperCollins*Publishers*

This is a work of fiction. Names, characters, places, and incidents are products of the author's imagination or are used fictitiously and are not to be construed as real. Any resemblance to actual events, locales, organizations, or persons, living or dead, is entirely coincidental.

HARPER

An Imprint of HarperCollins*Publishers*
10 East 53rd Street
New York, New York 10022-5299

Copyright © 2008 by Marcus Pelegrimas
ISBN: 978-0-06-114728-9

First Harper paperback printing: April 2008

HarperCollins® and Harper® are registered trademarks of Harper-Collins Publishers.

Printed in the United States of America

Visit Harper paperbacks on the World Wide Web at
www.harpercollins.com

10 9 8 7 6 5 4 3 2 1

In memory of my Uncle Bert

THE MAN FROM BOOT HILL
REAPER'S FEE

ONE

Middle Cross, Oregon
1885

Lester Peterson was a wanted man.

Although he'd gotten into his fair share of fights, Lester hadn't used his gun for anything more than doling out flesh wounds and killing a few horses. Then again, one of those horses was the cause for some of Lester's biggest headaches.

Back in eighty-one, Lester had needed to get out of Texas faster than his feet could carry him, and a horse was his only means of transportation into greener, northern pastures. Because of his lack of funds, Lester needed to be a little more creative when it came to getting his hands on a horse, so he stole one from a saloon outside of San Antonio. That horse had belonged to a wealthy rancher who, Lester figured, would easily see his way past the loss.

Lester was not only wrong about the rancher's forgiving nature, but he also underestimated the rancher's memory. A price was put on Lester's head, which only grew every month that he wasn't found. No matter how many other horses or how much money he would steal, Lester found himself running from that one mistake he'd made in Texas those years ago.

Some of the heat had died down since he'd made his way into Oregon. Even so, Lester figured that letting his guard down, even for a second, would be his undoing.

He was right.

A second ago, Lester had been strolling along the quiet street while savoring the cigar he'd just purchased after an overcooked steak. Before he knew what was happening to him, the cigar was being forced down his throat by a fist slamming into his face.

Lester staggered back until his shoulders bumped against the side of a building. His senses reeled from the shock of getting punched in the mouth. Red haze crept into the edges of Lester's vision and he felt as if the ground were tilting under his boots.

When he tried to breathe, Lester choked on his cigar.

When he reached up to dig the cigar from his mouth, Lester's fingers found a mess of blood.

"Howdy," someone said from just out of Lester's sight.

Even though Lester couldn't see the other man, he didn't have to guess the man's intentions. The loosened teeth in his jaw told him all he needed to know in that regard.

"You shon of a bidge!" Lester grunted through his aching jaw and mouthful of blood.

The other man laughed as if he'd just heard an amusing little joke. A second later, his hand clamped around Lester's neck so he could hold the newly bloodied face directly in front of him.

Now, the other man was all Lester could see. He might have only been an inch or two taller than Lester's five feet, ten inches, but the man seemed to loom over him like a mountain coated in battered denim. His face was narrow and his features were like shallow etchings scraped into the surface of a rock wall. His cheeks were all but flat, making his eyes look like deep gouges dug out of that same wall of stone. There was something glinting deep within them, and it wasn't anything Lester wanted to think about.

Holding Lester out a few inches away from him, the man nodded and looked him over the way a fisherman examined whatever hung at the end of his line. "Don't bother giving me any bullshit names, either. I know it's you, Peterson."

Realizing his mouth was hanging open, Lester closed it and swallowed the salty mix of blood and spit that had pooled on his tongue. When he tried to scowl, it hurt. When he tried to speak, it hurt even more. "Who the fug are you?"

The other man grinned and replied, "I'm the fellow that's going to be hauling your ass back to

Texas." He waited for a few seconds and then nodded again when he saw the look of panic spread across Lester's face. "That's right. You know exactly where you're going and why you're headed there."

"All this trouble for that goddamn horse?"

The man shrugged. "I guess he really cared for that horse."

"The vugging thing is dead, for Christ's sake!"

"Oh, now I wouldn't mention that when we get into Texas." He thought for a moment as he adjusted his grip so he had a hold of Lester's collar. "On second thought, maybe you should bring it up. It might just bump up the reward that's being offered for you."

Suddenly, Lester's eyes lit up. He was being hauled away from the wall, but there wasn't anything he could do about that. "I know something you might want to hear."

"You got a gun on you?" the man asked as he flipped open Lester's jacket. "Ah, there it is."

Lester reached for the pistol tucked under his belt, which caused the other man to respond.

In the blink of an eye, the man shoved Lester back with one hand, while drawing his own gun with the other. He stooped slightly with his pistol tucked in close to his body. His other arm was still outstretched to keep Lester at a distance.

Looking as if he didn't know what was going on, Lester shook his head and sputtered, "I was gonna give you my gun. Honest!"

"You'd better do that and be quick about it. I doubt that rancher would have much of a problem paying to see your corpse."

Lester's hand trembled as he moved it closer to the grip of his pistol. Extending his thumb and forefinger, he pinched the handle and wrangled it from under his belt. "See? Nice and easy."

The other man's eyes remained focused on Lester and the gun dangling from his fingers. The man's own hand snapped out to take the gun away from Lester so quickly that it took Lester a moment to realize that the gun was no longer in his possession. Now holding a gun in each hand, the other man let out the breath he'd been holding.

"There," Lester said as he wiped the sweat from his brow. "That wasn't so hard. Maybe we should get somewhere we can talk. There's folks walking around, you know."

"I know." Looking over to one of those folks, the man touched the brim of his hat with the barrel of Lester's pistol. "Afternoon, Mister Lowery."

The old man on the other side of the street squinted and then tossed a wave in response. "Afternoon, Mister Kinman."

Lester's eyes opened even wider. "You're Alan Kinman?"

"That's me."

Lester looked away from Kinman's face to watch Mr. Lowery turn a corner without so much as glancing over his shoulder.

Kinman chuckled and spun Lester around to

shove him face-first against the wall. "You don't seem to have many friends around here."

"If folks knew about you, they wouldn't be too happy to have you around, either."

"They know who I am. Who do you think told me where to find you? Seems your Thursday-night cigar is common knowledge. You see, honest folk like to keep an eye on a no-good horse thief like you."

"And you don't think they mind having a murderous bounty hunter in town?"

"I don't give a shit if they do or don't," Kinman replied. "I'll be leaving before long and that suits everyone just fine."

"Everyone but me," Lester muttered.

"Nothing about you matters, asshole."

Lester waited until the handcuffs were tightened around his wrists. The iron bracelets felt like weights keeping him at the bottom of a lake and jangled loudly as he was once again spun around, to face the street. "You may not be in for as much money as you think. The last notice I saw for a bounty on my head was almost a year old."

"This one's a month old," Kinman said as he took a folded piece of paper from his coat and shoved it directly in front of Lester's face.

The notice even smelled new. Although the likeness hadn't been touched up any since Lester had stolen that horse, the wording made it sound as if he'd killed a dozen men to get that animal, and the reward had been bumped up accordingly.

"Damn," Lester muttered. "I hadn't seen that one yet."

"You don't still have that horse, by any chance, do you?" Kinman asked. "I may get some more reward money if you do."

Spitting out some more blood along with a tooth, Lester said, "I told you, it's dead. If I did have it still, why the hell would I tell you, anyway?"

Kinman paused so he could fix a glare onto Lester that felt like two drills being slowly twisted through his face. The smile that flickered across Kinman's lips wavered slightly as he explained, "It's a long way to Texas, and there's plenty that could happen along the way. If you keep me happy, I may be in a better frame of mind."

Lester shrugged and did a bad job of trying to appear comfortable as he said, "No. That horse is dead, just like I told you."

"That's a shame. It must have been a hell of an animal."

"Not really. The damn thing could barely run. To be honest, I only stole it 'cause I figured the owner would be glad to get rid of it."

Kinman laughed under his breath as he shoved Lester ahead of him and grabbed hold of the iron between Lester's wrists. "Looks like you made a bad call on that one, my boy. I appreciate the honesty, though. I would have bet you were going to hand over any old horse in your possession just to clear the path for you a bit."

Anger flashed across Lester's face as he cursed

the fact that he hadn't thought of that trick on his own. He recovered fairly quickly by trying to turn around and get a look at Kinman. "I know something else that may be—"

"Just keep moving, asshole," Kinman snarled as he grinned to another local who crossed his path.

Even though he couldn't turn around, Lester kept fighting to look at Kinman over his shoulder. "I know something that may spark your interest," he said quickly.

"Save it for the ride. I ain't in the mood to hear your bullshit right now."

"It's not bullshit," Lester said. "It could be worth a lot of money."

"You got a horse or not?"

"Yeah, but—"

"Where is it?" Kinman snapped. "I want to get the hell out of this piss bucket of a town before nightfall."

"In the stable, at the other end of this street."

Glancing in that direction before taking one more step, Kinman didn't move until he spotted the small barn on the far corner. "You ain't got any friends in this town, you know. You try anything and everyone here will stand by and watch me put a bullet through your head."

"I'm not trying anything," Lester insisted. "Jesus Christ, will you just listen to me?"

"Fine. You got until we reach that stable. After that, I'm stuffing a gag in your mouth and not taking it out for another day."

Lester sucked in a few breaths as he quickly gauged the distance between himself and the stable. Already, Kinman had started walking faster, so Lester simply unleashed what he'd wanted to say in a torrent of urgent words.

"There's some money buried," Lester spat out. "Lots of it. I heard even some jewels. Diamonds, maybe. It's the haul from a big robbery a few years back, pulled by some known men who were all killed."

"All killed, huh?" Kinman grunted. "Then who buried the jewels?"

"Well . . . *almost* all were killed. At least one man walked away. Maybe even just one man."

"Boy, you sure do know your facts, Lester."

"I don't know why they left the money," Lester explained. "All I know is where it's at. I was gonna go after it myself as soon as I could make the ride without fear of being spotted somewhere along the way. I was also gonna round up some men to go along with me."

"Men you can trust, I suppose?"

"Yeah! That's right!"

"Bullshit," Kinman grunted. "I changed my mind. I want you to shut up starting right now."

Glancing toward the stable, which was only about twenty paces away, Lester planted his heels into the dirt and said, "The money was stolen by Barrett Cobb! You ever heard of him?"

Kinman stopped behind his prisoner just so he could take a look up and down the street. Since none of the few people looking back at him seemed interested in mounting a rescue, the bounty hunter replied, "Sure I heard of him. Any man in my line of work's heard of Barrett Cobb."

"Then you gotta know he stole that much and nobody ever caught him. His gang's pulled more and bigger jobs than most anyone else. The one I'm talking about was in newspapers and everything!"

Stepping in front of Lester, Kinman stared into his eyes and said, "I also know something else. Cobb's dead."

"He's the one holding onto that money," Lester insisted. "I'd bet my life on it."

"You may be doing just that if you don't pick up your damn feet and get moving."

Lester shook his head and kept talking before he could be threatened again. "I been hearing this same rumor from a whole bunch of people. Plenty of men were asking me to go along with them to find the money, but I couldn't go because I knew I couldn't stick my head out from where I been hiding."

"At least that's one thing you got right."

"Now that I been found, there ain't no reason why I shouldn't go after that money. Since you're the one that found me, you can go along. We'll split whatever we find and both get real rich!"

Kinman smiled and began to slowly nod. After mulling it over for a few seconds, he smiled a bit wider and then drove his knee into Lester's stomach. "You think I'm stupid? There ain't no way I'm about to give you an inch so you can try and run a mile. You don't know what the hell you're talking about. The only way you know a damn thing about Cobb is from whatever horse shit you picked up in a saloon. I tried to hunt Cobb down for years, and I know for a fact he ain't been heard from for so long that he's gotta be dead. Even those newspapers you talked about say that same thing. Besides, Cobb's last robbery went so bad, there weren't no survivors from his gang."

"Nick Graves survived."

Kinman was about to punch Lester in his mouth again just to shut him up. Pausing with his fist cocked back like a hammer, he asked, "What's Graves got to do with any of this?"

Anticipating the punch he was about to receive, Lester cowered away from Kinman. Tentatively, he looked up. "Graves is the one that put Cobb in the ground."

"How do you know?"

"Because he's the only one of the men who pulled that robbery with Cobb who survived it. Plenty of men seen Graves in the Dakotas after Cobb was killed."

Kinman's eyes took on a faraway look as he slowly lowered the arm that had previously been set to deliver the next punch into Lester's face. "That murderous son of a bitch may have even been the one to put Cobb down . . . Do you know that for certain?"

Seeing the frustration bubbling up behind Kinman's eyes, Lester quickly answered, "Graves knows for sure where Cobb is buried, but there's a few others who know as well."

"Let me guess. Some of those men you were talking to?"

Lester nodded. "They got no reason to lie. We was going to go and dig up that grave, on account of that's where those jewels and all that money is buried."

"Who started that rumor?"

"Men I can trust. They're my kin, so it's got a good chance of being true. Since them jewels was stolen, they ain't never been found. That money's buried right along with whatever's left of Barrett Cobb. I know it."

As much as Kinman wanted to knock out the rest of Lester's teeth just so he wouldn't have to listen to the man's voice, there were too many words that stuck in the back of Kinman's mind. He came to a complete stop a few paces away from the stable.

Lester may have been hurting, but he wasn't blind. A thoughtful look had come into the bounty hunter's eye, and Lester latched onto it like a tell from another man in a poker game. "If I'm right, we can both become rich."

"And I suppose you'd want me to let you go in exchange?"

"Only if this pans out. If I'm wrong, you can still take me to Texas. That asshole rancher hasn't forgotten about me by now, so he probably never will. That means I'm the only one with anything to lose here."

"What about these other men who filled your head with this nonsense?" Kinman asked. "I suppose they're going after this supposed stash of jewels, too."

"Yep, but there's a reason they came to me in the first place. I know a shortcut through the Badlands to get us in and out without catching much attention from the savages who frequent the area."

"Indians shouldn't be your biggest concern," Kinman said. "If you think you can make me a fool, you'll find yourself being dragged back to Texas by your balls."

Lester didn't even flinch. "When we find that treasure, you'll be more'n happy to cut me loose."

Rolling his eyes, Kinman shoved Lester toward the stable. "Let's get moving."

TWO

———◆———

Ocean, California

Ever since a bar had been built into the back of the Tin Pan Restaurant, business had been good. It wasn't a big enough bar to change the place into a saloon, but it was enough to attract a few more customers while giving the regulars an excuse to stick around a while longer after they were through with their meals. One drawback to the Tin Pan's newest addition, however, was the fact that some customers overstayed their welcome.

One prime example of such a customer was a cowboy named Switchback Gil. He was new in town, but everyone knew his name, mostly because he'd loudly introduced himself to everyone in the place when he'd arrived. After moving to the bar and having a few drinks, he introduced himself all over again.

"Why the hell's this place called Ocean anyway?" Gil grunted. "There ain't no water in sight."

The stout man who'd been hired on to tend the bar was in his late fifties and had lived in Ocean his entire life. Normally, he jumped at the chance to explain the town's history to newcomers. This time, however, he shrugged and said, "Don't rightly know."

"Aw, come on! You gotta know! And call me Gil. Switchback Gil's the name!"

Wincing at the stench of liquor that flowed from Gil's mouth as he kept flapping his gums, the barkeep said, "You mentioned that already."

"Then let's hear the story!"

As Gil's voice echoed throughout the restaurant, a door toward the back swung open. The woman who stepped through the doorway had long, dark hair pulled into a braid that hung to the small of her back. Her dress was simple enough, but not even a burlap sack could have kept her nicely proportioned curves from being noticed.

She carried a large book tucked under one arm and had a pencil in her hand. As she walked toward the bar, her eyes narrowed at the sight of Switchback Gil supporting himself with both hands against the edge of the polished wooden surface. "Could you two keep it down out here?" she asked in a friendly tone. "I'm trying to work through the finances."

As soon as Gil's eyes found her, they widened and slowly ran up and down her body. "Well, well," he slurred. "That's more like it. Why don't you come over here and keep me company?"

Shaking her head before looking away from Gil, she focused her attention on the barkeep. "I think our friend Switchback Gil has had enough," she said.

"You heard o' me?" Gil asked.

"Everyone on this block has heard of you by now," she replied. "You're talking loud enough to wake the dead."

There were a few chuckles from the diners scattered at some of the tables. It was just past eight o'clock, so most of the dinner crowd was long gone. The ones who remained were picking at their meals, savoring the special of the day.

Gil settled himself so his back was against the bar as he raised his hands. "Don't call the law on me. I'm just enjoying my firewater."

The woman nodded and showed Gil a genuine smile. "We're closing in a bit, but there's plenty of saloons on Eighth Street. They'll be open all night long."

"Will they have ladies as pretty as you over there?"

"Sure. Go see for yourself." With that, she nodded to the barkeep and turned toward the back room.

The barkeep responded to her nod by shifting his hand away from the polished axe handle that was kept under the bar to discourage drunks from abusing the Tin Pan's hospitality. When he looked away from Gil, the barkeep saw one of the regulars step up and place his hands flat upon the bar.

"I'd like a brandy," the man said. "And a glass of wine for my wife."

"Coming right up."

Gil let out a low whistle and took half a step away from the bar. "This is one of them fancy places, huh? No wonder you don't want the likes of me around."

"Nothing like that, mister," the barkeep said. "I mean . . . Gil. We're just about to close, is all."

"Yeah. You wouldn't want a bad element around here. Not when you've already got killers like Nick Graves lurking about."

The barkeep didn't flinch. He simply shrugged, shook his head and said, "Don't know who you're talking about."

"Sure," Gil said. "And I'm certain that lady who just poked her nose out here a moment ago ain't never heard of Graves, either."

The door to the back room hadn't fully closed, but now it swung open again. The woman stepped out with her hands placed firmly upon her hips. "What are you talking about?"

"Ain't you Catherine Weaver?" Gil asked.

"I am."

"From what I hear, it should be Catherine Graves by now."

"You got my name right the first time. Do I know you?"

Gil walked straight toward Catherine, but was stopped as the axe handle slapped against his chest just hard enough to freeze him in his tracks. The barkeep held the axe handle in his extended arm, which was more than strong enough to keep steady as Gil tried a few times to push past it.

"I'm not out to harm Nick," Gil said, "but I do need to have a word with him. I heard that you and him were married."

"Where'd you hear that?" Catherine asked.

"From someone who goes to services every Sunday with the preacher who performed the ceremony."

"Well, you heard wrong," she said.

Several of the customers glanced nervously at one another. A few of the older men got up and came closer, making sure Catherine knew they weren't about to go anywhere.

Gil tried to take a step forward, but again was pushed back by the axe handle. Only then did he look at the barkeep. "You know what's good for you, you'll take that stick away before it gets rammed up yer ass."

The barkeep's face didn't change, but his grip around the solid piece of wood tightened.

"You want me to fetch Sheriff Stilson?" the old regular at the bar asked.

Settling into the situation, Catherine walked toward the bar. "No need for that. This is obviously just a mistake. You wanted a brandy?"

"That's right, but—"

"You'll have your brandy. Your wife will have her wine, and Gil and I will have a friendly chat like two civilized people."

The barkeep looked at her and asked, "You sure about that?"

"Sure, I'm sure," Catherine replied. "If I wanted fights in my place, I would have opened a saloon. Still, I'm sure Gil won't mind if we take this outside."

Although he seemed a bit surprised by the sudden shift in the tone of the conversation, Gil nodded and hooked his thumbs under his belt. "That sounds just fine to me."

Catherine led the way out the front door and Gil was quick to follow. Outside, the sky was dark blue and the stars were appearing overhead like a mess of silver dust that had been tossed into the air. Knowing she wasn't about to lose Gil anytime soon, Catherine turned toward the corner and walked with a confident stride. "So," she said, "what brings you to Ocean?"

It took a bit of work, but Gil managed to match Catherine's pace so he could walk directly beside her. "I heard I could find Nick Graves here. I also heard that you'd know where to find him."

"You're not the first to come looking for that man. I wish I could help you."

"Some folks thought he was dead, but that's a hard thing to defend anymore. Graves used to be a wanted man. There were some vigilantes in Montana who spread the word about a price on his head from here all the way to the Mississippi. Hell, I even heard a bounty hunter from New York knew about the reward."

"I'm no bounty hunter," Catherine stated. "I run a restaurant. That's the only business I've ever been in."

"So you're saying all those men who wanted to have a word with you were wrong?"

"What men? The only one that's come around asking for me is you."

Gil glared down at her through narrowed eyes. Even though she was several inches shorter than him, Catherine carried herself as if she was on a level field with any man. "That's a damn lie, ma'am."

"Excuse me?"

Jumping ahead one step, Gil got in front of Catherine so he could stop her with a stiff hand on each of her shoulders. Once he'd brought her to a halt, Gil closed the gap between himself and Catherine so he could look her in the eyes and speak in a menacing snarl. "I said that's a damn lie and you know it."

Before Catherine could respond, there was a knock against the boardwalk, as if something heavy had been dropped a little further along the street. She and Gil both looked. They found the noise had been made by a single boot thumping against the boardwalk as a tall, lean figure stepped up from the street.

The figure wasn't close enough to listen to what Catherine and Gil were saying and it didn't make a move toward them. Instead, it stayed put and kept as still as a stone marker protruding from the hallowed ground of a cemetery.

"Why do you want to find this man so badly?" Catherine asked.

"All I want is to ask a question. I don't have a problem with Graves and I'm not after the price on his head. Nobody even needs to know it was you who told me where to find him."

Catherine let out a little breath and smiled up at Gil. "That's good to know."

"My brother works at a telegraph office not far from here and he told me about a message that was sent by someone who mentioned Graves by name and that he lived here. I got here quick, since there's so much money involved."

"Money?" Catherine asked. "What money?"

Gil grinned and said, "I knew that might cover some more ground with you. There's money to be had and I stand a hell of a chance of getting to it first if I can have a word with Graves. If things go my way, you'll get your share for steering me in the right direction."

"How do I know you'd come back to hold up your end?"

Looking down the street, Gil spotted the lean figure still standing in the same place. The only part of the figure that moved was the coat that was flapping around the man's legs.

When he spoke again, Gil lowered his voice and turned his head away from the figure. "I can give you an advance."

"What sort of advance?"

"How's a thousand dollars sound?"

Catherine's eyes widened and she pulled in a breath. "Come back tomorrow night," she said. "If I find out anything, I'll let you know."

Still studying her, Gil scowled and gnashed his teeth together. He stopped just short of speaking again when he glanced at the corner to find the dark figure walking slowly toward them. Each step thumped against the boardwalk and sent a rumble all the way up to Gil's knees. It was difficult to make out many details, but when the man got close enough, Gil caught sight of the badge pinned to his chest.

"Fine," Gil said. "But you'd better have something for me if I'm to waste so much time around here."

"You're free to leave whenever you like," Catherine offered.

"I'll find you tomorrow at that place of yours around the same time as now." Glancing toward the approaching figure, he added, "Make it a few hours earlier." With that, Gil crossed the street. As the lawman approached Catherine with quicker steps, Gil was more than happy to be on his way.

Catherine walked up to the man as Gil rounded a corner. Reaching out with both hands, she grabbed his coat, pulled him to her and planted a kiss squarely upon his lips.

"My hero," she whispered after leaning back just enough to get the words out.

Nick's hands went reflexively to Catherine's hips, but his eyes darted toward the corner Gil had just turned. Even though the other man was nowhere in sight, Nick watched that spot for a few more seconds.

"Come on," he said. "Let's get off this street."

THREE

———◆———

Nick and Catherine walked back to the Tin Pan and stepped inside just as the barkeep was about to lock the door. She said a few words to the barkeep and then held the door open so he could leave for the night. After giving her employee a quick wave, Catherine locked the door and pulled down the shade in the front window.

Leaning against the bar, Nick reached over the top and fished out a bottle of clear liquid. He used his other hand to get a glass, poured himself a healthy dose of the liquor and took a sip. "Sometimes I think it was a mistake to stay here," he said as the vodka worked its way through his system.

"No, you always think it's a mistake to stay here," Catherine said as she leaned against the bar next to him. "It's almost to the point where I think you regret marrying me."

Nick looked into her eyes and smiled. The gesture seemed odd for features as harsh as his, but it was genuine enough. A thick beard covered his face, making his cheeks seem fuller and rounded.

Cool, steely blue eyes took in the sight of her as he reached out to run a callused hand along the side of Catherine's face. "You're the only reason I'd even consider staying," he said. "You know that."

"Sure I do, but it's still nice to hear every now and then."

"Well, you just heard it."

After draining the glass, Nick set it down and reached for the bottle.

"You haven't had that much to drink in a while," Catherine said.

"You're the only place in town that bothers keeping any of this for me," Nick replied as he tapped the bottle of vodka with the edge of his glass. "I'd hate to see it go to waste. Are you going to tell me about that fellow you were talking to, or do I have to wait until you warm up to the subject?"

Catherine blinked and took a step back from the bar. Crossing her arms sternly, she said, "Sheriff Stilson must be working you awfully hard for you to be so cranky."

"He's got me walking the same rounds as before and I can't blame him for it. Even with what little he knows about me, it's a miracle he deputized me at all."

"The way you handled that bank robber who rode through here a few months ago should have been enough to convince anyone. That is . . . unless he came here because he knew you from your wild youth." Although she'd been kidding when she'd said that, Catherine quickly recognized the expression on Nick's face.

"*Did* he come here looking for you?" she asked.

Nick let a few seconds pass before he answered. "He won't be coming around here again."

"That's because he's buried in the cemetery."

"As far as Stilson knows, he is."

"What?" Catherine asked. "He isn't?"

Nick shrugged and waved the bottle as if he was about to pour. Before he could refill his glass, Catherine reached over and took the bottle from him.

"He isn't?" she repeated.

"I'm trying to live a quiet life here. Isn't that why I allowed you to talk me into wearing this ridiculous thing?"

Seeing that Nick was pointing to the badge on his chest, she replied, "That ridiculous thing earns you some respect and it puts people off your trail." She paused and shrugged before adding, "I thought it was a pretty good idea."

"It is," Nick said as he reached over to rub her cheek. "And it does put people off my trail, but that doesn't mean I'm safe from anyone else who comes through here looking for me. How long do you think it'll be before that man you were talking to finds out who I am and where I can be found most every day of the week?"

"You're out at that cemetery or your workshop more often than that parlor you run. A squirrel can't get within twenty yards of any of those places without you knowing about it." She patted Nick's hand and smiled lovingly. "Perhaps you should talk to Stilson about being a deputy in more than just title. It . . . probably pays better, you know."

"I'm doing the only work I know," Nick said. Looking away from her, he added, "Well, the only work that won't land me in jail, anyways. Things around here have been good. I'd rather not fool with that."

"Good for the town isn't exactly good for an undertaker, which is your chosen profession. You can still do that job when it's needed, but we could use a salary that doesn't require a steady stream of people dropping over."

"It's been a while since the last funeral," Nick said. "Some of the folks around here are bound to keel over sooner rather than later." He met Catherine's eyes and smirked. "When it rains, it pours."

She wasn't amused.

"All right, so maybe I just don't like wearing this thing." With that, Nick took hold of the badge and tore it off his shirt. He looked down at it and then flipped it over to find shreds of cotton hanging from the pin behind the star. "What did that fellow want?"

"Who?"

Looking up at her, Nick said, "The fellow who you were talking to outside not too long ago. The one who scampered off the moment he saw me coming."

Catherine took a deep breath and ran her finger along the top of the bar. After pausing for a while, she realized that Nick was still waiting for an answer. "He was asking about you."

Nick straightened up as his hand immediately drifted toward the gun at his side.

Watching him go through that simple, practiced motion was almost enough to bring tears to Catherine's eyes. Under most circumstances, she looked at him the way any wife would look at her husband. There were moments when she was exasperated and moments when she wanted to laugh at him, but all of those moments were shaded by the love that flowed so easily between them.

When Nick made that subtle reach for his gun, he became the man he'd been when they'd first crossed paths. That also drew her attention to the gnarled stubs that remained of the middle two fingers on his gun hand and the pieces of his left hand that had also been torn away. Even the parts of his hands that were intact were covered in old wounds that made them look as if they'd been cobbled together from spare parts.

The gun at his side wasn't much different. It had begun as a Schofield revolver but had been restructured into something else. Its handle was whittled down to less than half its original size. Catherine had seen the gun enough to know the barrel was gnarled and grooved as well, as if it had been heated, twisted and then allowed to cool.

Most people figured the gun was a cheap piece of garbage only used to fire a round at the occasional snake.

Those people would have been dead wrong.

Catherine had seen what that gun could do in the proper hands. In fact, there was only one hand for the pistol and it was the same hand that hovered over it now.

"What did he want with me?" Nick asked.

Snapping herself out of the silence that had enveloped her, Catherine replied, "He said he needed to ask you something, but didn't say what it was. I know it had something to do with a lot of money."

"How much is a lot?"

"So much that he was willing to hand over a thousand dollars as an advance if I could help steer him in the right direction."

"Are you serious?"

She nodded. "And that was without any bargaining on my part. I probably could have gotten a higher offer."

"Maybe, but collecting it would have been another matter."

"Just the fact that he offered that much with a straight face told me a lot. Or do you think it was all just a load of dung?"

Nick rubbed his chin and felt the fresh whiskers that had taken up residence there. Even through the beard, he could feel the scars and lines as if they were tracks left in freshly blown sand. "It wasn't dung," he muttered. "At least, not all of it. Even if he figured on killing you, he wouldn't have parted with that amount of money so easily. Not unless he was certain he could miss it if push came to shove."

Knowing better than to question Nick's instincts on the matter, Catherine told him, "He wanted to know where you were."

"What did you tell him?"

"To try back tomorrow. It was the best I could do with you coming up on us so fast like that. Do you think he could have been an outlaw?"

Nick chuckled coldly as he lowered his hand. "No man on the right side of the law bolts from a badge like that."

"Did he look familiar?" Catherine asked.

"Nope. I don't even know how the hell he found me."

Catherine closed her eyes for just a bit longer than it would take her to blink. A change drifted over her face like a stray cloud passing across the moon. "I think I may know how he found you."

"You do?"

"Back when you and Joseph Van Meter were riding together, someone came here looking for me. Well . . . I guess they were looking for me so they could get to you."

Nick nodded solemnly. "And they almost found you. If Sheriff Stilson hadn't covered our tracks, things might have turned out a whole lot worse."

"Well, it's my guess that whoever came looking sent a telegram about what he found . . . or didn't find. Someone at that telegraph office remembered you being mentioned, and that got around to someone else."

"Jesus Christ," Nick grumbled. "I wonder why anyone even bothers with newspapers and such when there's so many goddamn gossips in this world. Are you sure that's the man who sent the message?"

"No, but he's the only one to come around after you since you put on that badge."

Nick took some of the edge from his voice when he asked, "What else did he say?"

"Not much more than that. All he kept asking was where to find you."

Backing away from the bar, Nick placed his hand upon the gnarled grip of his pistol and said, "Then I suppose I shouldn't disappoint him."

Catherine turned to face him, but didn't move any closer. "Or you could just let him go. He didn't even recognize you when he saw you, so he'll probably just leave if I don't give him anything else better to do."

"Or he might not leave," Nick said. "Or . . . I might want to hear what he's got to say."

"Why in the hell would you want to hear what he's got to say? You just told me that he's probably on the wrong side of the law. That's not the life you lead anymore. You promised me that."

"What I promised was to take care of you the best way I know how. I've had a badge pinned to me for a little while, but I was earning money another way for most of my life before that and I'll remind you that the money back then was a whole lot more than any deputy's salary."

"No good can come from this, Nick!" Catherine said as she pounded the bar with her fist. "Everything's been going so well since you decided to stay here with me. The Tin Pan's prosperous. You're a respected man in your own field and now folks even respect you as a lawman even though all you do is make the rounds every so often. You're a part of this town, Nick."

"I'm a part of you," he said as he stepped up to her and held both of her hands in his. "But that might not be such a good thing."

Catherine recoiled as if she'd been slapped in the face. "How could you say that?"

"Because there's parts of who I am that will never fade. They'll never go away and I'll never be able to wash them off, no matter what I do, what I say or what I pin onto my shirt. Those things will become part of you too, and you don't deserve that kind of stain upon your soul."

Although she'd been fighting him at first, Catherine pulled her hands out of Nick's grasp so she could take hold of his face and make certain he didn't look away. "Knowing you is the best thing that has ever happened to me and if that brings some ghosts along with it, then so be it. I'll go wherever you want me to go if you'll have me."

"I know, Catherine." Nick gently eased out of her grasp. He let his hands linger on her for a few moments before taking them away as well. "But you shouldn't have to give up so much. You don't deserve that kind of life."

"And you do?"

Nick knew the answer to that and so did she. Neither of them wanted to say it out loud.

FOUR

The following day, Nick had plenty of work to do. Even though nobody had died, he was still short a few coffins after the outbreak of fever during the previous winter. His father had always taught him to prepare for the future and that meant spending the good times preparing for the worst. Because he was a coffin maker and undertaker, most folks' best times just happened to be his worst.

Nick had been raised watching grave markers spread across one hillside or another. His father had taught him how to build coffins and he'd picked up the rest of the undertaker's trade from a few others over the years. Most of his days were now spent at or near Ocean's cemetery, tending the grounds, caring for the folks who were there to serve their time beneath it.

Nick's workshop was a small shack filled with fresh pieces of lumber and the tools of his trade. It smelled of cedar, oak, varnish and wood chips, which always brought a smile to his face. That smile wasn't there at the moment, however. The stacks of empty coffins outside the shack were only growing taller, and each wooden box was the culmination of a few days' work that had yet to bear fruit.

The cemetery grounds were immaculate and every marker was cleaned off. In fact, several of the markers looked better now than when Nick had first carved them. He spent much of his quiet time making the letters more ornate or putting a brighter smile upon a cherub's face. Unfortunately, the dead couldn't express their appreciation by putting money in Nick's pockets.

Even though it was a beautiful morning, Nick didn't spend much of it in the tranquility of his own personal boot hill. There was other work to be done, and most of that was in his parlor.

Nick decided to walk into town. Even though Rasa or Kazys could have used the exercise, there was no reason to bother saddling up either of his horses. It wasn't a long walk, but Nick took his time. There was nobody waiting for him when he got there.

His parlor was dusty and had some cobwebs growing in the upper corners like moss spreading over the surface of a log. After sweeping them away, Nick rolled up his sleeves and got to work cleaning the rest of the place. He wiped off the display cases, straightened the chairs and arranged the Bibles in neat piles. When he was done, Nick stood at the front door so he could admire his handiwork.

"You should have sent word you were doing all this cleaning," Catherine said from just outside the door. "I would have helped."

Nick jumped and reflexively reached for his gun. Fortunately, he wasn't wearing his holster, or he might have cleared leather before realizing who was there. "Jesus, Catherine," he said. "Don't sneak up on me like that."

Grinning at the fact that she was the only one who could catch him off guard so easily, Catherine gave him a peck on the cheek and walked around him. There was a basket dangling from one of her arms and a bottle in each hand. "Sorry about that," she said, walking to the display cases where Bibles and invitation samples were kept. "I would have knocked, but I thought that might startle you more."

"What's this?"

"Lunch. What does it look like?"

"How did you know I'd be here?"

"You usually stop by here on Wednesdays." Glancing at him with a mischievous glint in her eyes, she asked, "Don't you know your own habits, Mister Graves?"

Nick had to stop and think for a moment before he realized that she was right. "I guess not. You haven't brought me lunch for a long time."

"Well, I can't be waiting around for you every day, but that doesn't mean I wouldn't mind doing so every now and then. I can't stay long, though." The farmers will be wanting lunch soon.

Digging through the mix of sandwiches and fruit in the basket, Nick selected one of each and said, "I'll take whatever I can get."

"You seem to be in a better mood. Did someone die?"

Considering how well she kept a straight face, Nick might have been the only man alive to know that she was kidding. "No. Nobody died, but I'm considering shooting someone just so I can get back in business."

She waved that off and picked out a sandwich for herself. "Nonsense. The Tin Pan's doing great. Even though the new bar brings in a few dregs, it's turned out to be a good investment. We can afford to wait around for the next funeral." Snapping her fingers excitedly, she added, "Missus Nordstrom looks fairly pale. We might be in for some prosperous times yet."

Nick shook his head and took a bite of an apple. "That's terrible."

"I know," Catherine replied with a crinkle of her nose. "I'm a devil."

They ate for a few more minutes without saying much of anything. It was good to savor the quiet times. Being in an undertaker's parlor didn't put a dent in either of them. They simply ate their lunch and then cleaned up when they were done.

After packing the remnants into the basket, Catherine said, "By the way, that man came by the restaurant for breakfast."

Nick bristled and didn't try to cover it. "What did you tell him?"

"I told him he might be able to catch sight of you at the gun shop."

That was the second time in two days Catherine had surprised him. Nick squinted as if he was trying to see through a fog before saying, "I thought you weren't going to have any part in that business."

"If I want us to work together, that's what we should do. Me hiding things from you and trying to undo them behind your back won't do anyone any good. All I ask is that you return the favor."

"Okay. Why the gun shop?"

"Because it's not close to my restaurant or this parlor. You could avoid it if you chose. Also, he talked about you like he only knew you from your wild days, so it seemed like the sort of place he would expect to find you. It was either that or the saloon, and I didn't want to set up anything with that much potential for a backfire."

Nick was speechless. All he could do was shake his head and laugh quietly under his breath.

"What's so funny?" Catherine asked.

"Are you sure you never met Barrett?"

"I'm sure. Why?"

"Because that's the same amount of thinking he put into every little thing he did."

"And I suppose you never planned ahead a step or two?"

Nick chuckled once again, but at his own expense. "I was more the kind to steam ahead and try to dodge some of the hell I kicked up along the way."

"Yes, well, try not to kick any up today. If you want to see what's on this fellow's mind, I know I can't stop you. If you'd like to keep things quiet for a change, avoid the gun shop and then chase him out of town wearing that badge of yours." Cautiously, she added, "You do still have the badge, don't you?"

"Yes."

"Good." Catherine took the basket and pointed to the bottles that were still on the counter. "That's sarsaparilla. You're not getting any of that vile liquor you forced me to buy until after business hours."

"Not vile," Nick corrected. "Vodka."

"Same difference."

With that, Catherine patted Nick's cheek and walked out of the parlor.

It was funny how such a simple thing as lunch could make such a big difference. In fact, Nick hadn't even realized how glum he'd been until the clouds had lifted. Now, when he looked around, he saw a prosperous business in a friendly town. That business had now been cleaned, which made it seem even better.

A bit of Nick's budding optimism faded when he thought about the other news that Catherine had brought. As attractive as the idea of chasing this stranger out of town seemed, Nick simply couldn't do it. There were too many possibilities attached. His old friend Barrett had taught him that much.

Then again, it was sometimes healthier to avoid Barrett's advice like the plague.

FIVE

"Give me all your money," Barrett said as he stomped into the cabin like a dog nosing its way through the back door. He wasn't normally a big man, but the layers of furs, coats, shirts and long johns he wore added a considerable amount of bulk to his frame.

Nick was asleep in a corner, huddled there in a position that might have been uncomfortable if he still had any feeling in his legs. As it was, the cold chewed at him all the way down to the bone. He was so cold, in fact, that reaching for his pistol was the first time the young man had ever heard his joints creak.

"Go to hell, asshole!" Nick snapped as he finally managed to take his gun from its holster.

Barrett didn't even flinch when he found himself staring down the barrel of Nick's pistol. His eyes were wide open and he trembled with something other than cold or fear. "Don't be such a cock-sucker, Nick. I'm serious."

"I am, too," Nick replied as he thumbed the hammer back. "Serious as hell. And you'll be dead as hell before you take the money I got."

"I helped steal most of that, too, you know."

"And you ain't stealing this."

Nick's face reflected anger as well as pain from awakening his previously deadened nerves. The shack wasn't much bigger than an outhouse, and had been put together so poorly that it let in more snow than it kept out. Nick's boots scraped against the floor as he fought to sit up. When he pressed his back against the wall for support, it caused the boards behind him to creak like an old man begging for mercy.

"The only one to steal from us is you, remember?" Barrett said with a grin.

"That was different. That was to get in one of the biggest poker games in the area."

"That's what you say about all of 'em, and when the hell are you gonna take my advice? Faro's where the real money's at."

Nick was tired of arguing. A stiff wind ripped over the side of the mountain and tore through the shack like a set of wolf's fangs ripping through an exposed neck. "What do you need money for?" Nick asked as he tucked his gun under the outer-most of the blankets wrapped around him. "We don't even got enough to pay for a hotel."

"How much do we have?"

After staring at Barrett for a few more seconds, Nick realized the other young man wasn't about to go anywhere. Nick let out a sigh and started going through the arduous motions of peeling off the blankets surrounding him like a cocoon. Once the blankets were gone, Nick was still wrapped up in a tangle of garments, ranging from an old sailor's coat to a few layers previously worn by federal infantry.

"I wanted to go into town," Nick grumbled. "I wanted to get someplace to stay. Even a back room in a goddamn saloon would be better than this."

"This," Barrett said, rubbing his hands together, "is perfect. Nobody knows it's here, so it'll make a perfect spot to hole up."

Nick stopped what he was doing and snapped his eyes back up to his friend. He'd known Barrett Cobb since they were both kids. They'd formed their first gang together. They'd run off to start robbing general stores together. They'd robbed armories and a train together. They'd also watched various members of their gang drop like flies when the shooting started.

At the moment, Barrett and Nick were the only members of their gang still in Colorado. The rest of his friends could have been dead or in Oklahoma, for all he knew. "You got something planned, Barrett?" Nick asked.

Barrett shrugged and didn't even try to cover the grin that was creeping onto his face. "Maybe, but it'll take some cash to get going."

"How much?"

"At least a hundred. Maybe two."

Nick's hands curled into fists inside his pockets. "If I had that much money, why the fuck would I be curled up in a ball in all this goddamn cold?"

"I don't know. Maybe you've been holding out."

"You calling me a thief?"

"No. I said maybe you were holding out. You know . . . for an emergency."

Slowly, Nick's scowl faded and he took one hand out of his pocket. Apart from a few scars and several calluses, it was in perfect working order. The whiskers on his face may have been long, but they weren't nearly thick enough to form a beard or come close to hiding the resignation on his face. He opened his fist to reveal a few wadded bills and some large coins. "There's twenty-four dollars and fifty cents."

Barrett scowled, but it was more good-natured than the expression that had darkened Nick's features. "I've got thirty. Seems like we were both holding out."

"I ain't handing it over until I hear what you got planned."

Ever since he was a kid, Barrett had never been able to contain his own excitement. Even now that he was in his early twenties, he seemed more like the boy who was jumping out of his skin to reveal his plot to sneak a peek into a whorehouse with a broken window without getting caught. "There's a bank less than two miles from here . . ."

"Oh no," Nick said. "Hell no!"

"What? Why? You didn't even hear what I've got to say!"

"I heard 'bank,' and that's enough. We're stuck out here because of that posse that tore after us after that bullshit in Leadville. We ain't heard from anyone else in the gang since then, and we ain't set to meet up with no one for another couple weeks."

Barrett listened to all of this without losing the grin on his face. He simply nodded, waited for Nick to run out of steam and then said, "It'll only take two of us to rob this bank."

Rubbing his ears with the palms of his hands, Nick winced at the pain that caused and then leaned forward to stare even harder at his friend. "What?"

"You heard me. I figured out a way for the two of us to rob this bank."

"You must be shit out of your mind."

The wind kicked up again and roared so hard that it rattled the entire shack around both of the young men huddled inside. Barrett started to speak, but was cut short as the cold seized up his lungs like a fist clamping around his chest. As the wind kept howling, neither of the two could move. When it finally let up, both young men slumped forward and vigorously rubbed their hands together.

"I'd like to see you swear around your pappy like that," Barrett said as he blew into his cupped hands.

"My pa ain't nothing but a goddamn gravedigger and he won't never be anything more than that. I already got more people who know my name than . . . them that . . . know his."

"All right, you'd better stop trying to talk. I think your tongue's frozen. Just sit there and hear me out." Even though Nick opened his mouth to speak, Barrett kept saying his piece before Nick could get rolling. "This bank I saw is a little place on the edge of Willhemene Pass. With the cold and all, there ain't been more than two or three folks working inside at any given time."

Suddenly, Nick found the strength required to lift himself and all those coats up off the floor. Once on his feet, he hunched over like a cobra eyeing an unsuspecting mouse. "You been into town enough times to gather all of that?"

"Yes," Barrett said. "I thought you would have figured that out since I've been gone so much."

"You said you was out getting wood and scouting for the law."

"I brought back wood and I've done plenty of scouting. Haven't you been listening?"

"You know what I been doing? I've been freezing my balls off out here in this goddamn shack while you've been warming yourself in a fire somewhere in town, which is where I wanted to be!"

There were only a few years separating Barrett and Nick, but the calmness in Barrett's eyes made that gap seem a whole lot wider. "You would've spent our money," Barrett said. As soon as those words were out, Barrett realized they'd been poorly chosen. He quickly added, "Besides, your face is the one the law's getting to know. I can still get around fairly well without being noticed."

Nick's eye twitched as he struggled to keep himself from lunging at Barrett's throat. As he thought about that first reward notice he'd seen with his likeness drawn on it, Nick felt his anger subside. "All right, then. But I still want to get into town to make up for it."

"I can show you the bank," Barrett said. "We should be able to live in fancy hotels for a while after knocking that one over." He paused and backed up a bit before adding, "I still need your money."

Nick actually laughed this time. "I ain't holding out on any more than what I already told you about. That means we're still a long ways from that hundred or two you said you needed. What the hell do you need that much for anyway?"

"The two of us can rob that bank, but only if we get one of the local law dogs on our side. I figure we'd need a pretty good bribe to get that done."

"You want me to hand over that much money to some fucking lawman? You must be crazy. How do you know one of these lawmen is even crooked?"

Barrett stomped his feet and rubbed his hands together as another gust of wind ripped through the shack. "There ain't many lawmen out there who can't be bought off. We may find one cheaper, but I just want to be prepared in case we need to kick in a little extra. Believe me, we'll make up our losses."

Nick cracked his knuckles and worked out some of the knots that had been frozen into his neck. "You got any prospects as far as these lawmen are concerned?"

"I found the one that looks to be the weakest link in the chain, and the one that's the strongest."

"Take me to both of them."

"Why?" Barrett asked.

"Because I'm going to save us a hundred dollars or so. Now, tell me the rest of this plan you thought up."

The deputy was the youngest one in town. He walked with his head hanging low and his arms tight against his body as if he was afraid of getting punched in the ribs at any moment. The hat and coat he wore were a bit too big for him. Every time a stiff breeze came along, it nearly plucked the hat from his head or knocked him over.

Main Street consisted of two short rows of store-fronts facing each other and very few people walking between them. Only a few carriages traveled the street throughout the day, leaving the sparse population of Willhemene Pass to huddle inside their homes or in one of the town's two saloons to keep warm.

A wind kicked up and howled between the buildings on either side of the street, filling the deputy's ears with a cold roar. That roar was more than loud enough to cover the sounds of footsteps rushing up behind him. When his hat was knocked off his head, the deputy assumed it was from the wind. If he'd bothered turning around, he would have seen Barrett standing there with his arm still outstretched.

"Damn," the deputy whispered as he rushed forward to chase his hat. He bent to pick it up as the wind died down. Suddenly, he could hear the second set of footsteps rushing toward him from the side.

Nick placed a hand flat upon the lawman's back to keep him from standing up. "Evening, Marshal," he said with a grin. The deputy was holding a rifle in his hand, but Nick kicked it down and stepped on the barrel to hold it against the ground.

To his credit, the deputy kept his bony fingers wrapped around the rifle even after the gun was trapped under Nick's boot. Once Nick put a bit more of his weight down though, the crushing pain shooting through the deputy's half-frozen fingers was too much to bear.

Nick shoved the deputy toward Barrett with one hand and scooped up the rifle with the other. "It's all right," he said as he glanced around to make sure they weren't being watched. "You're not the first one to fall for that trick. Now, how about you come along with us so we can have a little talk?"

The deputy flinched and looked over at Barrett when he realized what had happened. Although Barrett didn't have his own gun drawn, he had his hand upon his holster to make it clear that he could pull his weapon at any time.

"I'd suggest you do what he tells you," Barrett said through the bandanna wrapped around the lower portion of his face. "Or this could get real ugly."

Nick walked with an easy stride and dropped his arm around the deputy's shoulders as if they were just three friends headed out to get a drink. He kept the rifle in his grasp and pointed in the deputy's direction. "This won't take long, and you might just be glad you bumped into us."

They led the deputy away from the center of town and around a corner. It wasn't a very long walk before they found themselves in front of a darkened store, with a mountain range behind them. The sun had set some time ago, and the moonlight reflected off the snow.

Squinting into the pale shadows, Nick couldn't see another living thing for miles in that direction. The street was more than quiet enough to suit his purposes, so Nick grabbed the deputy by the throat with his left hand and used his right to jam the rifle's barrel into the lawman's gut.

The deputy looked even younger up close than he did from afar. His skin was pale and his cheeks had the sunken appearance of someone who had been deathly ill. With so much fear showing on his face, his eyes looked wider than the sockets that held them. "Who . . . who are you?"

"I'm the son of a bitch that's robbing your bank tomorrow," Nick snarled. "And if you know what's good for you, Marshal, you'll steer clear of it so I can do my business."

"I'm not a marshal. I'm just a—"

"I can see the deputy badge on your coat, you loco son of a bitch. I ain't blind. I'm just giving you credit for being smarter than another shit-for-brains deputy. No matter what badge you got on, you should be able to influence your fellow law dogs."

"The sheriff . . . he's the one who . . ." The deputy's voice caught in the back of his pinched throat as the rifle barrel was driven even further into his stomach.

Nick leaned forward to glare directly into the deputy's eyes, making certain most of his weight was behind the rifle. "Make up a reason for the law to be somewhere else around noon tomorrow. Find something to keep them busy. Think of something, or everyone inside that bank will be killed. You understand me?"

The deputy nodded weakly at first, but his head found a momentum of its own and was soon twitching up and down.

"Good," Nick said. "Now, do I even have to tell you to keep quiet about who gave you this idea when you see your law dog friends?"

The deputy shook his head wildly.

"Didn't think so." Nick started to turn away, but then shifted back around to fix his glare once more upon the deputy. His lips curled into a predator's snarl as his finger began to tighten around the rifle's trigger. "You sure I can count on you?"

"Yes, yes," the deputy wheezed. "Please. God, don't kill me."

Nick could smell the young lawman's fear and he pulled it all the way down to the bottom of his lungs as if he were savoring a beautiful woman's perfume. Once he'd had his fill, he nodded and backed away. "All right, then. Get the fuck out of my sight."

Those words might as well have been a fire lit under the deputy's backside, since they sent him scampering away from Barrett and Nick so quickly that he almost lost his footing several times. Even after the deputy had rounded the corner, his desperate steps could still be heard scraping against the frozen soil.

Nick was laughing as Barrett pulled the bandanna down from his face.

"Are you sure about this, Nick?" Barrett asked.

"Sure, I'm sure. Now, where's this weak link you were talking about?"

"In the saloon right down the street."

"Then let's get to him before that yellow little runt does. You'd better be the runt's shadow for a while, just to make sure."

Barrett took off in the direction the deputy had gone.

Nick had to keep himself from whistling as he stepped back onto Main Street to look for the saloon Barrett had mentioned. The town was laid out just as Barrett had described on their way in from their shack. The saloon was right where it should be, marked with the picture of the wolf's paw Barrett had described.

Shoving open the door, Nick stepped in and spotted Barrett's lawman. The man was about Nick's size and possibly a few years older. He kept himself upright by putting both elbows upon the edge of the bar and wore his badge pinned crookedly to his left collar.

"It's damn cold out there!" Nick said as he stomped into the saloon.

"It's always cold, mister," the bartender replied. "How about something to thaw the blood in yer veins?"

Nick stood beside the haggard man wearing the badge. "You cold, too?" he asked.

The man was barely sober enough to look up and spot the person beside him. "I ain't. . .cold enough to piss . . . in the . . . " were the only slurred words he could pronounce clearly.

Nick laughed and slapped the man on the back as if the babble actually meant something to him. He then slapped twenty dollars upon the bar. "This is for my drink as well as my friend's here," Nick said to the bartender. "Keep 'em coming!"

SIX

The bank was situated near the edge of town. It looked like something closer to a church or schoolhouse, since the building was small, square and had a tall, pointed roof. The two masked men approached it, one anxiously pulling the other along. The more eager of the two kicked open the bank's front door with his gun already in hand.

It was six minutes past noon.

"Hands where I can see 'em!" the first man shouted as he waved his gun at the three customers standing in front of the two teller windows. "You assholes behind that cage get all the money you can grab and stuff it into a sack!"

There was one young woman behind the cage separating the public and private halves of the bank. She already had her hands in the air and was trembling almost too much to hold them up. The other person behind the cage was a man in his fifties who wore a pair of round spectacles. He'd been sitting at a rolltop desk when the masked men entered and now stood up.

"You!" the first masked man snapped as he aimed directly at the old man behind the cage. "Open the safe and empty it into a sack."

"There is no safe," the man replied.

The first masked man shoved forward past a customer to stick his arm between two of the cage's bars. "Don't feed me any bullshit unless you want to die, old man!" he said as he thumbed back the hammer of his pistol.

"We've got cash in the drawers, but—"

The older man was cut short as the gun in the masked man's hand barked and sent a bullet through the female teller's side. Yelping and falling to the floor, the woman grabbed the fresh wound. Despite the pain, the bullet had caught more of her dress than it had of her skin.

"Don't try my patience, old man," the first masked man said.

The older man didn't have anything else left to say. Instead, he nodded and walked behind his desk to reveal a small safe hidden beneath a red sheet and a vase of flowers.

Until now, the second masked man hadn't done anything but stand in the doorway. When he started fidgeting, the first gunman walked over to him and pulled him inside.

"My partner's getting nervous," the first masked man said.

Just then, one of the customers spoke up. "Maybe that's because the law's outside," a young man with smooth features said as he pointed toward the window.

The first masked man looked out the window and nodded. "So they are. All three of them." Looking toward the cage, he asked, "How much you got for me?"

"The safe's not open yet," the old man replied.

The teller was already on her feet. She held up a single bag and whimpered, "This is all I could get."

"Toss it over."

She did as she was told and then leaned against her counter.

After scooping up the bag, the first gunman walked to the front door and patted his partner roughly upon the back. "What do you say? Feel like shooting your way out of here?"

The second gunman started to say something, but was cut off as the first one shoved him toward the steps leading to the street.

"Kiss my ass, law dogs!" the first masked man said as he fired a few shots at the approaching lawmen.

The sheriff was a barrel-chested man in his forties with a thick mustache drooping over his mouth. He fired the shotgun in his hand, missing the first masked man and startling the second. As the second masked man started to raise his arm, another blast caught him in the chest and dropped him straight to the ground.

The first masked man was already on his horse, thundering away from the bank. He rode down Main Street, allowing the lawmen to come after him.

The thunder of hooves beating against the ground and shots blasting through the air made it seem as if a storm had rolled in from the mountains to stir up some hell in Willhemene Pass. That storm rolled out of the town, leaving a body in the street and several confused locals standing with their mouths agape.

Inside the bank, the manager scrambled to the teller's side. "Are you all right?" he asked.

The woman pulled in a few breaths, pressed her hand to her side, but eventually nodded. "It's not so bad. At least, I don't think it is."

"We'll get you to Doc Whistler." Craning his neck to get a look past the teller through the bars to the front section of the bank, the manager shouted, "Can anyone hear me?"

Plenty of noise was coming from outside. One voice answered the manager's question, though. It belonged to the only customer who'd spoken to the masked men before they'd left.

The customer's steps echoed through the bank as his boots scraped against the floor. "Are you all right, ma'am?" the customer asked, peeking through the teller's window.

"It looks like a flesh wound, but I'm no doctor," the manager replied. "Are those robbers gone?"

The customer walked back to the door, looked

outside and then shut it behind him. The sound of the lock being turned rattled through the small one-room building.

"The law rode off to chase after that robber. Looks like they got one of them before they left, though," Barrett said in the same, calm voice he'd used to inform Nick about the sheriff and his men. He walked over to the cage and looked at the area behind it with mild interest. When he spotted the safe, he took a gun from under his coat and eased it between the bars.

The manager was in the process of helping the woman to the back door when he spotted Barrett pointing the gun at him. "What . . . what the hell is this?"

"Weren't you listening before?" Barrett asked. "It's a robbery. Now that we've got this place to ourselves, why don't you finish emptying that safe?"

The confusion written across the manager's face might have been funny under any other circumstances. In fact, Barrett knew that Nick would have been laughing if he was there to see it.

"But . . . we were . . ."

"Only told about two of us coming?" Barrett asked as a way to finish the manager's question. "Things change. Now get that money before I start making more noise."

The manager did what he was told; emptying the contents of the safe into another couple of bags as if he was in a daze.

Barrett took the bags, fitted them under his arms and then closed his coat over them. "Keep quiet until someone comes to get you," he told the two behind the cage. "My other partner outside's got an itchy trigger finger." With that, Barrett turned his back on the cage and walked out the front door. By the time he stepped outside, his gun was tucked away and a panicked look was on his face.

"Good Lord," exclaimed a local man who was kneeling next to the body of the masked man lying in the street.

Barrett and several other locals gathered around the body as the man kneeling beside it pulled the robber's mask off. When the face of the drunkard deputy was revealed, Barrett let out a relieved sigh. As the locals got a look for themselves and started nervously chattering, Barrett was able to slip away and walk down the street to the horse waiting for him there.

It was well past nightfall and there was still no trace of Nick. Barrett sat huddled in the shack they'd claimed as their own, rubbing his arms and watching the steam curl upward every time he let out a breath. The cold had been gnawing at him for hours and had chewed all the way down to the marrow in his bones.

Outside, a few hearty animals scampered through the snow. The wind wasn't as fierce as it had been earlier, but there was still a trickle of air seeping in through the walls. Barrett focused his eyes upon a spot on the floor just in front of his boots. As much as he wanted to go outside and watch for Nick, he knew he'd only last a matter of moments before his ears began to ache and his fingers went numb.

Instead of giving his eyes something to do, Barrett closed them and focused on what he could hear.

Barrett could never figure why, but winter nights always seemed to be especially quiet. Because of that, every footstep was a crash and every snowflake's landing was like a pebble knocking against a tin roof.

When he heard the sound of heavy steps crunching in the snow, Barrett's eyes snapped open and he jumped to his feet. Since he hadn't stretched his legs for a while, every joint in his body ignited with pain. Barrett simply gritted his teeth and drew his pistol.

There was someone outside.

Whoever it was, they were most definitely on a horse.

The lighter steps could just be heard scattered among the heavier ones, but as hard as Barrett tried, he couldn't decipher how many were out there.

The more he strained his ears listening, the louder each step got. Finally, he knew he had to take a look outside for himself. If it was a posse approaching the shack instead of Nick, showing himself now wouldn't make much difference anyway.

Barrett tightened his grip on his gun and steeled himself to look out through the shack's crooked window. Despite all the possible outcomes racing through his mind, Barrett kept going back to the one that ended with him catching a bullet in his face the moment he showed it to some approaching lawmen.

Letting out the breath he'd been holding, Barrett leaned to the side, looked out the window and found himself less than an inch away from Nick's smiling face.

"Jesus Christ," Barrett said as his finger clamped reflexively around his trigger and sent a bullet through the door.

Nick jumped away from the window and drew his own gun without even thinking about it. "What the hell?" he said as he took a quick look behind him and then around to either side.

Barrett charged outside, still holding his gun. "You scared the shit out of me, Nick. What the fuck were you thinking?"

"And that's coming from someone who's always telling me to watch my cussing?"

"Where the hell have you been?"

Nick didn't answer right away. Instead, he cocked his head to one side and held up a finger like an overly dramatic actor playing to his audience. "You hear that?"

"My ears are still ringing."

"The posse's on its way."

"You're not getting me twice," Barrett said.

As if on cue, the sounds of more hooves pounding against the snow could be heard rumbling through the air.

"You led them back here?!" Barrett said.

"I lost 'em a while ago, but they're combing this whole mountain. I thought I'd swing by here and get you out of here. I didn't think you'd fire a shot to let 'em know we're here, though."

There were plenty of things Barrett wanted to say and not one of them was of the friendly variety. As he quickly gathered his few possessions and saddled his horse, Barrett felt his heart slamming against the inside of his ribs as if it was trying to escape his chest.

"You got the money?" Nick asked.

"Yes, now let's get the hell out of here!"

Nick snapped his reins and got his horse moving past the shack toward a smaller trail he'd found the night before. As he rode down the narrow strip of dirt, which occasionally disappeared beneath the snow, he was smiling wide enough for his teeth to freeze. With the wind stirring again and the horses making their way down the narrow pass, Nick couldn't hear much of anything else. He still knew the posse was coming after him, though. Lawmen all put the same stench into the air, just as much as the one lying face up in the street when Nick had ridden away from that bank.

The path down the mountain may have been narrow, but it wasn't exactly treacherous. It led them down to a winding pass that would eventually link up with the trail leading to Denver. It had become second nature for Nick to avoid the main trails, so he turned away from that one and kept riding until he found a spot that suited him.

Barrett followed, but couldn't keep from squirming. Between trying to steer his horse through the darkness and shifting to get a look behind or around him, he rarely sat still long enough to allow his eyes to focus. He saw Nick's horse slow to a stop, so Barrett followed suit and climbed from his saddle as soon as he was able.

"Are they gone?" Barrett asked.

Nick swung off of his horse's back and strutted up to him so he could clap his friend on the back. "There's no way in hell them laws are gonna find us. Now let's see that money."

"We should wait until morning, or maybe until we're far enough away to—"

"To hell with all of that," Nick cut in. "I went through all this trouble, so I want to see the money."

Knowing better than to argue with him, Barrett fished out one of the two bags he'd been given by the bank manager and handed it over to Nick. "There's another just like it, but I'm not getting that one out until we can split it up."

Nick pulled open the bag and stuffed his hand inside like a kid reaching for the last cookie in the jar. When he took his hand back out, his fingers were wrapped tightly around a fat wad of cash. "Now this is what I call a perfect job."

"Perfect?" Barrett asked. "I wanted to buy off that crooked drunk so he could make sure there weren't any law around that bank. Instead, you went ahead and approached the deputy I specifically told you could be trouble."

Nick shook his head and slowly flipped through the money. "That was a small town, Barrett. The law was gonna be there no matter what. This way, we cut their numbers down by one and drew everyone out so you could waltz right out of there with the money. Perfect."

Even though Barrett was still more than a little aggravated, it was difficult for him to be angry with Nick. "It did turn out pretty well," he admitted.

"Did you have any trouble getting out of there?"

"No."

"And what about that deputy I left behind?" Nick asked.

"Dead."

"Serves him right. You know what it took to get him over to my way of thinking?"

Barrett shrugged.

"A few bottles of whiskey and a twenty-dollar advance on what we'd take away from that bank." Producing a folded bill from his shirt pocket, Nick added, "The dumb shit was too drunk to even ask for the twenty dollars up front. I'm surprised the law came at all, considering the chowder heads they got working for them."

"The only thing that surprises me is that you got away without forking over that bribe," Barrett said quietly. "Most men would sell out their own kin if the price was right. Men with badges ain't nothing more than assholes with the authority to shove someone around."

"Well that asshole won't be shovin' anyone around anymore."

Barrett winced slightly as he said, "That might bump up the price on our heads. He was still a lawman, after all, and you did shoot that woman."

"I didn't do nothing more than scratch her," Nick said confidently. "And that was just to let folks think I was serious. Besides, what's the problem? It worked, didn't it?"

"Yeah. It worked."

SEVEN

———◆———

Ocean, California
1885

Switchback Gil sat in a chair on the boardwalk with his legs propped up on a hitching rail. One hand was draped lazily across his belly as the other reached down for a cup of water on the ground beside him. From where he sat, he could look directly across the street at the gun shop, or up and down the street in any direction to see who was coming.

Gil strained his arm a bit more to reach his cup of water. When he still couldn't find it, he turned his head to look and see if he'd accidentally spilled it. What he found was a large figure standing beside and somewhat behind him. All he could make out was a leg and the flap of a dark coat. Before he could pull his legs down from the rail, the figure extended his arm.

"Here you go," the scratchy voice said as he handed Gil the cup of water.

When Gil looked down, he didn't pay much attention to the dented cup being handed to him. Instead, he focused on the gnarled, whittled-down fingers holding it. Gil got his legs down, but wasn't able to stand up before the cup was tossed away and he was hauled up by the front of his shirt.

Nick lifted Gil from his chair and set him right back down again. Although Gil's legs were a bit wobbly at first, he adjusted soon enough.

"You're Nick Graves," Gil announced.

"That's the rumor."

"I wanted to talk to you."

"I know. That's why I'm here. You want to spill it while we're young or would you rather dance around some more?"

Chuckling uneasily and brushing himself off, Gil kept his hand upon the gun holstered at his side. Hooking his thumb toward the street, he asked, "You want to take a walk? I'd rather not do my talking where anyone can overhear."

Nick glanced at the street and couldn't find any strangers waiting for them. In fact, he couldn't see much of anyone else in the area. "Sure." Just to be safe, Nick stepped into the street and started walking in the opposite direction to where Gil had pointed.

Gil scrambled to his feet and followed him. "I wanted to ask about your friend, Barrett Cobb," he said quickly.

Stopping in his tracks, Nick turned to him and said, "Barrett's dead."

"I . . . uh . . . I know. At least, that's what I

heard." Gil wrung his hands as he started walking again.

This time, Nick was the one who had to do the catching up. He did so with long, powerful strides and easily overtook the smaller man.

"I heard them boys in Montana got to you," Gil said, motioning toward Nick's hand. "Guess that rumor was true, too."

"You asked about Barrett. What the hell do you want to know about him?" Nick growled.

Glancing around nervously, Gil hooked his thumb toward an alley. "It'd be best if we talked in pri—"

"We'll talk right here," Nick said in a tone that made Gil flinch. "Say what you came to say and do it quick."

"You were his friend. Cobb's, I mean."

"Yeah."

"Word is that you may be the one who gave him the Reaper's Fee."

Nick's brow furrowed as he drilled straight through Gil's skull with his eyes. "What's that supposed to mean?" he asked, unable to recall Barrett ever using that term.

Leaning forward on the balls of his feet, Gil said, "You buried him with the money that was stolen on his last job. Some folks say you helped him steal it. Some say you were the one to bury him, since there weren't nobody alive who'd care enough about Cobb to . . . well . . . to go through all that trouble."

"You talk like you know an awful lot."

Gil nodded and grinned as if he was about to reach around and pat himself on the back.

"What's this 'Reaper's Fee'?" Nick asked.

"It's just the name someone came up with for what's supposed to be in that coffin with Barrett Cobb. You know . . . like the money he'd pay to the Reaper when he came a-callin'."

Nick's face might as well have been carved out of stone. His expression was a cold slap that knocked Gil's grin right off his face.

"Even though I don't believe you had anything to do with that robbery," Gil said as he glanced down at the gun hanging from Nick's battered holster, "my bet is that you'd know something about it. I hear you were the only man Cobb called his friend . . . although there are some folks who say you might have been the one to kill him."

"Barrett was like my brother," Nick said.

"Hell, I'd like to kill my brother every now and then. Ain't nothing wrong with that."

Despite everything running through Nick's mind at that moment, he couldn't help but look at Gil with outright confusion. "Just who the hell are you, and where the hell did you hear all of this?"

"Didn't the lady tell you? I'm Switchback Gil."

Nick recognized the tone in Gil's voice, as well as the arrogant posture that meant that Gil fully expected his name to strike a chord with anyone who heard it. Seeing that proud display made Nick feel as if he were looking at a faded picture of himself, back when he was young and full of his own brand of hellfire.

"That name don't mean shit to me, boy," Nick said. "Now tell me who filled your head with all of those rumors."

"Word's been getting around about that stash you buried. The company that owned them jewels has been out looking for them and they say you were wrapped up in the robbery."

"Folks say I'm wrapped up in plenty of things."

"Are they all lying?" Gil asked.

Nick didn't respond to that right away. As the memories flooded through his mind, Nick had to stand there and let them run their course before he said, "Not all of them."

"Then you know what I'm talking about. But that was in the past," Gil quickly added. "A blind man could see you ain't in any condition to be a threat no more. That's what I was trying to tell the folks that came around talking about them jewels."

"How thoughtful of you," Nick said dryly.

"There ain't many men as thoughtful as me. Most are just chasing off after the tales that are being spread without doing any scouting ahead. I hear there's been graves dug up all the way from here to the Dakotas and everywhere in between."

"That's not a very wise way to go about things. Not with so many Indians in those parts."

Gil smirked and snapped his fingers. "That's exactly what I thought."

"Are you going to tell me why you came out here to waste so much of my time?" Nick asked.

To Nick's surprise, Gil actually stepped up to him and looked him squarely in the eyes. "I want you to tell me where I can find that grave. After that, I'll be on my way and you can have all the time you need to think about how lucky you were that I found you instead of some of them others that are out there looking."

"What others?"

"There's a price on your head, old man. Didn't you know that?"

Nick found himself grinning at the sound of that. Although he knew there were some gray strands in his hair and a few silvery whiskers in his beard, he hadn't exactly thought of himself as old just yet. Then again, he could recall pinning that same moniker on men younger than himself when he'd been around Gil's age.

If Gil had been concerned with privacy before, his own confidence had wiped that worry away. Now he stood in the street and glared directly into Nick's eyes, bowing his shoulders like the proverbial cock of the walk. "You may have been a real bad man all them years ago," he said. "But that was all them years ago. I've heard about some of the things you done from a cousin that lives up in Montana. He knows some real good stories about Nicolai Graves."

"I barely ever hear people call me by my given

name anymore. Most folks just say Nick. That's good to hear."

"Glad you like it," Gil said with a smug grin. "From what my cousin tells me, you were shot up, ran out of Virginia City and left for dead by the vigilantes up there."

"I wasn't the only one."

"Not by a stretch, but you're one of the most famous ones."

"There was a time," Nick said fondly, "when it would have done me good to hear that."

Gil nodded and then took a step back so he could square his shoulders to Nick. "Yeah? Well you can look back on the old days all you want after you tell me where to find that grave."

"Barrett was my friend. Why would I tell you something like that?"

"Because it'd be real bad for you if you didn't." As he said that, Gil pressed the palm of his hand against his holstered gun as the muscles in his jaw flexed beneath the skin of his face.

Nick kept his head down and his eyes on Gil. He could hear a few people walking along the street to his right, but he didn't bother looking in that direction. It was too late to be concerned with appearances. As Nick's hand brushed aside his coat to give him better access to his gun, he asked, "You sure you want to do it this way, boy?"

"You could just tell me what I want to know and

that'd be it. If you think I'm gonna start shaking because you got a gun strapped around your waist, you got another thing comin'. That piece of shit you got there couldn't even kill a snake if you jammed the barrel down its mouth. Hell, the holster alone looks old enough to start rotting away if I gave it another few minutes."

There were so many scars on Nick's hands that he could barely feel the handle of the modified Schofield pistol. The leather of the holster was so worn and had been tooled so much that it was more like a piece of him. "Who else is going after that grave?" Nick asked. "I want names."

"Well, it doesn't matter if you heard of them or not. If I was you, I'd pile my things into a wagon and get out of this town, because there's gonna be more coming around looking for you."

"There always are."

"Once I find them jewels, they'll stop coming and you can live out the rest of your years in peace."

"I can't allow that," Nick said calmly.

Gil cocked his head and leaned forward a bit. "What did you just say?"

"You heard me, boy. I can't allow anyone to defile my friend's grave. Especially not some wet-behind-the-ears prick like you."

Gil heard that just fine. His face contorted into an angry mask and he drew in a deep breath until his chest was puffed out, pulling himself up to his full height.

Nick, on the other hand, remained in the same

relaxed posture he'd taken since the conversation had begun.

"I'm finding them jewels one way or another," Gil said. "You can tell me where the grave is or I could get it from that pretty lady who owns that restaurant. She seemed to know all there was to know about you."

"That's not the path you wanna take," Nick said calmly.

"I won't have to if you stop strutting like you got some stones between yer legs and answer the question you were asked."

Nick let out a discouraged breath, blinked once and then drew his gun. The inside of his holster had been tooled with curved ridges that interlocked with the grooves twisting around the barrel of his modified Schofield. When the gun was brought up, the grip shifted directly into Nick's palm. Most men wouldn't have much use for such a feature, but most men also had all their fingers. The modification allowed Nick to make up some of the speed he'd lost when his gun hand had been mangled. His own skill and instinct, combined with a loosened trigger, gave Nick enough speed to clear leather and fire a shot before Gil could utter one more sarcastic word.

The shot cracked through the air and punched a hole through Gil's chest. It was a little right of center, which meant Gil was still drawing breath and able to look down as his body absorbed the impact. Although Gil had drawn his own pistol out of pure reflex, he wasn't able to lift his arm before Nick's second shot drilled through his heart.

Gil's eyes were open wide and his face bore a look of surprise that wasn't at all unfamiliar to Nick. He'd seen that same look on plenty of other men's faces. Seeing it now, Nick's ears were filled with the echoes of his own youthful laughter that might have followed such an easy kill.

Nick wasn't laughing now. Instead, he kept his gun in hand and his eyes on Gil until the other man's legs finally buckled and he crumpled to the ground.

Looking up, Nick saw several familiar faces staring back at him. Shop owners looked through their windows and a young man driving a wagon pulled back on his reins before his horses pulled him any closer to the spot where the shots had been fired.

Nick met every one of the eyes that were watching him. Some were frightened. Some were surprised. Some were just confused. All of them were waiting for an explanation. Most folks who saw such a thing just wanted to know what the other man had done or who he was.

Rather than take time to explain himself, Nick walked away.

There wasn't enough time for explanations.

EIGHT

———————•———————

"Someone's going to dig up a dead body?" Catherine gasped. "Are you sure about this?"

Nick was in their bedroom, stuffing clothes into a saddlebag and nodding his head. "Pretty damn sure."

"Someone's going to dig up Barrett?"

"Yes and for the tenth time, yes."

Catherine stood in the doorway with her arms folded. She blinked and then rubbed her eyes with the heel of her hand. "Sorry, but I just can't believe someone would do that."

"I can."

"Why?"

"Because," Nick said, "I'm the one who buried those jewels in the casket along with him."

Frozen right down to the expression on her face, Catherine had to wait until she was forced to draw a breath before she could speak. "Why on earth would you do that?" she asked. "It's not like Barrett needs the money."

"Barrett lived to pull off those jobs of his and he

wound up dying for it," Nick explained. "The least I could do was let him have the money since I was the one to put an end to his career." Pausing to close his eyes for a moment, he added, "Since I was the one to put an end to him."

"You told me about what happened between you and him," Catherine said. "Barrett didn't give you a choice. You had to shoot him. That was years ago, Nick. Don't let what happened ruin you any more than it already has."

"They're calling it the Reaper's Fee," Nick said as if he hadn't even heard what Catherine was saying. "They gave it a nice little nickname and talked it up in all the saloons. I don't know who found out about the money or who spread this shit around, but I'll be damned if I'm going to let a bunch of ignorant, money-hungry shit heads dig up my friend."

"It doesn't matter if they do." Seeing that her words had no impact, Catherine walked over to step directly in front of Nick. "Did you hear me? I said it doesn't matter if they do dig him up. They're the ones who'll have that on their souls. Not you."

"Do you honestly believe that there's a God in the clouds somewhere who keeps track of these things so we don't have to?"

Catherine looked back at him and nodded solemnly. "Yes. I do."

Just then, Nick felt like a heel for asking that question as if it was a joke. Although Catherine made plenty of exceptions in order to live as his wife, she'd always kept her religion wrapped up securely inside of her. It wasn't ever forced down Nick's throat, but it was still there all the same.

"Sorry," Nick said. "I didn't mean it that way."

"Yes you did, but that's all right. I want you to tell me why you want to follow up on this so badly."

Nick stopped what he was doing and took a moment to compose his thoughts. At first, he figured he would just give her the short version, which would be more than he would give to anyone else. Then Nick remembered that Catherine wasn't just anyone else. The biggest difference between her and the rest of humanity was that she would actually listen to what he had to say.

"I've never had many friends," Nick said, "but Barrett was one of them. I may have had to be the one to send him off, but I sure as hell won't let someone disgrace him by digging him up and stealing what I gave to him."

"But those jewels . . . they're stolen. Aren't they?" Catherine asked.

"Whether they're stolen or if they belonged to his granddaddy doesn't matter. Whether he was a thief or a preacher doesn't matter. Whether he spent his last days shoveling dirt or trying to kill me doesn't matter. All that matters is that he was my friend and now he's dead. I've been earning my living as a mourner all these years, sending folks off to meet their Maker and carving their headstones. The least I can do is mourn my friend and see that he rests in peace."

Catherine didn't say anything for a while. She reached out to rub his arm as he was talking and kept her hand on him when he was through. Now, she gave his hand a squeeze and said, "I understand."

Nick blinked and waited for another shoe to drop. When it was clear there was nothing else coming, he asked, "You do?"

She nodded. "I may not agree, but I understand. If you've got to leave, then . . ." Catherine kept herself from finishing what she'd been saying when she heard a horse ride up to the front of the house and come to a stop.

Even before the horse had settled down, its rider slid from the saddle and landed loudly enough for the impact of his boots to be heard inside the house. "Nick? You in there?" a familiar voice called out.

Voicing the same words that were going through Nick's head, Catherine whispered, "It's Sheriff Stilson."

Nick felt the old impulse to bolt, which was exactly what he would have done in his younger days when a lawman came knocking at his door. Old habits were hard to break, but Nick choked down the reflex and let out a strained breath. "Whatever I say, you just keep quiet," he cautioned Catherine.

Catherine's face had been neutral before, but she now looked more worried with each second that passed. "What's the matter, Nick?"

"Stilson isn't here for a social call."

"Why? What happened?"

"You remember Switchback Gill?" Nick asked.

"Yes."

"He backed me into a corner and I had to kill him."

Catherine's eyes closed for a second before she started to nod. "If you need to leave, you'd better do it now."

At first, Nick was surprised. Then, he smiled and rubbed Catherine's shoulders. "That's awfully nice of you, but I'm going to face Stilson and tell him what happened."

"Why not just tell him that Gil was a threat? Plenty of folks from the Tin Pan will back you up."

As Catherine waited for an answer, Stilson knocked on the door.

"Stilson's a good man," Nick said quickly. "He's helped me plenty, but . . ."

"Never mind," Catherine said quickly. "You do what you need to do and get going. Just promise me you'll come home."

"Of course I promise."

With that, Nick took Catherine in his arms and kissed her as if he hadn't seen her for a year. Their mouths parted for a moment so their eyes could take in the sight of each other, and then Nick kissed her as if he wasn't going to see her for another year. Stilson knocked again, so Nick cut himself short and forced himself to go to the door. When he opened it, he must have still been a little flushed in the face.

"Oh," Stilson said. "Did I interrupt anything?"

"No, Sheriff."

"I guess you know why I'm here."

"It's either about the Jeffrey boys breaking those windows," Nick replied, "or that man I shot across from Don's gun shop."

Chuckling despite his best attempts not to, Stilson nodded and took his hat off so he could run his hand over his balding head. "It'd be the second one. I'd like to know why I heard about it from Don before hearing about it from you."

"The bastard made some threats that I had to check on before going through the proper chain of command."

"He say something against Catherine?" Stilson asked.

"Not specifically, but he threatened my wife and family."

"Why would he do something like that?"

"Because I recognized his face from a gang of thieves in the Dakotas and let him know he should think twice before starting any trouble around here," Nick said.

"You think he was planning a robbery?"

Nick shrugged. "I don't know if he was planning anything, Sheriff. I do know I put him on a friendly notice, he didn't like it too much, and then he decided to threaten my family."

"When did the shooting start?"

Without flinching, Nick replied, "The second he went for his gun."

Stilson kept his eyes on Nick for a few more seconds. His eyes were intense and calculating as he mulled over what he'd heard. Finally, he nodded and said, "Apart from the words that passed between you, I guess that matches up with what Don and the rest of them told me. I wish you would have come to me with this first, though. At the very least, you could have said something to the folks who saw you gun that fellow down. They was all plenty scared."

"I bet they were. Sorry about that."

As the sheriff kept his eyes on him, Nick could feel the lawman sizing him up. He'd felt it plenty of times before whenever he, Barrett and the rest of his old gang had ridden into a town, whether they were there to get something to eat or burn the whole place to the ground. In the old days, Nick might have had a few choice words to say under all that scrutiny. Now he stood there and let the other man come to whatever assumption he saw fit.

"Take a walk down there and clean up the mess," Stilson finally said. "You are the undertaker, after all. While you're at it, make it known who that asshole was. It'll do folks good to know he only got what was comin' to him. As for the rest of it, I suppose you did what needed to be done. Every lawman gets shit tossed his way, but that don't mean he needs to stand by and take it. If you say he went for his gun, then I believe you."

Hearing the pause in Stilson's voice, Nick replied, "He went for his gun, all right."

There was no lie to be seen upon Nick's face, so the sheriff nodded. "Then that's that. I'll expect you at my office to let me know when the street's cleaned up."

"Yes, sir."

Stilson put his hat back on and walked to his horse. After climbing into the saddle, he tossed a wave over his shoulder and rode back to town.

After making sure the lawman was gone, Nick closed the door and turned around to find Catherine standing in the same spot where he'd left her.

"Sounds like that went pretty well," she said from the bedroom's doorway.

"I think it did."

"It also sounds like you've got some work to do. Or were you planning on heading out before following that through?"

Nick shook his head. "I ain't about to shirk my duties, but I'll be leaving town after that."

"You're headed for the Dakotas?"

Nick nodded. "Yep. Barrett's grave is in the Badlands."

"What do you intend on doing once you get there?"

"I guess that depends on what I find. I'm hoping

to just take down any marker I might've left and see to it that nobody's able to find that grave even if they know where to look. If I find something different . . . then I'll just have to play whatever cards I'm dealt."

"How long will you be gone?"

Nick felt his stomach clench as the answer jumped into his head. "I can't say for certain, but it'll be a while. It's a long way to the Dakotas and I may have to make some odd turns to avoid cutting through too much Indian territory."

To Nick's surprise, Catherine smiled. She began tugging at the ribbons and strings that kept her dress cinched in tightly against the ample curves of her body. "Then maybe you should see to some of your other duties before you go. A husband can't just leave his wife for that long without giving her something to remember him by."

"No," Nick said as he walked to her. "He sure can't."

Catherine turned within his arms and pulled him into the bedroom.

Switchback Gil was still in the street when Nick finally got around to cleaning up. Someone had draped a blanket over the body, and the bit of street traffic, walking or riding, curved around it as if Gil were a rock in the middle of the road. Nick felt a little bad, simply because his duties as an undertaker were to make certain the departed weren't put through such indignities.

Then again, considering the kind of man Gil had been and what Nick had been doing in the meantime, the slip in professionalism was easily overlooked. Nick came along with his wagon, boxed Gil up into one of the coffins he'd made, and hauled it to his cemetery.

After spending a lifetime digging man-sized holes in the ground, Nick put Gil under a few feet of soil in no time at all. Since he knew it would be difficult to leave if he saw Catherine again, he decided against taking his wagon back and simply left it next to his workshop at the edge of the cemetery.

Nick saddled up Kazys, the younger of his two horses, and unhitched Rasa from the wagon. After scratching the older girl behind the ears, he led the horse in the direction of his house and gave her a smack on the rump. She would be able to find her way home.

As he watched, Nick couldn't help but be a little jealous.

NINE

Nick hated being on a train.

It wasn't a fear that some folks had of being hitched to a steam engine rolling over two iron bars. It wasn't a fear of Indians derailing the whole locomotive and sending him to a fiery death. It wasn't any sort of fear at all. It was more like a vicious annoyance at the entire process.

Sitting upon a bench that rattled beneath him for hours on end, Nick clenched his eyes shut as tightly as he clenched his fists. He knew there was no other way to get from California to the Dakotas with enough time to have a prayer of finding Barrett's grave ahead of the treasure hunters. If he'd ridden Kazys any farther than the train station, he would be in for the journey that had tested the resolve of so many wagon trains back in the great westward rush.

As much as Nick loved his new homeland, he sometimes cursed it for being so damn big. With that thought, Nick caught himself slipping into the mind-set he'd had when he'd looked at this country

for the first time. The tight confines of the passenger car and the constant motion of everything
around him were all too similar to the cramped
quarters of the leaky ship that had deposited Nick
and his father at Boston Harbor.

As a child, Nick and his parents had taken a
boat from the country where he'd been born. So
much had happened since then and so much had
changed that those days seemed more like a story
that someone had once told to him than a
memory.

To Nick's childish eyes, the ship had seemed as
big as a town even though he was forced to spend
most of his time in a space as big as a box. It was
stuffed to bursting with so many bodies that the
stench of them still lingered in the back of his
nose. Most of those bodies had been alive, but
that changed once a sickness swept through the
passengers stuffed below the decks. To this day,
Nick didn't know if those passengers were
supposed to be on that boat or if they'd been
allowed to board thanks to a corrupt captain
who'd taken their money and given them rotten
rations in return.

In the end, none of that truly mattered. The passengers had gotten sicker as the boat drew closer to
the Boston shore. By the time it bumped against
Nick's new homeland, the vessel was lighter thanks
to the dozens of bodies that had been dumped
overboard.

One of those bodies had belonged to Nick's

mother. After that, he'd told his father that he never wanted to see an ocean again. Although they'd had their differences over the years, the old man had kept his word and took Nick to grow up in the middle of the New World.

Nick sifted through his memories and tried not to think about the long train ride that was still ahead of him. His mood improved a bit, however, once he discovered the dining car while stretching his legs. When meals weren't being served, some of the tables were occupied by men who'd set up card games or women who wanted to get away from the occasionally rowdy general population of passengers.

Nick found a slightly more comfortable chair against a window that allowed him to watch the land roll past him in a blur of greens and browns. It was a softer time of day when the sun bathed the terrain in a red glow to make the window seem more like a painting. The easy smile on Nick's face lasted right up until he opened the window and caught a hot cinder in his eye. Shutting the window angrily, Nick swore he could hear someone laughing at him from one of the other tables.

Taking a moment to figure his distance to the Badlands, Nick toyed with the idea of stopping the train by any means necessary, taking Kazys from the livery car, and riding the rest of the way. The estimate Nick arrived at wasn't to his liking. The train ride would be long enough. If he rode to the Dakotas the more familiar way, he might as well let any number of grave robbers take their shot at Barrett's inheritance.

Nick got up from his chair and walked to the back of the car. The cool wind he felt when stepping between cars only reminded him of being in the saddle when Kazys had built up a full head of steam. When he found the sleeper car, he looked for a conductor.

"How much for a bed?" Nick asked.

The conductor was a happy fellow who walked the row of every car as if he was touring his own Promised Land. "Let me check to see if there are any left," he said. After flipping through a few pages on his small pad of paper, he tapped it with his finger and chirped, "We've got one open. It's . . ."

"I'll take it," Nick cut in as the conductor was trying to figure out which door to point to.

Nick didn't care how much he would have to pay for the compartment. When he heard the price, he handed some money over to the conductor and dragged himself through the narrow doorway.

The compartment wasn't much more than a closet with a view. There was a cot hanging from a wall, a window and a stool. Nick sat down on the cot, pulled the shade over the window and then closed his eyes. He drifted off to sleep eventually, but didn't get any better of a rest than when he'd dozed off while sitting on one of the benches with the rest of the passengers.

Whatever he'd paid for the room, Nick vowed he wouldn't pay it again.

* * *

Hours dragged into days.

Towns came and went.

The sun made its rounds in the sky.

There were plenty of stops and starts along the way. After a while, Nick stopped keeping track of them, since doing so only reminded him of how much longer he had to be cooped up in that damn crate on wheels. Just because he wasn't paying complete attention, however, didn't mean that he hadn't grown to learn the subtle sounds and feel of the train itself.

When it rattled and squealed this time, Nick knew something was wrong.

He was sitting on the bench that seemed to give him the fewest splinters, his head leaning against the window. As the train shook and the wheels screeched, Nick rubbed his eyes and forced himself to focus upon the window. Unlike the other times when he'd felt the train slow, there wasn't a station or even a platform in sight.

Cautiously opening the window, Nick looked outside. Since he didn't have any point of reference, it would have been just as helpful to guess where he was on the map by the position of the clouds in the sky.

"Hey," Nick said to the conductor who hurried down the aisle. "What's happening?"

"Just making a stop," the conductor replied.

"Where are we?"

"Wyoming."

"Where in Wyoming?" Nick growled.

For the first time since the train had left California, the conductor actually reacted to the gruff tone in Nick's voice. "Sir, you'll just have to stay here and be patient. I'm going to find out right now." With that, the conductor moved along to push his way past the rest of the anxious passengers.

Nick let out an aggravated sigh, but he couldn't blame the conductor for being terse. Even though he was sure someone in uniform would make some sort of announcement before too long, Nick wasn't very good at waiting. He also wasn't inclined to trust men in uniforms.

Nick's first impulse was to sit back down and try to think of something else while things were straightened out. That kept him appeased for all of three seconds before he was once more shifting and aching to get up.

He couldn't quite figure out what was bothering him until he took another long, deep breath.

Smoke.

He smelled smoke.

He hadn't been completely certain at first, but now that he'd pulled in enough of it for the taste to collect at the back of his throat, he would have staked his life on it. Nick went to the window again and looked outside. All he could see was the Wyoming landscape, and that didn't give him anything to go on. When he opened the window and stuck his head outside to get a look further up the tracks, the first things he saw were the backs of the heads of all the other people who were doing the same thing.

Even so, all Nick had to do was crane his neck to look upward in order to see the trail of black smoke snaking into the sky.

"God damn," Nick muttered as he tried to pull his head back into the train without losing an ear.

As he got up from his seat, Nick had to shove his way through a small crowd as more and more passengers struggled to get to a spot where they could get a better view of whatever was holding them up. Nick lost more patience with each step he took. Most of those other passengers seemed to be more concerned with finding another way to trip him up rather than the scent of smoke growing thicker in the air.

By the time he made it to the door leading out of the car, Nick practically exploded through it. Rather than step into the next car, he stepped to the edge of the iron grate separating him from a drop off the train. Nick held onto the grate and leaned out until he was well beyond the row of curious heads poking out from various windows. What he saw was almost enough to make him lose his grip on the rusted iron bar.

There was a fairly good-sized town in the distance, which was swarming with activity. People ran to and fro. Horses bolted in every direction and the sounds of screaming voices could occasionally be heard. All of that sunk into Nick's senses while his eyes soaked up the sight of the flames that engulfed an entire section of town.

"Good God," Nick whispered.

Now that he was outside, the smoke in the air was almost thick enough to choke on. He wondered just how long those flames had been burning. Nick wanted to ask someone what was going on. Part of him even considered hopping off the train while it was stopped so he could go find out.

The longer he watched those flames, the harder it was for him to look away.

They formed a constantly moving shape that leaped up and then dropped back down again. The air around the fire wavered as heat billowed out like an extension of the black plumes of smoke. The roar of the flames rubbed against Nick's ears, mingling with the high pitch of panicked screams.

The door to the next car came open and the conductor stepped through in such a hurry that he didn't even notice Nick was standing there.

"What's going on here?" Nick asked.

Jumping at the sound of Nick's voice, the conductor replied, "Town's on fire," and started pulling open the door to the car Nick had just left.

"I can see that. Did we stop to lend a hand?"

The conductor chuckled and leaned over the side to get another look for himself. "Doesn't look like there's much we can do about it. We stopped because the tracks are blocked. I didn't see exactly

what's blocking us, but I hear it's quite a mess."
He reached out once more for the door's handle,
paused and looked at Nick again. "I'd like to avoid
frightening the passengers any more than necessary. I'd appreciate it if you didn't . . . uh . . . fan
the flames, so to speak."

Recognizing an opportunity when he heard one,
Nick asked, "How much longer are we going to be
stuck on this train?"

"To be honest, I couldn't say. I got word that the
town's station isn't allowing anyone to leave the
trains."

"What?"

"There's some sort of riot going on." Squinting
at Nick, the conductor added, "Couldn't you hear
the gunshots? I thought that's why you were out
here."

Ever since the train had first gotten up to full
speed, Nick hadn't been able to hear much of anything else besides the roar of the engine, the grind-
ing of the wheels and the screaming of the kids in
the passenger cars. For the sake of this conversation, however, he nodded and said, "Of course I
heard them. I'd like to have a look for myself instead of sitting out here and waiting for the bullets
to start breaking windows."

"We might be stuck until they clear the track,
but that shouldn't take too long. At least we have
sleeper compartments."

"You let me and my horse out here and I'd sure
appreciate it."

The conductor blinked once and then said, "I just told you that we're not letting anyone disembark."

"Then maybe I should consider it my civic duty to let folks know exactly what's going on. If they ask my opinion, perhaps I should tell them whatever I may have gathered from talking to you. I'm sure they'd love to get the real story."

"You do that and I can have you detained," the conductor said sternly.

Nick dug into his pocket and pulled out a few dollars. Tucking them into the conductor's pocket, he said, "Then how about you do a favor for someone in a real hurry?"

"Fine," the conductor snapped. "If you're some sort of goddamn looter, you'll be shot on sight anyhow. Head to the livery car and I'll let you out."

Nick smiled for the first time since he'd been cooped up in that train. "That was easier than I expected."

"I've got more than enough to do without worrying about some lunatic who wants to make things worse," the conductor replied as the good humor drifted back into his voice. "You already paid for your ticket, so you can get off whenever you like. Try to keep quiet about this, though."

"You worried about catching hell from the engineer?" Nick asked.

"No. I'm worried that you might start a rush of more folks wanting to get off this train."

"Even with the shots and the fire?"

Rolling his eyes and nodding, the conductor said, "You'd be amazed at how stupid folks get when they get scared."

That drew Nick's eyes back toward the chaos happening in the town. "Maybe. Maybe not."

"If you don't make it back before we get moving again, you're on your own. I can give you a slip so you can catch the next train and that can carry you the rest of the way into Cheyenne. That is where you were headed, right?"

"That's right."

"You sure about this, mister? Things look awfully rough out there."

"I wouldn't have them any other way."

TEN

The town's name was Rock Springs. Nick read it on a sign that was still in pristine condition not too far ahead of the train. When he looked over his shoulder, he saw the side of the livery car was already shut tight. There were still plenty of folks sticking their heads out the windows and Nick could only imagine the questions they were throwing at that poor conductor who'd given the okay for Nick to leave.

Kazys must have hated the train ride as much as Nick, because the horse had bounded from the car without even noticing that the ramp hadn't been lowered. Only the shots, the screams and the roaring fire ahead brought the horse to a stop. Nick tugged on the reins to settle Kazys down a bit, and made a bit more progress by rubbing the horse's ear.

"It's all right, boy," Nick said. "I ain't out of my mind. When you see this much hell in front of you, it's always better to be on the move instead of cooped up in a goddamn box."

Kazys let out a gruff breath and shook his head.

"Or, maybe I am a little out of my head," Nick added. "Either way, at least we're off that train."

When he closed his eyes, Nick actually felt his nerves settle. The sounds drifting from Rock Springs weren't exactly comforting, but they beat the hell out of rattling around with the rest of the passengers like a bunch of moths knocking against the inside of a crate.

When he opened his eyes, Nick focused on bits and pieces of the chaotic picture in front of him. In the old days, Nick hadn't been too interested in fires that he hadn't started. After spending some time living in a town rather than robbing it, Nick knew that every spare hand could be put to good use in a situation like this. Considering the shots that he heard crackling through the air, Nick figured he could be of some use in other aspects as well.

Just as he was about to snap his reins, Nick heard a shot come from somewhere a hell of a lot closer than the town. In fact, the sound of the shot was accompanied by the whistle of a bullet whipping past his head. Nick reflexively hunkered down and snapped Kazys's reins to get the horse moving.

"That's right!" someone shouted from not too far away. "You better keep runnin,' you Chink bastard!"

Another shot was fired at Nick's back as he touched his heels to Kazys's sides and rode back toward the tracks. Now that he was moving along the tracks, Nick got a much better view of what had brought the locomotive to a stop. A wrecked wagon with only two wheels lay piled upon the tracks. The front end of that wagon was wedged into the ground and there were several other piles of broken planks and lumber around the wreck.

Nick's attention was quickly diverted to the men who were circling the wreck. A few of those men were on foot and running back to the train. Another three were on horseback and they seemed to be defending the obstruction. Every one of those riders held guns and one of them had taken a shot at Nick.

The first man to get close to Nick wasn't one of the armed riders. He ran toward the train, waving his arms, wearing a dirty pair of coveralls and a filthy bandanna wrapped around his neck. "Get the hell away from there!" he shouted. "Those men are crazy!"

Nick rode around so that he was between the man in the coveralls and the ones doing the shooting. After drawing his pistol, Nick took a few shots at the men on horseback. That scattered them just long enough for Nick to rein Kazys to a stop and offer his hand to the man in the coveralls.

"You trying to get back to that train?" Nick asked.

The man took Nick's hand and climbed onto Kazys's back behind him. "Hell yes. I'm the engineer. Them others and I were just trying to see about clearing that track." He winced as Nick fired a few more shots to keep the other horsemen at bay. "They'll be killed if they don't get back."

"I've got you with me, so you're heading back first," Nick said as he pointed Kazys toward the train and snapped his reins. "I'll see what I can do for the rest after that."

"Better be quick. There's plenty more of them crazy bastards around here."

Nick had plenty of questions by the time they reached the train, but the engineer climbed down from the saddle and scrambled up into his spot behind the train's controls. Nick lost sight of him, but figured he was as safe as he could be, wrapped up in all that iron. Turning Kazys back around, Nick got the horse moving toward the wreck.

Two of the other horsemen were now riding straight toward Nick. Between them, there was another man dressed in a similar fashion as the engineer. The other man in coveralls ran as fast as his legs would carry him. Since he knew all of those gunmen's horses could run a lot faster than a fellow in coveralls, Nick charged straight toward the other two.

Bullets hissed through the air as the two men on horseback fired at Nick again and again.

Nick kept his head down and his gun ready, but didn't pull his trigger. Although the bullets around him were getting closer, they were still far enough off the mark for him to remain confident. Once he had a clean shot, Nick lifted his gun and fired as if he was simply pointing to the spot where he wanted the bullet to go.

The lead from Nick's modified Schofield clipped one of the horseman's elbows, spinning his entire body around as if an unseen claw had taken a swipe at him. Between the bullet and the movement of his own horse, it was less than a second before the gunman lost his balance completely and dropped to the ground. He landed with a thump, tried to get up and then flopped down again, letting out a pained groan.

Flipping the reins to his gun hand so he could pull them to the right, Nick rode around the man in coveralls and offered his left arm. The man grabbed onto his arm and held on so tightly that Nick thought it might get pulled from its socket. Some pain flared in Nick's shoulder but ended as soon as the man hauled himself up onto the saddle.

"Go!" the man shouted as he lay awkwardly across Kazys's rump.

"You all right back there?" Nick asked.

"Just go!"

Nick fired a shot at the other rider, who'd turned away from him as soon as his partner had been dropped.

Once he was within a yard or two of the train, Nick came to a stop and let the man slide off of Kazys's backside. "How many more of you are out there?" Nick asked.

"Just one," he replied after seeing the engineer

climb down from his cabin. "If he ain't already dead."

That was all Nick needed to hear. He turned Kazys around, snapped the reins and got the horse moving toward the wreck. This time, however, he couldn't see the other horseman or the other member of the train's crew. Nick held his gun at the ready as he pulled back on the reins to keep Kazys from charging straight into an ambush.

When he saw something big moving around behind the wreck, Nick reflexively fired a shot at it. He pulled his aim slightly to one side, which caused a chunk of wood fly into the air. That was enough to force the horseman out from where he'd been hiding. Just then, the third horseman swung around the other side of the wreck while firing his gun at a short fellow wearing work pants and a dirty shirt.

Nick fired to scare the rider away from the remaining member of the train's crew, but all he did was catch the rider's attention.

The rider fired a quick shot at Nick, shouting, "Go to hell with the rest of yer Chink friends!"

Although the rider was a god-awful shot, Nick wasn't about to stand by until he got lucky. He shifted his aim, pulled his trigger and felt the modified Schofield buck against his palm. Nick's shot caught the rider in the chest and knocked him straight back and off his horse as if he'd been kicked by a mule.

Seeing that was more than enough to send the

other rider in the opposite direction. As he dug his heels into his horse's sides, the rider shouted, "You're dead, asshole! You and all those goddamn Chinks are dead!"

Nick rode up to the man in the work clothes and offered his hand. This time, he was able to get the man somewhat situated on Kazys's back rather than draping him over the horse like a sack of flour. "Are you hurt?" Nick asked.

"My arm's shot, but I'll be all right. Just get me out of here."

Nick wasn't about to argue. He brought the man back to the train. The other two were there waiting for him, so Nick asked, "What was all that about?"

"We were just going to see about clearing the track," the engineer replied. "The three of us headed out there to have a look when them sons of bitches rode up and fired at us."

"Why'd they do that?"

"I don't know. What I do know is that I ain't about to sit here any longer than I have to. I'll drive straight through that mess rather than stay put and get shot at."

Nick glanced around and said, "Looks like they're gone for now, but I wouldn't count on them staying away for long. I'll see what I can do about that mess."

"You already done plenty, mister," the conductor said as the other two men nodded in agreement.

"Well, I'm not done yet. Neither are you men. I'll need at least one of you to come along with me. My guess is you're the man I'm after," Nick said while nodding to the second man he'd brought to the train. "You don't look wounded."

"I ain't," the man replied. "At least, not yet."

Nick had already replaced the spent shells in his Schofield with fresh ones from his gun belt. "Good. I'll try to keep it that way. Come on."

Even though he didn't seem too excited by the prospect of heading back out there, the worker nodded and climbed onto Kazys's back behind Nick.

"What's your name?" Nick asked.

"Earl."

"Hang on, Earl. I didn't save your life just to toss it away again."

"I sure hope not."

Nick barely had to shake the reins to get Kazys moving again. Between the shooting and all the people climbing on and off of him, the horse was more than a little anxious. Using that in his favor, Nick got over to the wreck and circled it a few times in a matter of seconds.

From what he could see, the wagon's rear wheels were mostly intact. The garbage piled up around the wagon made it look a whole lot worse than it was, but the front axle was most definitely beyond repair.

"Clear away that wood," Nick said as he climbed down from the saddle.

Earl dropped down beside him and immediately got to work. "That's what I was doing when those assholes showed up shooting the hell out of this place."

"Then go ahead and commence. I think I can move this wagon a bit."

"It won't have to be more than maybe five feet or so," Earl said as he picked up another large hunk of wood and tossed it away from the tracks. "As long as the wagon's wheels are clear, the train should be able to push the rest of it aside."

"Sounds like a plan."

Nick led Kazys around to the back of the wagon and then took the rope that was hanging from his saddle. He looped one end of the rope several times around the saddle horn and then dropped to one knee so he could tie the other end around the wagon's rear axle. Even though his knots were strong and Kazys had pulled loads a lot bigger than this one, Nick still wasn't happy with the sight in front of him.

"You think that'll work?" Earl asked as he tossed away the last large piece of lumber and brushed himself off.

Nick shook his head. "I don't know, but we'll need to do more than stand here thinking about it."

Just then, Nick spotted what could have been the armed horsemen riding around for another attack. One of them was slumped in his saddle as if he'd taken a hard fall, and the other was anxiously pointing toward the wrecked wagon. Unfortunately, there were more horsemen gathering around those other two.

"If we're gonna get this done, we need to do it quick," Nick said.

Earl ran around to the front of the wagon. "Come on over here," he said as he lowered himself to get his shoulder beneath one end of the singletree, the pivoting crosspiece to which the tracings of a harness would normally fasten. "The two of us should be able to get this thing rolling."

Even as Nick positioned himself, he had his doubts about lifting all that weight. Then again, the wagon didn't look half as imposing without so much extra lumber piled around it. By the time he got his shoulder in place and his feet planted, Nick realized that the wagon was about the same size as the one he'd left with Catherine.

"On three," Earl said. "One. . .two. . ."

"Wait a minute," Nick interrupted. Before Earl could ask about the delay, Nick drew his gun and fired a few rounds at the horsemen.

There were half a dozen of them gathered not too far away and they scattered as hot lead was sent flying in their direction.

"All right," Nick said as he got his shoulder back into place. "Three!"

With that, both men began straightening their legs while letting out a long, strained breath.

Nick could feel his muscles burning under his

skin as if every last one of them had been doused
in kerosene and put to a match. He kept the pain
going, however, by forcing his legs to straighten
even more as he fought to lift his part of the
wagon.

Beside Nick, Earl lowered his head and raised
the singletree just enough to cause the wheel on his
side to budge. "Come on!" he shouted. "Just a bit
more."

Knowing that he'd only have to start all over
again if he gave up now, Nick gritted his teeth and
raised his side some more. Fortunately for him and
all of his muscles, Nick now had his side of the
wagon as high off the ground as Earl's. Nick lifted
his chin and let out a gruff holler toward the
back.

Kazys responded to Nick's voice and immediately started moving in the direction he'd been
pointed. As soon as the horse took up the slack in
the rope tied to his saddle horn, Kazys dug his
hooves into the dirt and pulled even harder.

With the combined efforts of one horse and two
men, the wagon groaned and rumbled away from
the tracks. Nick could feel his knees aching with
every shuffling fraction of a step he took. Earl
didn't seem to be doing much better, but he struggled through until the wagon had rolled another
couple of feet.

"That should be . . . good enough," Earl said.

Just to be safe, Nick kept pushing for a bit longer.
"All right," he said. "Lower it."

Both men stopped and eased the wagon down again. As soon as he was free from under the splintered wood, Nick ran around to let Kazys know he could stop pulling. Nick untied the rope from the saddle horn and tossed it away. By this time, the nearby horsemen had begun firing at him.

"Is that good enough?" Nick asked.

"Should be," Earl said. "Now, let's get the hell out of here!"

Nick didn't need to be told twice. He climbed into the saddle and Earl climbed on behind him. As he snapped the reins, Nick fired a few shots at the horsemen. He didn't even bother to see if he'd hit anything before facing forward and urging Kazys to go faster.

The horse got them to the train in a matter of seconds and Earl climbed up into the cab of the locomotive. Already, smoke was pouring from the pistons stack and the other men inside the engine were hurrying about their tasks.

"If you're coming along, you'd best hop on board," the engineer said. "If I get going, I ain't about to slow down until I get far away from here!"

"Go on ahead," Nick said. "I'll cover your back."

"You sure about that?"

"Yeah. Just go."

The engineer leaned out to quickly shake Nick's hand. Before Nick could back away from the engine, it was already beginning to roll forward.

Nick reloaded his gun, rode ahead of the train and crossed the tracks. Some of the horsemen were working their way toward him, but backed up as soon as they saw Nick heading in their direction. They fired a few nervous shots as they gathered their courage. Instead of waiting for them to work themselves into a lather, Nick touched his heels to Kazys's sides and charged forward with his gun blazing.

Nick stormed straight into the armed horsemen as if he fully intended on riding over the barrels of their drawn guns. He started by firing a few shots over their heads, which scared a few of them off. The ones who kept their composure enough to hold their ground and take aim were the first to be shot from their saddles.

Two of the horsemen dropped before the train smashed through the rest of the refuse blocking the track. The wagon was knocked aside and rolled away as broken crates and splintered boards were sent flying.

For a few seconds, every one of Nick's senses felt like they were burning.

Once the train passed, Nick was left to feel the heat of the nearby fires drifting over his face. In a strange way, he preferred that to sitting next to that damn window.

ELEVEN

───────◆───────

Nick didn't pull back on his reins until he was in town. Rock Springs wasn't the biggest town he'd seen, but it was spread out enough for him to find a section that wasn't in chaos. Even with the flames turning the sky a dull orange in spots, the streets where Nick came to a stop were fairly quiet. Holding his gun at the ready, Nick shifted in his saddle to look for a target.

All he found were some frightened folks trying to hide from him.

After holstering his gun, Nick moved along and turned a corner so he could get another look at the train tracks. Now that the train had moved on, the horsemen didn't seem too interested in guarding the area. Before Nick could move on, however, he saw a pair of men shuffling toward the tracks. They waved at someone who was out of Nick's line of sight.

Sure enough, another old wagon was slowly creeping toward the tracks.

"Son of a bitch," Nick muttered.

The stubborn streak inside of him wanted nothing more than to chase those men away and roll that wagon over their backs.

The rest of him knew that another set of nameless men would probably just show up a little later to roll another old wagon into that very same spot.

With a sigh that he'd only heard come out of his father when the old man's patience had been stretched to its limit, Nick turned his back on the railroad tracks and rode into Rock Springs.

"You should've stayed on that train, mister."

Nick looked toward the sound of that voice and didn't see anyone right away. Then, after taking a second and third glance, he spotted an old woman sitting on a nearby porch. She was so small that she barely stood out as being separate from the chair she occupied.

"It looked like you had some trouble," Nick said. "I saw the fires."

"Yeah?" the old lady huffed. "What business is it of yours?"

Nick didn't really know what to say to that.

"Are you one of the Federals?" she asked. Lifting her head seemed to require more energy than the old lady had, but she strained and grunted through the task anyway. After examining Nick's face through clouded eyes, she slumped back into her chair and added, "You sure as hell don't look like no Chinese."

"Some men were blocking up the railroad tracks.

They were spouting off about Chinese, too. What the hell is going on here?"

"You ain't heard?"

A large group of men marching down the street carrying shotguns caught Nick's eye. His hand dropped reflexively to the gun at his side, but he didn't clear leather.

As the men got closer, their gaze drifted toward Nick. A few of them shifted and the barrels of their shotguns wandered in his direction, but then they looked away. Without saying a word, they kept right on moving and then finally turned a corner.

"No need to get so fidgety," the old woman said. "They ain't after you."

"How do you know?"

She looked up at him as if Nick had just asked her how she knew where the ground was. "Because you ain't Chinese," she said.

"Hasn't anyone around here seen a Chinaman before?"

"They seen too many of 'em. That's the problem," she said, rocking back and forth in her chair. "The mining company decided to replace all the local boys with Chinese to keep their profits up. Them slope-eyed workers take less money and don't mind putting good men out of work."

"Doesn't sound like the Chinese had much of a choice in the matter."

The woman looked up at Nick as if she was about to spit on him. Then she shrugged and said,

"Maybe not. Either way, it don't matter much anymore. Most of Chinatown's burnt down."

Looking over to the glow of flames in the distance, Nick muttered, "That'll learn 'em."

"That'll drive 'em the hell out of town is what it'll do," she said angrily. "And it'll show the mining companies that we won't sit back and let good folks get run out of their jobs just so a few cents can be saved on hiring workers that don't belong around here no how."

"I heard shooting," Nick said. "My guess is that the mining companies are letting you know what they think about your little statement."

"Ain't my statement. I'm just sitting here watching how things turn out. The statement you're hearing would be Francis Hale's."

"Who's he?"

"Used to be the foreman of some organized miners or something like that. Now, he's the fellow that's putting up ten dollars of his own money for every dead Chinese that's brought to him."

"Jesus," Nick said.

The old woman shook her head and scratched her chin. "Jesus ain't anywhere near Rock Springs, mister. Not for right now, anyway."

Gritting his teeth, Nick asked, "What about the railroad tracks?"

"What about 'em?"

"They're being blocked. Why's that?"

She shrugged. "I just sit here and watch." The old woman laughed until she hacked a mess up in the back of her throat. After spitting onto the ground, she said again, "You want my opinion, you should'a stayed on that train. What the hell would possess you to stay here?"

Before Nick could come up with an answer, the old woman stared down at his mangled hands and grinned. Nodding, she said, "Ah, I see you been through your share of hell already. Once you been tossed into the fire, it ain't easy to live outside of it."

As much as Nick wanted to refute what she was saying, he simply couldn't. Her words struck like a set of fangs that sank into him and only drove in deeper the more he tried to be rid of them.

"You'll probably want to see Mister Hale," she said. "Most of the men who got the sand to keep walking these bloody streets want to see him. He's at the Central Mining Office, down the street. Just head that way and make a right. You can't miss it, seeing as how it's one of the only damned things on that street that ain't burned down yet."

Something within the old woman's scratchy voice struck him like a kick in the backside. It was the tone used by any mother or grandmother to shoo her little ones out of the kitchen, only this time it was being used to move someone toward a riot. Before Nick could take more than a few steps away, he stopped and turned back around to face her.

"Have there been others coming through here looking for this kind of work?" he asked.

"What kind? Mining or shooting Chinese?"

"The second one," Nick replied with a distasteful snarl.

"More'n I care to admit." When she spoke those last few words, the old woman showed the first traces of genuine sorrow. At that moment, the fire seemed to cast her face in a deeper glow and the twitches in the corners of her eyes were perfectly timed to the gunshots being fired in the distance.

Finding a stable for Kazys wasn't as difficult as Nick had expected. All he needed to do was head away from the noise and flames, find a spot that wasn't under attack and look for a livery with horses inside of it. As long as other folks had a vested interest in the place, Nick figured that was as safe as he was apt to get. Since the stable he'd found wasn't anywhere near Chinatown, Nick hoped it would be suitable for a just a little while.

Of course, he knew he could always keep the saddle on Kazys's back and put Rock Springs far behind him. In fact, that's exactly what nearly every piece of good sense in his head was screaming at him to do. Under other circumstances, he might have followed that advice to the letter. But Nick had already been shot at, chased down and nearly killed by the lunatics of Rock Springs. None of that sat too well with him and the notion of letting those assholes get away with what they were doing sat like a rock in the bottom of his gut.

As much as he would have liked to preach the

loftier motives, Nick knew there was one thing in particular that kept him from leaving Rock Springs. That town had a major railroad line rolling right through it. Without that railroad line, it could be months before Nick found his way back home again. Riding back to California wasn't impossible, but it sure as hell wouldn't be ideal, and it could very well be the last ride of Kazys's life.

Keeping those things in mind, Nick patted the horse's nose as he shut the gate on the stall Kazys was forced to share with another stallion. The Arabian in there with Kazys was a fine animal and wouldn't have been left there unless his owner had some confidence in the facility. He didn't seem to mind Kazys being in there with him, so that's where Nick left him.

Nick stuck his head outside to make certain nobody had seen him enter the stable, just in case there were some looters who weren't interested in Chinatown. As far as he could tell, the streets were empty.

Retracing his steps so he could follow the directions the old lady had given him, Nick moved from one street to another. He could feel the heat from the raging fires on his skin. The sound of the flames was a constant roar that reminded him of how the sea had sounded from within the battered hull of a ship. For the moment, the screams had faded away. The gunshots, however, erupted every so often like a pack of firecrackers that had been tossed into the street.

Nick's eyes narrowed to try and focus on some shapes that were moving within a darkened building across the street. Turning on the balls of his feet, he crouched down and slapped his hand against the grip of his modified Schofield. As much as he tried to see more, all Nick could make out was a pair of figures crawling toward the front. Nick moved cautiously toward them.

"Don't kill us!" one of the men said. "Please. We will leave. Just don't shoot again."

"I never shot the first time," Nick said. "What happened to you?"

The man fought to move forward another few steps, reached out with one hand and then fell face-first onto the boardwalk just outside the door.

Nick could hear repressed sobbing coming from behind the unmoving figure. He stepped forward and only had to look at the face of the person lying on the ground to know there was nothing he could do to help him. He'd seen plenty of Chinamen in his day, but Nick Graves had seen even more dead men. The figure lying in the doorway was both.

Kneeling over the body, Nick looked further into the shadows and spotted the second figure huddled against a wall. "What happened?" Nick demanded. "Who did this?"

"You know who did it!" the woman shouted as she snapped her head forward just far enough for her to be seen. "You come here to take his body for money! Just take it and take me, too, if that's what you want."

Nick found himself backing away from the dead man.

"Take him!" she screamed.

Suddenly, from deeper within the building, there came the sound of wood cracking and splintering under what sounded like the blow of a large hammer. Heavy steps thudded through the room, causing the woman to sob and scramble on all fours away from the sound.

Stepping over the dead body, Nick found himself inside a modestly decorated home. There were a few pieces of furniture here and there, as well as a couple of exotic statues and small paintings. Nick recognized the style of the decorations as Chinese, but didn't know much more about them than that. He didn't have to know a thing about the Chinese woman cowering on the floor to know she was scared out of her mind.

Her mouth was moving but no words came out. Her eyes were clenched shut and she was curled up in a ball as if every single one of her muscles had seized up.

"There you are," said a man who walked into the room from somewhere in the back of the house. "I knew you wouldn't leave this place all by yourself."

The man who spoke had a face full of stubble and a thick, untrimmed mustache hanging down over his lip. His voice filled the room like swamp gas and was tainted by a thick Louisiana accent. "Who might you be?" he asked Nick.

"I'm new in town," Nick said.

"Heard the commotion, did ya?"

"Sure did. My train was stuck here and I needed to make sure it keeps moving along."

"Yours too?" he asked with a surprised look on his face. "My train got stopped not too long ago. Then again, with all that's been happening, it's kinda hard to say just how long I been here."

Nick had spotted the gun in the man's hand the moment the guy entered the room. Now all he wanted was to position himself between the gun and the Chinese woman before they were introduced to each other in a violent fashion.

"That one dead?" the man asked as he nodded toward the body lying half in and half out of the house.

"Yeah," Nick replied.

"Good." Without another word or even a shift in his expression, the man brought his arm up an inch or so and fired a shot into the Chinese woman's head. "You carry the heavier of the two and I'll split the reward with you."

Nick wanted nothing more than to draw his gun and put that killer down like the mad dog he was. He kept himself in check, though he was shocked at what he'd just seen. Although the other man's gun arm had been fast, what had caught Nick off guard even more was the complete lack of expression on the gunman's face. He killed that woman as if he was just stretching his arm, before Nick could do a damn thing about it.

Unfortunately, it was too late to save either of the Chinese people lying on the floor. Their killer was obviously in on whatever insanity was going on in Rock Springs, which made Nick want to play along to see what more he could do than just take a shot at this one man.

The man nodded and grinned when he saw Nick stoop down to heft the Chinese man's body over his shoulder. "Don't worry about splitting the reward. There's plenty more of them Chinese runnin' about."

"I'd like to know who I'm splitting it with."

"Name's Alan Kinman. Pleased to meet ya."

TWELVE

———◆———

After taking a few odd turns and cutting through a couple of alleys, Nick found himself walking straight toward the Central Mining Company. Kinman led him there as if he'd been born and raised in Rock Springs. Whenever shooting sparked up along the way, Kinman didn't even flinch. As they got closer to the raging fires, he seemed to revel in the heat.

Nick followed Kinman's lead right up to the mining office's front stoop. Once there, Kinman dropped the Chinese woman's body onto the boards as if he was delivering a sack of grain. Although Nick wanted to follow suit, he couldn't force himself to be so disrespectful. He was quick about it, but he set the man down gently and shut his eyelids.

"We got two more for ya," Kinman shouted into the office.

In response to that announcement, a tall man with dark bushy hair walked outside. His face was decorated with a slender mustache and a sprout of whiskers just beneath the middle of his bottom lip. He smiled as if his teeth were a bit too big for his jaw and nodded approvingly when he saw the fresh kills piled upon his porch. "You sure as hell do, Alan. I'm starting to think you're trying to wring me of every dollar I got."

"You don't wanna pay, you'd better let me know right now, because I intend on heading right back out after this."

The man stuck a few fingers into the pocket of an expensive pearl gray vest and dug out a wad of bills. "I got you covered for a while longer," he said as he peeled twenty dollars off of the wad. "Who's your friend?"

"Don't know," Kinman said. "I didn't ask."

"I'm Nicolai," Nick said in a clipped tone, hoping they didn't pry any further.

They didn't.

"Francis Hale," the man in the nice suit said. "I'm the founder of this feast. I take it you're new to town?"

"Just arrived."

"Not by train, I know that for damn sure," Francis said smugly.

"I'm passing through on my way to Cheyenne," Nick said. "I won't be staying long."

"Just collecting on some easy money, eh? Well, just know that you're lending a hand to a hell of a good cause. The folks who think they can slap some damn Chinese devils into a spot that used to be filled by an honest Christian will remember what's been happening here in Rock Springs. Once the Federals try to get here with the next shipment of them Chink bastards, they'll be begging for the way things used to be."

Nick glanced over to his right, where Kinman was standing. The rough-looking man rubbed a hand over the harsh stubble on top of his head. Dirt was smeared upon his scalp and face, but wasn't thick enough to mask the annoyed expression that showed up as he rolled his eyes.

"He can make all the faces he wants," Francis said, pointing at Kinman. "He don't live here. He don't know how many good men gave all their good years to work in these mines, only to have their livelihoods stripped away on account of some slant-eyes who'll do it cheaper."

"You really think the Federals will listen to this?" Nick asked. Although he'd been expecting to catch some hell for the question, Nick wanted to see how Francis would deliver his answer.

Surprisingly enough, Francis grinned and said, "They will when they try to ship in their troops and replacement workers on a stretch of blown-up track. And they sure as hell will take notice when the only Chinese that're left in this town are the dead ones piled up behind this very building."

"If you're done with your speech," Kinman said, "then we've got some more bodies to collect."

Francis nodded and held onto the edges of his vest like a politician posing for the camera. "I won't stand in your way. Just be careful, because

Sheriff Young is out with the rest of the fucking Chinese sympathizers to make our job harder."

Turning his back to the mining office and leading Nick into the street, Kinman looked over and grumbled under his breath, "Them sympathizers he's talking about would be the Fire Brigade and they're mainly out to douse the flames that the assholes on Hale's payroll got started."

"What about the rest of what he was saying?" Nick asked.

Kinman led him down the street a way before glancing over at Nick. "You'll have to refresh my memory. Hale talks an awful lot and if he ain't talking about money, I ain't listening."

"I wouldn't let him hear you say that," Nick told him. "He seems like the sort to get upset when he hears his men bad-mouthing him that way."

After letting out a quick grunt of a laugh, Kinman said, "I've only been in town for less than a day and I sure as hell ain't one of his men. I was on an eastbound train just like you that got stopped. Only reason I got off is because Hale was shouting that there was money to be made."

"That's a hell of a lot better than the reception I got," Nick told him. "All I heard was gunshots. How'd you get your train moving again?"

"I didn't. Hale stopped us and fed everyone his line about the mining companies and the Chinese. There was one fella who meant to come here, so he got off. I figured I was close enough to my destination that I could ride my horse the rest of the way if it meant earning some money while I was here. After that, Hale gave the word and his boys cleared the track." Kinman lowered his voice a bit as he asked, "That ain't how it happened for you?"

Nick shook his head. "The tracks are blocked off and guarded by armed men. I had to fight through those assholes just so the train could pass."

"And you didn't ride along with it?"

"Nah," Nick replied with a forced smirk. "I always did have a weakness for fireworks."

"You want my opinion, I'd say you made a hell of a good choice. There's some real money to be made here."

"Ten dollars a head for killing Chinamen? I can think of a lot easier ways to make a lot more money."

"What about a thousand dollars for blowing those Federals to hell?"

Whether he was thinking about collecting the money or not, Nick couldn't help but be startled by that. "A thousand?"

"And for becoming a man wanted for disrupting government process or whatever the hell else they try to call it once it's done. Basically, you'd be taking a bullet for Hale once folks start spreadin' the blame around."

"Is that kind of heat worth a thousand dollars?"

"It is if you do it right," Kinman said. "The way

I got it figured, we might not even be spotted before this thing is done. The money will still be ours and we're the hell out of this shit hole."

"We?"

Holding out his hand, Kinman nodded once and said, "Sure. You got a stomach for this."

"What makes you so sure?"

"First of all, you got off that train of yours when everyone else had to have been shaking in their boots and crying for mercy." As Kinman took a breath, a distant rumble marked the collapse of a building in another part of town. "Second," he said without so much as looking in the direction of the rumble, "the way you hefted that body over your shoulder. It shows you ain't the squeamish sort."

"I've worked with plenty of dead folks."

"Yeah. I just bet you have."

Pausing for a moment, Nick said, "I'm a mourner."

"A what?"

Even though there was a more official and complete explanation, Nick let it slide with, "It's like an undertaker." Once that was said, Nick took a more careful look at the hand Kinman was still extending to him. His fingers were curled around a messy wad of money. Nick snatched it from him and worked his fingers through the bills. His half of the money was all there. As much as he wanted to toss it into the street or even back into Kinman's face, Nick shoved the cash into his pocket.

"Oh, I see," Kinman said. "So, do most under-takers see folks get shot right in front of them?" Glancing over at Nick as they walked another couple of paces, Kinman waited before answering his own question. "I didn't think so. Whatever your line of work is, I'd say you're the man I'm looking for. At least, for the hour or two it'll take to get this cakewalk over and done with."

"You call this a cakewalk?" Nick asked.

"For me and you? Sure. For them . . ." Kinman said as he nodded ahead to where a small group of people was huddled, ". . . not hardly."

Nick could tell the group had already seen him and Kinman coming. There were four of them crammed into a small alcove between a laundry and a store displaying men's suits. All of them were Chinese and dressed in black or gray pants with simple white shirts. Two were children and the other two were a man and woman who'd posi-tioned themselves to try and keep the little ones from view.

Kinman walked with his hand resting upon his holstered gun. His arm looked relaxed, but the muscles from his shoulder all the way down to his fingertips were as tense as bowstrings. Nick knew that much because he'd walked that same way plenty of times and could recognize it in someone else. If he had any doubts, all Nick had to do was look at the hungry sparkle in Kinman's eyes.

"See what I mean?" Kinman whispered. "Plenty of money to be made here."

Nick reached out to hold him back with an out-stretched arm. As soon as Kinman's eyes snapped toward him, Nick said, "Let me take these."

"Sure," Kinman replied. "We was gonna split the money anyhow. Better make it quick, though. They already seen us comin'."

Nick's eyes darted up and down, left and right before centering back upon his main target. In the space of a few heartbeats, Nick had sized up as much as he could regarding the people around him, what could go wrong and routes that could best be used for escape. Even as he was looking for all of those things, Nick could feel the other man getting more and more anxious beside him.

"Stand back," Nick said as he stepped forward and in front of Kinman. Drawing his pistol, Nick took aim and fired a shot as he moved toward the Chinese family cowering at the mouth of the narrow alley.

Nick's shot punched into the wall several inches to the left of the Chinese man's head. Fixing his eyes upon him, Nick rushed forward with his gun held in front of him and his chin stuck out even farther. Sure enough, it was the Chinese man's first impulse to take a swing at Nick with a balled fist.

Even though the punch had some strength behind it, there wasn't nearly enough to put Nick down. Nick snapped his head back just long enough to get a look behind him. Kinman was standing a few paces back to watch the show. When Nick looked back at the Chinese man, he hissed, "Hit me again."

The Chinese man was so stunned that Nick wondered if he even understood English. Either the man understood just fine or he was fighting mad, because he quickly took another swing at Nick.

As that punch glanced off his jaw, Nick got a better look at the rest of the family as well as the spot they were in. The opening between the buildings could barely be called an alley. It was so narrow that the two children were just able to squeeze into it. The Chinese woman looked as though she might be able to squeeze through, but the man would have a bit more trouble.

"Run," Nick said as he gave the Chinese man a punch that wasn't much more than a tap on the chest. "Find somewhere to hide and don't come out till this passes over."

"You will shoot," the Chinese man said.

"Just over your heads as you go." He could feel Kinman's patience wearing thin, so Nick made some noise by slamming his shoulder against the wall, adding, "I could have killed you already. Just hit me, run and make it look good."

The Chinese man looked past Nick at Kinman. That was enough to spur him on, and he delivered a chopping blow to Nick's stomach that legitimately doubled him over. From there, the man shoved his wife in front of him so they could both throw themselves into the narrow alleyway.

As he straightened up, Nick saw Kinman moving up next to him. Nick acted as if he didn't know where the other man was so he could pass off his next move as an accident. He let out a few vicious curses, stepped back and knocked into Kinman along the way. Bringing up his pistol, Nick stepped back and fired into the alley. His first shot hissed straight down the alley and well over the family's heads. His next shot tore through the side of one building and his third sent a bunch of splinters flying from the other wall.

Besides causing a whole lot of noise, Nick's shots also filled the narrow space between the buildings with gritty black smoke. A lot more of it rolled straight back into the faces of the two men still standing at the front of the opening.

Nick's eyes narrowed reflexively as the burned powder drifted into his face. Since he couldn't see much more than a bit of movement within the alley, he knew that Kinman must have been similarly impaired.

"Dammit," Nick snarled as the echoes of his gunshots died away. "I'll crawl in there after them."

Kinman clapped a hand on Nick's shoulder and pulled him back a bit. "Don't bother," he said. "These Chinese are like rats. They got hidey-holes all over the goddamn place. Going after them now is just asking to walk into a shotgun blast or some other ambush."

"Sorry about that."

"Don't worry about it. There's plenty more where they came from. You want in on that railroad job?" Kinman asked.

"Sure. I could use the money."

"Let's do some more hunting and then we can go back to Hale's place for dynamite. Where you headed from here, Nicolai?"

"Up into the Dakotas."

Kinman smirked and said, "What a coincidence. So am I."

THIRTEEN

Kinman was right. There were plenty more Chinese to be found inside of Rock Springs. As he and Nick made their way up and down the streets, it got harder and harder for Nick to pretend that he didn't see someone hiding in a doorway or rushing into a building. More than once, Nick thought he would be called out on his attempts to draw Kinman's attention away from those desperate faces.

Fortunately for those frightened souls, Kinman seemed more intent on talking up Hale's plan to blow up the railroad tracks. As he spelled out the plan to Nick, he acted as if he was sharing the details of a surprise birthday party. Nick listened, nodded and kept looking for another way to keep from having to put another local in harm's way.

"I need a drink," Nick said as they walked down another street.

Kinman shook his head and replied, "You're out of luck there. The saloons are closed."

"What? Why would they be closed?"

"The barkeeps are trying to keep from adding fuel to the fire by getting these arsonists liquored up. Don't try talking your way in either, because I gave it my best shot. Some of these saloon owners say they're trying to settle things down, but my guess is that most of them just don't want to be blamed for making things worse."

Nick nodded and looked at the darkened windows of the nearest saloon with newfound respect. "They may be onto something," he said.

"They're just covering their asses." Kinman grunted. "I'm inclined to toss a brick through one of these goddamn windows just so I can get my hands on a bottle. In fact . . ."

Recognizing the glint in the man's eye from all the other times he'd been around dangerous men with too much time on their hands, Nick reached into his inner jacket pocket and took out a dented flask. "Here," he said, handing the flask to Kinman. "Maybe this'll help."

Kinman looked at the flask and then back up at Nick. "I thought you wanted to head into a saloon to get a drink."

"I just didn't want to take a dent out of my personal supply."

Kinman seemed more than a little skeptical. But once he screwed open the flask and sniffed the contents, he grinned and nodded. "Ah. Now I see. This ain't your typical gutter-brewed whiskey."

"I can't even find it in most saloons," Nick said. "Sometimes, there ain't anyone in town who's ever heard of vodka."

Kinman tipped the flask back just enough for a healthy taste of the clear liquor. His eyes closed as the liquid heat worked its way through him and warmed his stomach. "That's a hell of a treat," he said, handing back the flask. "Thanks."

Nick took a drink as well, savoring the taste and the feel of the liquor the way some folks savor a cigar or a finely cooked meal. When he let out the breath he'd been holding, Nick felt as if he were exhaling steam from the potent liquor burning its path down his throat.

"Seems like the fires are being put out," Nick said as he put the flask back into his pocket.

Kinman nodded and spared a quick glance toward the section of town that had been ablaze. "Maybe we do got the saloon keepers to thank for that. The men who set them fires only burned down Chinese houses."

"Houses?" Nick asked. "Not businesses?"

Shaking his head, Kinman replied, "Chinese businesses may have a few white investors. Chinese laundries may have some white folks' clothes hanging in the back. Nope, they just stuck to the houses because that's where they could burn down the most Chinese with the least bit of fuss."

Nick felt his stomach shift within him in a way that had nothing to do with the vodka. He was taken slightly aback when he found the same disgusted look upon Kinman's face. "Why would you take money from someone like Hale?" Nick asked.

"Why wouldn't I? You think someone else wouldn't just step up and do what I done? It's easy work and it was gettin' done with or without me. Sheriff Young's got his hands full with the fires and the assholes setting them for now, but he'll crack down on Hale so hard that prick won't know what hit him."

"What about the Federals?" Nick asked.

Kinman looked over at him. "Those Federals will roll into town sooner or later," he said. "All we need to do is make it later rather than sooner and we can ride outta here as rich men."

"It could be messy if any Federals get hurt."

"Not if nobody knows who did the hurtin'." As Kinman broke into laughter, he slapped Nick on the back and added, "We'll just skin that rabbit when we get to it, as my grandpappy used to say. Speakin' of rabbits, it looks like the Chinese rabbits are all back in their holes. Let's get to work on our other business."

The town had fallen into an eerie sort of calm. More folks were poking their heads out of their doorways and walking the streets, and there were more lawmen making their rounds. Nick figured that many of the men wearing badges were newly deputized or even part of a posse meant to regain order. The look in their eyes said they were both anxious to use their guns and afraid at the same time.

Kinman must have picked up on the same thing, because he became more and more silent as the folks around him got the courage to walk outside again. Even though the night air was filled with more cautious voices and less with gunfire, Kinman glanced around as if he was suspicious of every face he saw.

"Don't let these folks get too good a look at you," he said. "Once the law gets here, they'll be apt to tell them about every stranger they've seen."

"They've got to know about Hale," Nick said. "A man like that surely hasn't been silent while this mess was brewing."

"Oh sure. And I'm positive none of these folks pointed out a Chinese or two to Hale out of spite. I'm also sure none of these folks happen to be miners as well and are looking to get anyone but Hale into trouble for this bloodbath."

Nick nodded and choked down his disgust for his fellow man. "Point taken. Where are we headed?"

"There's a hardware store just up the street. Hale said he'd meet us there with the supplies we need."

True to his word, the hardware store was up the street and marked by a single lantern glowing in the window. As he approached the store, Nick felt like he'd been swept up by a passing twister and tossed a hundred feet into the air. Where he'd been before didn't matter, and he was too busy to think about where he was headed. Looking back on it, Nick might have thought a week or two had passed since he'd been sitting on that train aching for a way to get off of it. Now that the twister had come, all he could do was try to position himself for the best landing he could manage.

As he followed Kinman around to the back of the store, Nick was reminded of something Barrett had once told him. His friend's words drifted through his head like a phantom breeze, bringing a hint of a smile to his face.

"A man don't get rich without taking a wrong turn now and then," Barrett had said during one of the many wrong turns their old gang had taken. "He's gotta follow his nose no matter where it leads."

"Most folks know better than to live life like that," Nick had said at the time.

Barrett had looked at him and nodded. "That's why most folks are dirt poor, breaking their backs and cursing every minute they got to spend on this earth without the sand to do a damn thing about it."

At the time, Nick had liked the sound of that.

Now, it struck him as true but not quite as amusing.

He knew there was something important brewing in Rock Springs the moment he'd spotted the flames. Getting off the train was a bonus, but

Nick had to admit he would have preferred to be one of the other folks that Barrett had talked about. At least that way he would still be on his way to Cheyenne with only a few loud children and smelly old men to gripe about instead of carrying an armful of guns and a crate loaded with dynamite.

Those things were handed over by a trio of men with faces that were so dirty, they might never have been clean. Those stern faces were unwilling to meet Nick or Kinman's eyes as they followed through on Hale's commands. Hale, on the other hand, couldn't have been happier.

"These are the only weapons we could get on such short notice," Hale said. "But that shouldn't be a concern to . . . men like yourselves."

"Yeah." Kinman grunted as he selected one of the shotguns from the pile and hefted it over his shoulder. "We got plenty of guns already. You need help with that crate?"

Nick got his fingers under the crate and lifted it. Since the crate was less than half the size of one of the coffins he'd built over the years, he managed to get the crate up onto his shoulder without much trouble.

"I got it," Nick said.

Hale nodded enthusiastically and pulled a watch from his pocket. "Good, good. You'd better get moving, then."

"Aren't you coming along with us?" Nick asked.

Suddenly, Hale didn't feel like smiling. "Why

would I do that? You know what you need to do. Just do it. If I was going to do the job, I wouldn't need to pay you men."

"The locals are starting to walk about," Nick said. "The fires are being put out and the law's even coming around."

When he saw Hale look in his direction, Kinman nodded. "He's right. It's not like we can walk down the street with a load like this and not expect to be noticed."

"Jesus Christ," Hale grumbled. "I might as well—"

"Might as well what?" Nick snapped. "Kill these folks your own self instead of piling up their bodies? Plant this dynamite yourself instead of sitting back and watching the explosions? Or maybe take some of the blame yourself rather than paying us to take it for you. Yeah. Maybe you should do it yourself."

Hale obviously wasn't pleased to hear what Nick had to say, but some of the indignant fire had left his eyes. In fact, Hale seemed to become downright uncomfortable the longer he stood there in front of the two men. Finally, he said, "I see what you mean. Fine, then. Let me get my wagon and I can take you to the tracks. I might even know a spot where you can take your time in planting that dynamite without being spotted."

"See now?" Kinman said triumphantly. "Seems like ol' Nick might know what he's talking about after all."

Hale ran across the street to a small lot where a few horses and wagons were kept. After getting a single horse tied to a small cart, Hale motioned for the others to meet him down the street. As soon as he drew to a stop in front of the Central Mining Office, Hale's men loaded the wagon and Kinman climbed onto the seat beside him.

"Actually, I could just tell you where to go . . ." Hale started to say. Once he got a look at the glare Nick was shooting at him, he added, "You're right. It would be quicker if I just took you there myself."

"Bring the payment," Nick said.

Hale froze with his mouth hanging open. After clearing his throat and trying to regain his composure in front of the rest of his men, he asked, "Why?"

"Because I don't intend on staying here," Nick replied. "You may fancy shitting on your own doorstep, but I'm moving on as soon as this job is over."

"I need to bring you back to town anyway, so why don't you just—"

"You don't need to bring me anywhere." Nick cut in. "I'm going to get my horse and then we'll move along. I left him in a stable not far from here."

Hale opened and closed his mouth a few times and even got out a few sputtering breaths without managing to form any words. Finally, he looked over at Kinman and said, "You vouched for this man?"

"Actually," Kinman said, "I think he's making a good point. If the Federals are on their way, they could arrive at any moment."

"They won't be here for a while yet!"

"Can you guarantee that?"

Kinman's question hung in the air like the acrid smoke drifting in from Chinatown. Hale looked around at the few other men taking orders from him, but none of them had anything to offer.

Looking back at Nick, Hale had a coldness in his eyes. It wasn't cold enough to make Nick turn away.

"Get the money, Cy," Hale said. As one of his men ran off to follow through on the command, Hale said, "Get your horse, Nicolai."

Nick straightened a bit and cocked his head to one side. The look he gave Hale was the same one he'd given countless other times in his youth. So far, no man had lived to see that look more than once.

"If you don't mind," Hale said to make quick amends. Although he tried to keep the same serious look in his eyes, he was unable to maintain the edge in his tone. "Since I'll be carrying this much cash on me, I'd appreciate it if we stayed together until the job is done."

Taking his sweet time before nodding slightly, Nick turned and walked to the stable where Kazys was waiting.

FOURTEEN

———◆———

Nick and Kinman rode their own horses while Hale and two of his men rode in the small wagon. With the fires being put out slowly but surely, the night was reclaiming Rock Springs with its thick blanket of darkness. Even so, the smell of burnt gunpowder and spilled blood still hung heavily in the air.

Hale snapped his reins and got the wagon rolling ahead of Nick and Kinman. Just when he was about to mention how empty the streets were, he spotted someone standing at a window and tipped his hat to them. He kept quiet for the rest of the ride.

When Hale steered off the road and toward a cluster of trees, Nick thought the man's hands had slipped from the reins. But rather than roll straight into the greenery, the horse nosed aside some branches to reveal a narrow trail that looked only slightly wider than a footpath. Nick made certain both the wagon and Kinman were ahead of him before he ventured into those trees.

The trail was mercifully short. Every step of the way, Nick got swatted in the face by low-hanging branches. Wooden barbs clawed at his arms and snagged at his sleeves when he tried to brush them out of the way. When he managed to wipe the dust and pollen from his eyes, Nick was looking at a wide stretch of land with a set of railroad tracks running straight down the middle of it. Hale was practically standing on top of the wagon as he snapped the reins to drive it to a spot beside the tracks. As soon as his brake was set, he jumped down from his seat.

"All right," Hale said. "This is the spot. I don't think anyone got a look at what was in that wagon, and they sure didn't get much of a look at you two, so I'll be on my way."

"What's the hurry?" Nick asked.

Hale started to reach for his horse to unhitch it. "I'm paying you men to do this job and that's what you'll do. If I wanted to do it myself, I could have saved the money." He stared at Nick and Kinman. "What are you men waiting for? Get to work!"

"I think the plans are about to change," Kinman said.

The fear had already taken hold of Hale's features as he started backing toward his men, who were beside the wagon. Hale bumped against Cy, who was the closer of the two. "You two stand to make some easy money," he said. "Don't ruin it by doing something stupid."

Kinman chuckled and said, "Stupid, huh? By stupid, do you mean being the ones to set this dynamite so your men here can witness it? Or do you mean stupid as in being the ones hunted by the army for killing its soldiers while you do whatever the hell you want right here?"

Watching the two men talk, Nick learned plenty from their faces. He learned even more from the faces of the men Hale had brought along with him. Although Hale looked more scared than anything else, Cy and the other gunman wore the expressions of men getting ready to make a move.

"Or maybe you just got a guilty conscience," Kinman added. "Perhaps you're just the sort of fellow who don't like getting his hands dirty. You could be the sort who just likes to plan the deeds and reap the benefits afterward."

"You're the one who killed those Chinamen," Hale said defiantly.

"That's right. And they barely put up a fight. You could have done it your own self if you weren't sitting in your office while your own town was on fire. Tell me something, Hale. Did you have enough sand to start even one of them fires or did you just watch from behind a window somewhere with the rest of the women?"

Hale's face twitched and the muscles in his jaw tensed. After a few stuttering hisses, he managed to part his lips enough to speak to the men who'd ridden alongside him. "Blow this asshole's head off."

Kinman smirked and brought up his pistol in a quick, fluid motion. He took aim and prepared to fire with plenty of time to spare, but didn't manage to get his shot off before his pistol was knocked off target. When he turned toward the man who'd swatted his hand to one side, there was an angry fire raging in his eyes.

"What in the hell are you doing?" Kinman growled.

Nick leaned to one side and used the same hand that had swatted Kinman's gun to point toward Hale and his men. "Watch where you're shooting!" was all he had time to say before pulling hard on his reins and steering Kazys away.

In the space of a heartbeat, Kinman turned to where Nick had been pointing and saw why Nick had stepped in. Both of Hale's gunmen stood in front of and within spitting distance of the wagon, which had enough dynamite to turn a healthy section of railroad tracks into twisted metal. Ducking low, Kinman swore under his breath and snapped his reins to move out of the gunmen's line of fire.

Even though Hale and his men were nowhere near as quick on the draw as Kinman or Nick, they'd had plenty of time to pull their triggers by now. Gunshots cracked through the air and lead hissed past Nick and Kinman. Fortunately, the men doing the firing were just as rattled by Nick's sudden actions as Kinman had been. Their shots went wild and sailed harmlessly into the night.

The biggest struggle for Nick was to keep from drawing his gun. He left the modified Schofield in its holster so he could have both hands free. He rode around the wagon and reached out, snagging the horse's bridle to take control of Hale's wagon.

"Get away from there, God dammit," Hale said as he turned and aimed at Nick.

All those years of lugging coffins paid off, as Nick was able to pull his feet out of the stirrups, get clear of Kazys's back and pull himself onto the other horse, just as Hale's shot whizzed over his head.

Meanwhile, the other two gunmen kept firing as Kinman raced around them. They knew better than to empty their cylinders too quickly and still had a few rounds each by the time their target came to a stop.

Dropping from his saddle, Kinman turned toward the gunmen. His boots slammed against the dirt, but the sound of the impact was masked by a shot from his pistol. The bullet caught Cy in the shoulder, twisted him in his saddle and knocked him off of his horse. Kinman wasted no time in shifting his aim to the other gunman. Now that he'd steadied himself, he took proper aim and sent a round straight through that one's face.

Cy heard the solid thump of the body hitting the dirt, and that told him all he needed to know. He gritted his teeth and fired his remaining shots at Kinman, who had gotten into a prone position.

Grinning like a kid in the middle of a game of tag, Kinman pushed himself to the left and rolled toward Hale's wagon.

Cy's hammer dropped onto the back of an empty brass casing.

Kinman kept his aim on Cy as he got himself back onto his feet. When Cy dropped his gun and held up his hands, Kinman shook his head. "Too late for all that," he said. Before Cy could speak a word in his own defense, Kinman pulled the trigger and sent his final bullet into Cy's chest.

Nick wasn't able to hear what Kinman said, but the shot blasted through the air so close to the horses that it got the animals shaking their heads and stomping their hooves. Hale, too, had fired off his remaining rounds and was cursing loudly. Nick poked his head up to get a look at him and had to quickly duck as Hale threw his gun at him.

"I've come too far to stop now!" Hale said as he climbed into the driver's seat. "I wasn't the one to start this riot, but I sure as hell won't let it pass without making some progress."

Nick pulled himself up onto the wagon and immediately caught Hale's fist in his jaw. The impact was barely hard enough to turn Nick's head.

"It's not a riot," Nick said. "It's a damned massacre!"

"Call it what you want. This town's a powder keg thanks to those filthy Chinamen!"

As he cocked his arm back, Nick said, "Whatever this town is, you're only making it worse." He drove his fist into the middle of Hale's face.

Blood spewed from Hale's nose, which was now flattened awkwardly against his head. He turned onto his belly so he was draped over the back of the wagon's seat and his legs were pointed toward the anxious horse. Digging into his pocket, he said, "You and Kinman have already done enough! All this shooting must have drawn a crowd."

Nick glanced back in the direction from which they'd come and saw plenty of movement among the trees and neighboring buildings. He couldn't be sure how many folks were watching from back there, but he could feel those eyes fixed upon him. They'd been given one hell of a show.

When he turned around again, Nick was treated to a sight that made his own eyes widen.

Hale had twisted around onto his side. His face was contorted into a twisted, grinning mask and his fingers were pinched around a single lit match. "Back the hell away from me or we both get blown sky-high," he said in a disturbingly calm tone.

"Your men are already dead," Nick said. "No need for you to join them."

"We'll all join them unless you do what I say. I've brought this too far to back up now."

"Go on and do what he says," Kinman said from a few yards away.

Nick only had to shift his eyes a bit to get a look at Kinman. Keeping Hale in the edge of his vision,

Nick saw Kinman step forward while casually re-loading his pistol.

"There's enough dynamite to kill us all," Nick warned.

Kinman shrugged. "Then standing here or there won't make much difference. Might as well do what he says so we don't have to die in the name of some greedy Chinese."

Hale smirked and slithered away from Nick until his back was against the edge of the driver's seat. "That's right. This town's in the grip of a cleansing fire and it needs to burn until all the wickedness is purged. I only represent the good, honest workers of Rock Springs, who are trying to provide for their families."

"Those Chinese have families, too," Nick said.

"And they've got their jobs at these mines as well as at plenty of others. The line was crossed when they were set up to replace good Christian workers and put them out of their jobs."

"Take it up with the mining companies."

"Save your breath," Kinman said before Hale could reply. "Let Hale do what he's gonna do. Better that than have some more good workers suffer."

"That's absolutely right," Hale said. He contin-ued to look at Nick as the match in his hand burned down to his fingers. Flailing like a trout that had been dropped onto dry land, Hale squirmed over the back of the seat and landed on one of the crates of dynamite. His hands buried themselves into his pockets and then came out with another few matches.

Nick let out an aggravated breath, just managing to release the horse's tracings as he climbed down from the wagon before Hale started another little fire.

"What about the money?" Kinman asked. "You put on your show and we're the ones who'll take the blame no matter what, so we might as well get our payment."

Hale grunted as he righted himself with his back against the side of the wagon. "Quite right," he wheezed. He reached into another pocket to take out a bundle of money. Tossing the cash at Kinman, Hale said, "Take it and go. When you read about the history we've made here today, you'll thank me for letting you be a part of it."

Nick was already on Kazys's back and riding away from the wagon. As soon as he'd collected the money and stuffed it into his own pocket, Kinman followed suit.

"Mark my words!" Hale shouted as he made his way back to the driver's seat. "This is a historical day!" Smiling victoriously and sitting like a king upon his throne, Hale snapped his reins. As soon as the leather cracked against its flank, the horse bolted and pulled free of the wagon.

"What the hell?" Hale grunted.

Nick drew his pistol and fired at the back of the wagon. His first bullet drilled through the wooden panel without a result. His next shots, combined

with gunfire from Kinman, were more than enough
to ignite the dynamite.

It seemed to spool out like a series of pictures
that slowly passed in front of Nick's eyes. First, he
saw the flash of orange light from the back of the
wagon. Next, he saw bits of wood fly out in every
direction. Everything after that was a blur.

Nick's ears were ringing so badly that he wasn't
exactly certain if he'd heard the explosion or not.
Heat from the fire washed over him until he found
himself wondering if he'd fired too soon and would
perish in the flames right along with Hale. Despite
all the heat, Nick swore he could feel the cold
touch of the Reaper's skeletal hand closing around
the back of his neck. It wasn't the first time he'd
felt the grazing touch of those fingers, but Nick
casually wondered if it would be his last.

And in a flash, those thoughts were forced out of
Nick's head as he was flung straight back into the
world of the living.

The rest of the dynamite went up in a thunder-
ous roar, but Nick and Kinman were riding away
from it as quickly as their horses could take them.
Nick didn't recall snapping his reins, but he also
didn't recall covering enough ground to get where
he was now.

Flames crackled and sputtered, but there wasn't
much of the wagon left to burn. Nick found himself on the other side of the railroad tracks, watching charred wooden hunks hit the ground. Kazys
was panting like a dog that had been left out in the

sun. The horse's sides swelled like a set of bellows against Nick's legs.

For a while, Nick could only hear his own heart beating. Then, the sounds of his own breathing rushed through his ears. After that, the rest of the world made itself known to him as shouts and clanging bells rippled through the air.

The fire brigade was coming. Nick could see a large wagon racing from town toward the explosion. Now that he'd collected most of his wits, Nick looked down to find the railroad tracks still crossing the ground in front of him. They were a bit cluttered, but otherwise fine.

All Nick could think about was the trainload of Federals still bound for Rock Springs. Despite the grit in his teeth, smoke in his eyes and ringing in his ears, Nick couldn't help but smile. When he finally caught sight of Kinman riding up to him, Nick saw a similar grin on the man's face.

"Crazy bastard got what was coming to him!" Kinman shouted so he could be heard above the ringing in his own ears. "Let's get the hell out of here, before the rest of his men get here!"

Nick wished he could stay long enough to see the Federal troops blast apart any of Hale's remaining gunmen. Then again, those gunmen could very well be just a bunch of angry locals who'd been pushed too far by their circumstances and whipped into a frenzy by a man who liked the taste of blood. That part struck a little too close to home for Nick's tastes.

Pulling on Kazys's reins, Nick pointed the horse eastward and touched his heels to the animal's sides. Kazys was more than willing to get moving again and thc smoking remains of the wagon were soon lost behind him.

On his way out of town, Nick spotted more than a few grateful Chinese faces looking out at him from darkened windows. He hoped the Federal train would arrive before the situation in Rock Springs could get any worse.

FIFTEEN

Nick's mind wandered as he rode out of Rock Springs. Tearing out of a town with the grit of smoke in the back of his throat and the law possibly on his heels was nothing new to him. In fact, running away sometimes felt more natural than walking. He was ashamed to consider that it was more natural than any of the skills his father had taught him.

After taking a moment to get his bearings, Nick steered Kazys toward the northeast, making certain head away from Rock Springs. He couldn't be precise, but that put the Dakotas more or less in front of him.

When he heard another horse coming in his direction, Nick reflexively reached for his gun. He stopped short of clearing leather as Kinman drew to a stop a good distance away from him.

"Keep riding that way and I'll catch up to you," Kinman shouted.

Nick waved him off and kept moving. "Don't bother. I've got business to tend to."

"Yeah," Kinman grunted. "So do I."

* * *

Rock Springs felt as noisy and crowded as a saloon, even at the late hour that Kinman returned to it. Folks walked the streets, talking hurriedly to each other or shouting out to familiar faces they passed along their way. Lawmen rode in pairs either dragging someone to jail or keeping their eyes out for another man to toss into a cell.

All Kinman had to do was keep his head down and his gun out of sight. He wasn't too worried about being recognized, since the only men who'd been close enough to spot him before the wagon exploded were either dead or miles away.

Staying well away from the smoldering Chinatown district, Kinman rode to a small house behind a blacksmith's shop. A quick glance into one of the windows made him fairly certain that the little house was still empty. He wasn't too worried if the owners had stopped by, though. Kinman only hoped that none of them had needed to relieve themselves before heading out again.

Kinman rode around the house, swung out of his saddle, and walked over to an outhouse that leaned partially against a tree. The narrow shack wasn't quite as tall as Kinman, himself, and was decorated with a star pattern cutout in the door. Stopping with his hand on the knotted rope threaded through the door, Kinman peeked through the star-shaped hole.

Lester looked right back at him.

"You done in there?" Kinman asked.

Although Lester glared intently at Kinman, he didn't even try to make a sound. After all the screaming he'd done already, he knew well enough that the bandanna that had been stuffed into his mouth was more than enough to keep him from being heard.

Kinman pulled open the door to admire his handiwork. Lester was just as he'd left him: both ankles bound tightly together and both arms tied to up and stuck between his legs. Using his boot to shove Lester's legs aside, Kinman double-checked that the rope was also still looped through the hole he'd knocked in the commode. Sure enough, if Lester wanted to go anywhere, he would have had to drag the entire outhouse along with him.

"Damn, Lester," Kinman said with a wince. "What the hell have you been eating?"

Lester glared silently at Kinman over the bandanna hanging from his mouth.

"Anyone been around here since I left?"

When he saw that Lester wasn't moving a muscle, Kinman placed his right hand upon his holstered pistol and used his left to pull the bandanna from Lester's mouth.

"Are you out of your goddamn mind?" Lester snapped the instant he was able. "This whole town's going to hell and you decide to take off and stretch your legs?"

"Not just stretch my legs, Lester. I turned a pretty profit as well."

"Doing what? Setting fires? I've been smelling smoke the whole time I was in here. You know those flames we saw when our train was stopped? I think they're still burning somewhere."

Kinman's grip tightened around the bandanna he'd used to silence his prisoner, but his spirits were too high for him to put the dirty cloth back into use. "You're gonna have to be quiet, now. There's something I need to talk about."

"Now you wanna be polite? Now you wanna be neighborly? Why don't you start off by untying me and then we'll see how polite and neighborly I can . . ." Lester's words trailed off when he heard the subtle brush of iron against leather and found himself looking down the barrel of Kinman's gun. "You were saying?" Lester squeaked.

Leaning against the outhouse door, Kinman announced, "I've acquired a partner for our little venture into the Badlands. His name's Nicolai Graves."

As much as he wanted to respond to that, Lester found himself without enough breath to utter a single word. Filling his lungs was difficult work. It was also not very rewarding considering where he was sitting. "You mean the same Nick Graves who used to ride with Barrett Cobb?"

Kinman nodded.

"This is the Barrett Cobb whose grave we're going to see," Lester pointed out. "You do realize that?"

"Oh, I sure do realize it. And it just so happens that Graves the *man* might turn out to be every bit as valuable as the grave we're out to find. Whatever you say is buried in that coffin—"

"It's in there," Lester said quickly. "I swear it!"

Kinman nodded and patted the air as if he was calming a frantic child. "We'll see about that when we get there. But whatever it is, it's the same as what it was when that last bit of dirt was thrown on top of it. Over the last few years, the price on Nick Graves' head has only been getting better."

Lester squinted and cocked his head to one side. "Why? I hear that Graves was nearly killed when he was run out of Montana. Lord knows he ain't been leading no gang like he used to."

"I don't give a rat's ass if he pissed off Jesus Christ himself, and all three wise men are the ones putting up the money. All I do care about is that the money's being put up by some very reliable sources. Even if I can't coax a bit more out when the time comes, the reward is pretty damn good as it stands."

"Wait a second," Lester said as he suddenly hopped up as if he meant to stand. Before his legs could straighten, he found the limit of the rope tying him to the commode and was jerked right back down again. Even as his ass bumped against the splintered wood, the smile remained upon his face. "You wouldn't be here if it weren't for me. Shouldn't I get a percentage of the reward, too?"

Despite Kinman's good humor, there was no way for him to hide the murderous glint that came into his eye. "You telling me you had something to do with those crazy fools blocking the railroad tracks?"

"No."

"Then maybe you had some way of making certain Graves and I crossed paths once we were both stuck in this mess?"

As much as he wanted to say otherwise, Lester shook his head. "Nope."

"Oh. Then shut yer damn mouth and count yourself lucky that I haven't put a bullet through your skull and dragged your carcass in for the reward."

"Where's Graves now?"

"Headed to the Badlands."

Lester looked at Kinman and waited for a few seconds. When he realized there wasn't anything else coming, he asked, "You let him go?"

Kinman nodded. "I'll catch up with him as soon as I get you out of here."

Tugging at his ropes, Lester strained to get up. "Then what are we waiting for? If he gets too far ahead, he may—"

"He may get an extra couple of hours on his own before I catch up to him again." Tapping the side of his nose, Kinman added, "I got his scent now, just like I got yours. I know where he's headed and there ain't too many ways to get there from here. My only question now is whether you're comin' along as a partner or as baggage."

"Things would be plenty easier if I came along as a partner."

Kinman narrowed his eyes and smirked. "You really think so?"

"All right, but I can be a good partner. I've got no reason to cross you."

"Don't take me for a fool, Lester. I don't like it."

"I'm not taking you for anything. I can help!"

"That's what I want to hear. You tell me how you can help and maybe I'll see my way clear to letting you leave this shithouse alive."

Lester's eyes widened. Suddenly, he looked around at the dirty walls surrounding him as if he'd found himself inside of a coffin. As his brain seized up under the pressure, he saw Kinman slowly lift his pistol and begin rolling the cylinder against his other palm.

"I'm waiting," Kinman said quietly.

"I . . . uh . . . I can keep an eye on Graves when you're not around!"

"Don't need that. I keep track of slippery cusses like that one for a living."

"I can watch your back in case Graves decides to take a shot at you."

Kinman chuckled under his breath. "You'd work extra hard to make sure I don't come to any harm so I can drag your ass in for the reward? I already told you I don't like being taken for a damn fool.

In fact, I don't know if there is a reason why I should keep you alive."

Lester laughed uncomfortably at first, thinking that Kinman was just turning the screws a bit tighter. Then he saw the bounty hunter's eyes become as cold as two chunks of ice as he pointed his gun again, and Lester knew there wasn't an ounce of bluff in what he'd said.

"I can find that grave!" Lester spat out. "I can take you straight to it in case things go wrong and you lose sight of . . ." Seeing that he wasn't getting anywhere with that one, Lester added, "You could kill Graves any time you want! Let him get you close and then shoot him. He can be the baggage and I can take you the rest of the way! I could even work on him to give you a better shot at him!"

Suddenly, the ice in Kinman's eyes began to melt. "You just might be onto something there."

Lester was curled up with his knees against his chest and his arms crossed in front of him. His face was twisted into a frightened wince as if he'd already been shot. Slowly, his muscles relaxed and he blinked uneasily. "Yeah? I mean . . . yeah!"

"You can lend a hand in setting up Graves after we find that cash buried out in the Badlands. You do that and you might even be in for a cut of the reward. That would be a nice little nest egg waiting for you once you get out of jail."

"Or you could keep all the reward and just let me go," Lester squeaked.

Kinman's eyes narrowed again.

"You can even keep a bigger cut of whatever we find buried with Cobb," Lester offered. "If I pull my weight, you can let me go with just enough money to get me across the border and you can ride off with that treasure and whatever money you get from Graves."

For the next several seconds, Kinman stood rooted to his spot. His face became an unreadable mask that seemed to collect more and more shadows around its edges. The gun in his hand didn't waver. From the way he held it, it could be holstered just as quickly as it could be used to blow Lester's head off his shoulders.

Finally, Kinman nodded and said, "I've got something in mind for you."

Lester wanted to ask what it was, but couldn't muster up enough breath to push the question out. The sounds drifting in from the rest of the town weren't as loud as they had been before, but there were still enough shouts and gunshots to make Lester wince at every last one of them.

"You play your cards right," Kinman snarled, "and you could live a comfortable life once you cross whichever border you have your eyes on. Cross me, and I'll see to it that you pray for a bullet in your head."

Nodding as if he meant to shake his head free of his neck, Lester said, "Sure! That sounds like a great deal."

But Kinman didn't move. "I know you're plannin' on how to escape or how to stab me in the back, but get that shit out of your head right now. Unless you think you can kill me, just go along with our plan and I'll cut you free. Even if you do manage to get away from me, I'll make it my life's work to track you down and gut you slow enough for you to feel every second of it."

"Wh . . . what's the plan?"

"There'll be time to discuss that on the ride outta here."

"Is there another train coming?" Lester asked.

"Yeah, but we won't want any part of it. There's plenty of horses around here for us to choose from. This place has got bigger things to worry about than a couple stolen animals. All I need to know is whether or not I can count on you to do the smart thing."

The enthusiasm had faded from Lester's face and was replaced by a frightened, almost sickened expression. After a bit of consideration, he nodded. "All right. Count me in."

Kinman holstered his gun and reached around to take out the blade sheathed at the small of his back. With one quick swipe, he cut the rope that had tied Lester to the outhouse. "Let's get outta here before this town tears itself apart."

Even though Lester could straighten up and move his arms, he didn't follow Kinman.

After taking a few steps away from the outhouse, Kinman looked over his shoulder and asked, "Ain't you coming?"

"Actually," Lester replied sheepishly. "I could use a few more minutes in here. Uh . . . alone."

Kinman grinned and kicked the door shut as he walked away so Lester could let his fear and nervousness work themselves out of his system.

SIXTEEN

———◆———

After all that had happened in the short time he'd been in Rock Springs, Nick found it hard to believe just how quickly he'd passed through that town. Compared to all the commotion that was flooding through that place, the quiet of hiding out in the middle of nowhere was a welcome relief.

As much as Nick would have liked to find a spot that was just off the trail and big enough for a campsite, he wasn't eager to be found by anyone following him. There was always the possibility of some lawman trying to catch up to him, thinking that Nick had meant to blow up those railroad tracks. What bothered him more than that was the possibility of crossing Kinman's path.

Nick didn't have to see the man shooting innocent Chinese to know that Kinman had put together a good-sized pile of bodies. Watching that wagon blow to pieces had been like Christmas morning for Kinman. The glee etched across Kinman's face had been almost enough to turn

Nick's stomach. It was very similar to the grin worn by the man who'd mutilated Nick's hands.

Nick led Kazys a little further off the trail as he did his best to focus on the ground directly in front of him instead of the ground he'd left behind.

Walking ahead of the horse, Nick kept his eyes trained upon the shadow-covered terrain. His fingers were clenched around Kazys's reins and the horse followed him without question. Before too long, the crunch of their steps against the ground washed away the echoes floating through Nick's mind in the same manner as a steady current washed the rocks from a riverbed.

Nick picked a spot to camp simply by running out of steam on a flat section of land. He wound up a good way from the trail and far enough away from Rock Springs to feel comfortable, so he tied Kazys off and took his bedroll from the saddle.

After he'd had some jerky and stretched out on his bedroll, Nick figured that all the trouble he'd gone through had been worth it just to get the hell off that train. Staying on would have only prolonged his misery just to gain a few more miles. Nick might not have been in Cheyenne, but he wasn't far off from the Badlands. He figured it should be a few days' ride at the most. He would be riding by himself, which made the extra time plenty worthwhile.

Nick strapped his holster over his belly, slid his hat so that it covered most of his face and lay back with his head propped up on his balled-up coat. Compared to the rest he'd tried to get with his head bouncing in that damn train, it was like floating on a cloud.

"I thought you said you'd know where to find him," Lester said.

The sun's rays were barely working their way across the sky, giving it the first orange hues of dawn. The air smelled fresh and there was a cool breeze blowing in from the west. Despite all of that pleasantness, Kinman still managed to flash a murderous glare at Lester.

Reflexively, Lester turned away.

"I do know where to find him," Kinman muttered. "I just couldn't exactly see every track in the dirt when it was dark."

"Well, the sun's up now. I just hope our friend Graves hasn't gone too far."

Kinman rode slowly with his eyes trained upon the ground. One hand was always resting upon the grip of his rifle, which lay across his lap. His other hand held the reins in a loose grip, allowing him to guide his horse as if by thought alone. "He can't be far from here," he said to himself as much as to Lester. "He either made camp last night or will make camp before too much longer. Either way, that'll allow us to catch up."

"We got to make camp, too, you know." The confidence in Lester's voice was no longer there when he added, "Don't we?"

The look he got from Kinman didn't inspire any confidence.

"We don't make camp," Kinman snarled, "until we find Graves."

"But . . . the horses need rest."

"We haven't been working them that hard."

Lester gnashed his teeth together and shifted uncomfortably. After weighing his options, he said, "Then I need rest! We haven't gotten out of our saddles since we left that shooting gallery of a town." Twisting around to get a look behind him, Lester let out a troubled moan. "We're still not far enough away from there, if you ask me."

"Nobody asked you."

Since Kinman seemed more interested in the ground under his feet than the conversation at hand, Lester stood up in his stirrups and made a show of looking left and right. "I don't see him or anyone else around here. Maybe you're just trying to get me to agree to giving you most of the money we're set to find."

"You think so? Then maybe I should just shoot you and take you back into Rock Springs. I'll bet they'd know where to go to turn your carcass in." Surprisingly enough, there wasn't a scowl on Kinman's face when he turned around. "Don't piss yourself just yet, Lester. I think I just found what I was after."

"Really?"

Kinman drew his horse to a stop and climbed down from the saddle. Lester would have liked to climb down with him, but his feet were tied to his stirrups, which were also connected by another rope that crossed underneath the horse they'd stolen for him to ride. Leaning forward, Lester stared intently at where Kinman was going.

"You see Graves somewhere?" Lester asked. "I told you we shouldn't have circled town so much when we left."

Ignoring the other man's ramblings, Kinman walked to a small patch of open ground that was just a little way from the trail. He reached a spot where the dirt had been smoothed out and ran the tips of his fingers along the earth. Kinman looked around slowly, taking in everything. When he spotted the deep set of horse's tracks, he grinned and nodded.

"What'd you find?" Lester asked. "Where is he? I don't see nobody."

Standing up but not moving from his spot, Kinman turned and studied every inch of ground in the vicinity one more time. Only then did he allow himself to disturb another speck of dirt with his own boot. "He was here," Kinman said as he walked back to where his horse was standing.

"How do you know it was him?"

Plenty of things rushed through Kinman's head that would serve as good answers to that question. Things ranging from the freshness of the tracks to the direction they were headed would have been good enough. There were also things like instinct and a knowledge that he'd gained after spending years of hunting down his fellow man that would shed some light on the matter. With all those things in mind, Kinman simply looked over to Lester and grunted, "It don't matter how I know. I just do."

Lester's instincts told him a few things as well. Namely, that it wasn't a good idea to press the matter any further. "All right," he said. "I was just askin'."

Although the tone in his voice left no room for doubt, Kinman didn't turn his back on the spot he'd found. He bent at the knees so he could run his hands into the upper layers of dirt. In a matter of seconds, his fingertips found a few scraps of food and the remnants of what had to have been a very small fire. Those things were enough to tell him that Nick had been trying to stay out of sight when he'd stopped there.

If he'd been waiting for Kinman to arrive, Graves wouldn't have minded building a larger fire. In fact, he might have built a sizeable one to make certain he was spotted. There was always the argument that Graves wouldn't have been anxious to be seen considering the circumstances in which they'd left Rock Springs, but any man should have known that the law in that town would have had their hands full with more important matters.

Kinman nodded to himself and straightened up.

Graves had been there, all right. There wasn't a doubt in his mind. Now, the trick would be to catch up to him without drawing too much suspicion.

"Looks like he headed to the northeast," Lester said. "I can see some horse tracks from here."

Kinman looked in that direction. His eyes followed the tracks, which he'd spotted less than a second after he'd spotted the campsite itself. The imprints were fairly fresh, which meant they'd probably been put down when the sun wasn't even high enough in the sky to chase away the shadows. They seemed to be evenly spaced, so the horse wasn't taking off in a rush. That either meant the rider was taking his sweet time, or was level-headed enough to walk when he knew damn well he should have been running.

Of course, there was always the third option. Nick Graves could have put down those tracks to give the impression of the first two possibilities. Having lost Graves' trail so many times over the years, Kinman knew that was a distinct possibility. He also knew it was useless to try and second-guess his prey's motives while standing still.

"Jesus Christ," Lester mumbled. "A slug could've gotten to the Dakotas by now."

Kinman wheeled around quickly enough to make Lester twitch in his saddle. As he climbed onto his own horse's back, Kinman said, "For the first time, I agree with you." He then snapped his reins and got moving.

Since Lester's horse was tied to Kinman's saddle horn, the other man had no choice but to follow.

Nick pulled in a lungful of air as the wind whipped past his head. Gripping the reins in a fist, he hunkered down low over Kazys's neck and leaned into the torrent of wind caused by the horse's galloping stride. The thunder of Kazys's hooves reminded him of the rumble of the train's engine that had carried them both all the way from California. At the moment, it was hard for him to believe that Kazys couldn't have covered that same amount of ground in half the time.

The entire country was spread out in front of him like a giant multicolored blanket. Mountains, rivers, plains and forests all rushed past him in a continuous display. As more dusty wind blasted his face, Nick grinned and choked down the grit that had collected in his throat.

The scenery was starting to look more familiar. Although he wasn't one for memorizing trails or shortcuts, he always had a good sense of where he was going. When he and Barrett had ridden together, the rest of the gang always knew that Barrett could figure out the quickest way to get where they were going and Nick could always get them home.

Nick was still amazed that he was the one riding back into the Dakotas wearing a few streaks of gray in his hair and Barrett was the one cooling his heels under several feet of dirt. No gambling man would have bet on Nick living through his twenties.

Kazys kept charging forward as if he was trying to rip away the upper layers of earth with his hooves. Nick steered away from the main trail at his first opportunity, while looking for the spot where he could eventually circle back onto the main course.

The tracks had grown deeper and farther apart. That caught Kinman's eye right away, telling him that Nick was moving faster. Even though there weren't many sets of fresh tracks in sight, Kinman had to trust his instinct that the ones he was following truly belonged to Nick Graves.

There were plenty of Indians in these parts. There were also scouts, messengers, couriers, and any number of men who might be riding by themselves and traveling in a rush. Come to think of it, Kinman guessed that anyone wanting to stay ahead of the Crow or Sioux would be riding pretty damn quickly right about now.

Even as all that raced through his mind, Kinman didn't consider slowing down. There were times when a man needed to be careful and there were times when he needed to throw himself headlong into whatever path he'd chosen. This was one of the latter times and Kinman raced down his own path, not caring whether it led to a coffin full of jewels or a slow death.

There was no time to worry about what lay in between.

SEVENTEEN

———————◆———————

The next few days were spent with Nick doing one of two things: looking ahead or looking behind. Everything else fell to the wayside. While looking ahead, he tried to gauge where he was in relation to where he wanted to be. As Kazys took him out of Wyoming and into the Dakotas, the horse was having a harder time maintaining the pace he'd set when he bolted out of Rock Springs.

Nick wasn't about to jeopardize the animal's health, but he also wasn't about to jeopardize his own by allowing himself to fall too close to the men who were chasing him. Kinman's presence was always nagging at the back of Nick's mind. He could feel the other man closing in on him, even though he couldn't see or hear him coming. Nick had been hunted for too many years to overlook that anxious feeling in the bottom of his gut.

Kinman pulled back on his reins and slowed down gradually enough for Lester's horse to get the hint. The bounty hunter's chest was heaving as if he'd run the last couple of miles on foot, and his eyes darted back and forth within their sockets.

"What's the matter?" Lester asked. "Did you lose him?"

Still glancing around, Kinman slowed his horse so he was directly beside Lester's. He reached to his belt and drew the hunting knife that was sheathed there.

Lester squirmed reflexively in his saddle. "All right, fine!" he squealed. "You didn't lose him!"

But none of Lester's pleading was about to stay Kinman's hand. Seeing that, Lester clenched his eyes shut and waited to feel the blade cut through his flesh. Although he did feel the cool touch of sharpened steel, it was only for a second as it glanced between his wrists.

When he opened his eyes again, Lester found the ropes tying his hands to the saddle had been cut. The rope connecting his ankles was the next to go. Kinman leaned down and swiped the blade through the rope as if it was warm butter, causing both ends to drop down and brush against the ground. Even Lester's horse seemed surprised to have the rope removed, since it had gotten used to feeling them on its belly for all these miles.

"What's the meaning of this?" Lester asked tentatively.

"Don't you remember what we talked about? I said I had plans for you."

"Yeah, I remember."

"Now's the time to see those plans through."

Lester gathered up his courage and glanced up the trail. When he looked back at Kinman, there was a glimmer of hope in his eyes. "We're still going after them jewels?"

"Of course," Kinman said with a humorless chuckle. "That is, unless you're about to tell me there ain't no buried treasure."

"Oh, it's there!"

"Then ride on ahead. I'll be right behind you."

Although Lester faced forward and gathered up his reins, he restrained himself from snapping the leather and setting his horse into motion. Every muscle in his body wanted to move forward. His legs tensed against the horse's sides. His chest tensed. Even his head stretched forward as if he was anticipating the wind being in his face. Soon, however, he seemed more like a turkey stretching his neck along the chopping block.

"We should probably stick together," Lester said. "This is Indian country, ain't it?"

Kinman nodded. "Sioux."

"You think them Sioux'll be happy scalping me and just let you pass?"

"Hell no. If the Sioux are out for scalps, then they'll get both of us. It won't matter too much whether we're separate or in one spot."

"I guess that's true. Why are you letting me go?"

"We're crossing into the Badlands and we need to split up. Graves is bound to be watching his back right about now, but he's only looking for me."

"What if he sees me first?" Lester asked.

"That's what you should hope for. He's never met you, has he?"

"Not that I recall."

"Good," Kinman said. "Then he's got every reason to treat you like he'd treat anyone else. Don't tell him who you are, just to be on the safe side. Keep him occupied until I've snuck around behind him. If he sees me, the plan's the same, only it's you doing the sneaking while Graves comes after me. You've got the easy job, since I'll be doing most of the fighting either way."

"Do you think Graves knows you're after him?"

Kinman shrugged and replied, "I don't think so, but I ain't about to bet my life on it. You'll ride ahead, but we won't be too far apart. When one of us hears shooting, the other comes in to lend a hand. That's how you're earning your freedom, remember? You play your cards right, and I may still throw you a percentage of whatever we find in that coffin you've been going on about."

Eventually, Lester started to nod. "All right."

"Don't look so cautious, Lester. I could've killed you at any time if I wanted you dead. You bolt from me like a coward now, and I can still catch you any time I please. I ain't got no doubt about that. Do you?"

Lester studied Kinman's eyes for a second. That was all it took for him to get the answer he needed. "Nope," he said.

"Good. That proves you're a smart fellow. Now get moving toward that ridge," Kinman said, pointing to the east. "I'm heading up north and will keep riding that way for a mile or so."

Lester swallowed and nodded as all the color drained from his face.

"What's eating you now?" Kinman asked.

"I feel more like bait in a trap right about now."

"At least you're still live bait."

Seeing Kinman's hand inch a bit closer to his gun, Lester pointed his horse to the east and snapped the reins. Even with the sense that he might get shot in the back at any second, Lester did feel good to be somewhat on his own. It wasn't long before he'd worked most of the kinks out of his arms and legs so he could keep moving in time to the horse's motions. Soon he built up some speed and was racing toward the ridge Kinman had pointed out.

When he looked over his shoulder, Lester didn't see more than a cloud of dust to indicate the bounty hunter had been there.

He tapped his heels against his horse's sides and let out a sharp yell to get the animal moving even faster. For the first minute or so, Lester wasn't even looking for Graves. Instead, he kept his eyes open for a sign of Kinman's approach or a good spot to make a sharp turn before the bounty hunter got there.

What he found when he cleared the ridge was something that put a whole other kind of dread into Lester's gut. The cold touch of it seeped down like a poison that had been slipped into his water and it spread out in all directions once it got to his stomach.

"Oh shit," Lester said under his breath when he spotted the row of horses approaching him from the left. He wasn't close enough to see the riders' faces, but he could most definitely spot the feathers tied to their heads, saddles and rifle barrels.

Lester counted four Indians, but knew there would be more coming from a small village he could see less than a mile or so away.

"Son of a bitch knew this was gonna happen," Lester rasped as he bunched up his reins and used them to whip his horse's flank. "I don't know how he knew, but he knew. I'm sure of it."

Muttering a silent prayer, Lester steered away from the Indians and hoped that would be enough to get them off his tail. Sometimes, all they wanted to do was scare folks away from their villages or sacred burial grounds. Lester was no expert on the matter, but he had enough common sense to know when to give the savages a wide berth. Since he'd caught sight of the village, he figured they were just a couple of braves out to gain a reputation by putting the fright into a white man.

Lester's horse was breathing heavily and slowing down. He let the animal ease up a bit so he could turn and take a quick peek over his shoulder. The Indians were even closer than he'd thought, and were gaining ground fast.

"Come on, you sack of bones." Lester grunted as he turned back around and whipped the horse's side. "Get your ass moving or we're both dead."

Lester knew better than to think his horse could understand him. The horse may not have even been able to hear him over the pounding of its own hooves or the sound of Indians sweeping in on him like a plague of locusts.

Every bit of sense in Lester's head told him to take a shot at those Indians before they got any closer. If he'd had a gun on him, he might have done that very thing. Even if he had a knife, he was getting desperate enough to turn and throw it at the first feathered head he could find.

Since he didn't even have anything in his pockets to throw, Lester snapped his reins again and hoped his horse wouldn't keel over before carrying him far enough away for those savages to lose interest.

Nick used his dented spyglass to watch the Indians ride closer. He knew they'd be coming, since he'd been the one to ride past their village close enough to draw their attention. Just for good measure, he'd kept on riding to the nearby burial ground so that he would lead Kinman or whoever was following him straight through the spot where no paleface should go.

Having ridden through this section of the Badlands several times throughout the years, Nick knew that most anyone heeding the warnings they

were given were allowed to change their course
without too much trouble.

Anyone who pushed the Sioux further than that
deserved whatever they got.

But Nick didn't see any surprised lawmen when
he looked through the spyglass. He didn't even see
Kinman. What he saw was a stranger who looked
as if he was about to piss his pants because he was
so afraid of the wild-eyed Indians coming his way.
More than that, the frightened stranger seemed to
be unarmed.

"Aw hell," Nick muttered.

Since he'd gone through so much trouble to keep
himself distanced from anyone that had been
following him, Nick studied the surrounding area
just to make certain he wasn't being drawn out.
Not only was Nick soon convinced that the stranger
was genuinely terrified, but he cursed himself for
waiting so long when the man might just be ready
to stumble into some serious trouble. So far, the
Sioux scouts were only shouting and firing a few
warning shots over the stranger's head. The longer
the stranger held his course, however, the madder
the scouts became. In no time at all, Nick was
certain they'd start aiming their shots just low
enough to draw blood.

Nick snapped his reins and got Kazys moving
along a path to intercept the stranger. He was
careful not to draw his gun. In fact, he rode with
his back straight and his arms held at an angle so

anyone could readily see that he was only holding the reins in his fists.

As soon as Nick was visible to the Indians, he could hear them yelling back and forth to one another. He knew a bit of the Sioux's tongue, but not enough to fully understand what they were saying. Nick didn't need a translator, however, to tell that the scouts weren't saying much of anything good.

Nick snapped his reins again and tapped his heels against Kazys's sides. The horse didn't appreciate the extra prodding, but responded by adding a bit more steam to his strides.

Using a method Barrett had always talked about, Nick continued to keep his back straight and his shoulders squared. He felt like he was doing a poor impersonation of paintings he'd seen of various Indian riders, but Nick kept up the brave front as he came to a stop in the middle of the space between the stranger and the approaching Indians.

For some reason, the stranger tugged on his reins and circled back around to Nick rather than riding on. "What the hell are you doing?" Lester asked breathlessly.

Nick held his hands up and out as he said, "Just don't make any more sudden moves. Point your nose south and keep riding."

"But I'm not headed south."

"That doesn't matter," Nick snarled, doing his

best to keep his temper from flaring up. "Just go that way and I'll try to make sure you get away from here in one piece."

Nick felt as if he was speaking a different language. Lester just wouldn't follow his directions. As his frustration bubbled to the surface, Nick dropped his hands and gestured to the stranger to get moving.

Unfortunately, Nick's movements got more of a reaction from the Sioux than from Lester.

One of the Sioux raised a clenched fist, and the others fanned out, immediately surrounding Nick and Lester. A few of them carried bows with arrows already notched and drawn back to be fired. The remaining seven riders brandished rifles decorated with beaded strips of leather, strips of fur and a few long feathers.

"What's your plan?" Lester whispered.

Nick kept his face passive, but the aggravation was more than clear in his voice. "My plan was to hold them off so you could get away. Since you're so intent on staying here, maybe you'd like to come up with something else."

"I . . . uh . . ."

"Didn't think so," Nick snapped. "What the hell are you doing here anyway?"

After scouring his brain for a suitable lie, the best Lester could come up with was, "Just passing through."

"And you just happened to be following me?" Nick asked.

Although Lester managed to shake his head, he couldn't get any words out.

"We can settle that later, I guess," Nick said. "That is, if either of us is drawing breath once this is over."

EIGHTEEN

———•———

The Indians surrounded Nick and Lester without once taking their eyes off of them. Their dark faces were painted sparsely with a few lines here and there. Feathers and bits of bone rattled from strings and leather straps hanging from armbands, headbands and rifle barrels. One of the Indians barked out a few words, which fell upon at least one set of ignorant ears.

"What the hell did he just say?" Lester asked.

Nick kept his eyes locked upon the one who'd spoken as he replied, "I'm not sure. Let me try something." With that, Nick uttered a string of syllables that only made Lester wince.

"You speak their language?" Lester asked.

"We'll find out in a moment."

The Indian who'd spoken was of average height and had a lean, powerful build. His face and chest were marked by a few more stripes and symbols than the other riders, whom he commanded with subtle nods or flicks of his hand. After listening to Nick, he seemed to regard him with a bit more interest.

Lester shifted uncomfortably in his saddle and grunted. "Can you get them to—"

"Shut up," Nick snapped.

The leader of the Indians nodded and glanced away from Lester as if he didn't mean to look at him again. Now focused completely upon Nick, he spoke in a low, steady voice.

Nick kept his face calm and his eyes leveled at the lead Indian. In some situations, his mannerisms might have seemed threatening or imposing. In this instance, however, Nick was merely giving what he was getting. He showed strength to the Indians and didn't back away from them, but he also didn't make a move in the wrong direction.

Although he didn't understand every word of what the Indians' leader said, Nick caught enough to have his initial suspicions confirmed. "They're Sioux," Nick said to Lester. "They live in that village and don't like visitors racing through here on their land."

"Don't these Injuns know their damn place?" Lester muttered.

A few of the Indians glanced at Lester and tightened their grip on their weapons. Lester noticed this immediately and leaned back in his saddle, while his hand drifted toward the spot where his gun should have been. The fact that his gun wasn't there didn't seem to matter. The Indians responded by raising rifles to shoulders and drawing their arrows back, waiting for the order to attack.

Knowing he had less than a second or two to keep things from boiling over, Nick twisted around in his saddle and did the first thing he could think of. His arm snapped out like a whip, catching Lester across the upper chest. Even though he hadn't intended on hurting the other man, Nick's blow had enough muscle behind it to knock Lester backward until he was wobbling in the saddle.

Lester started to pull himself up again, but slipped and toppled off his horse. Landing with a solid thump, Lester's shoulders slammed against the ground. One leg dangled away from the animal and one foot was snagged in its stirrup.

Wheezing, as most of the breath was knocked from his lungs, Lester struggled to pull his leg free, a steady stream of obscenities flowing from his mouth.

Despite the vulgarities Lester spewed, the Indians seemed anything but offended. In fact, they lowered their weapons and watched Lester's struggle with smiles growing on their faces.

Nick took advantage of the moment by reciting one of the other Sioux phrases he'd learned throughout his years of hiding in Indian country. He knew his grammar wasn't the best, but the effort was appreciated and the riders were more than willing to cut him a little slack.

As a show of good faith, the leader of the Sioux looked at Nick and spoke in words that both of the white men could understand.

"Leave here now and steer away from our sacred grounds."

"No problem," Nick said.

"Where you go from here?"

"Northeast."

The Sioux leader looked in that direction and nodded. "Keep your friend in line and we will let you pass."

"I'd appreciate that."

Lester watched all of this while still dangling by one leg from his stirrup. After one more tug, he managed to free his ankle so he could drop the rest of the way onto the ground. Just as he was about to get to his feet, Lester saw the Indians ride around him so they could get another look, laughing under their breaths. After satisfying their curiosity, the Indians pointed their horses back toward the village and rode away. Even though he didn't appreciate being the butt of a joke, Lester let it pass.

Nick waited until all the Sioux had gone before climbing down from his saddle and rushing over to Lester. Extending a hand toward the fallen man, Nick said, "Sorry about that, but they would have killed us if they thought you were about to start any trouble."

"I don't even got a gun."

"You were acting like you had one, and that was almost enough to get us killed. I had to let them know I was keeping you in line. Hope it didn't hurt too bad."

Accepting the hand Nick offered, Lester pulled himself to his feet and cautiously put his weight on the foot that had been caught up in the stirrup. "You surprised me more'n anything else," he said, ignoring the throbbing pain in his chest. "And I think I just twisted my ankle. Guess that makes me lucky."

"That makes us both lucky. Why were you following me, anyhow?"

Lester dusted himself off as he struggled to come up with an answer. To buy an additional few seconds, he took a step and winced in pain as if his ankle was bothering him. After all of that, he replied, "I wasn't following you."

"Yes you were," Nick said. "I left the trail, took a few turns after that and you were still behind me when I passed that village."

"What I meant was I wasn't meaning to follow YOU. I'm supposed to meet up with a friend of mine from Cheyenne and I mistook you for him."

Nick studied Lester for a few seconds. His hand rested upon the grip of his holstered pistol and remained there as if it hadn't decided what to do next.

Blinking as another thought hit him like a rock against the back of his head, Lester added, "My friend was coming in on a train from California. He must have gotten held up somewhere along the way. At least, I hope he wasn't held up, but you know what I mean."

"Actually," Nick said, "I do know what you mean. It seems like lots of trains were getting stopped in Rock Springs."

"Really? That must be it, then."

Nick nodded, mulling over what he'd heard. Eventually, he took his hand away from his pistol and walked back over to Kazys. "You should probably head back the way you came so you can meet your friend. You may even want to go to Rock Springs, although I'd advise you to wait a day or two. Things should be cleared up there by then."

Climbing into his own saddle, Lester started to speak but was cut off as pain lanced through his leg. In his haste to get onto his horse, he'd put all of his weight onto the ankle that had been snagged in the stirrup.

"You sure you're all right?" Nick asked.

Lester nodded and took a few breaths to steady himself. "Yeah. I was just hoping you'd let me ride with you for a piece."

Glancing toward the village, Nick saw that the Sioux had already stopped and formed a line that was well within range for rifle and bow shots. "We're still being watched," Nick warned. "I don't think those Sioux are anxious for a fight, but they're plenty anxious for us to leave."

"Then let's get the hell out of here," Lester said. "I just don't want to ride all the way back to Rock Springs when my friend is probably waiting for me in the opposite direction."

Despite the things that came to Nick's mind, the main thing he could think about was the group of Sioux that were watching them like hawks. Even when he'd ridden with killers and vigilantes, Nick had learned to never turn his nose up at Indian hospitality. Favors like that didn't come along too often and they were never to be taken lightly.

"Fine," Nick said quickly. "Just keep your hands where they can be seen and don't even think about straying from my side. There's a burial ground not far from here and if we so much as look at it, we're in for a war."

"Lead on, my friend. Lead on."

Despite the reservations he had, Nick led on. He kept Lester beside him and the Sioux's horses in his sight for as long as he could. The Indians barely even moved as Nick and Lester rode away. They remained in their formation until both men's horses had built up some speed. When Nick looked behind him again, the Sioux were gone.

Just to be on the safe side, Nick kept riding into the Badlands. It was rugged and beautiful country, which he'd passed through several times. Still, for every stretch of land that he knew like the back of his hand, there was another stretch that Nick didn't even recognize.

In his younger years, Nick and Barrett had used the Badlands as their own personal refuge. It was a good spot for meeting up with other members of his gang to plan jobs or split up the fruits of their labor. It was also easy to charge through and shake off anyone following them in much the same way that Nick had shaken Lester.

Even now, Nick glanced around at the rocky terrain and picked out caves where he could sleep and peaks he could use as lookout posts. The land hadn't changed much in the time that he'd been away. It was still a dangerous ride for anyone who didn't know their way, and a haven for everyone else. Barrett had loved the Badlands. That was why Nick had buried him there.

Steering Kazys toward a gravel-covered ridge, Nick pulled back on his reins and brought the horse to a stop. Lester was more than happy to follow suit.

"This is where we part ways," Nick said.

Lester blinked and looked around as if he was expecting another ambush. "What? Here? We're in the middle of nowhere!"

"I gave you the chance to leave before, but you didn't take it."

"I know, but that was when them Injuns were about to kill us," Lester whined.

"They're not going to kill us as long as we don't stray where we're not supposed to be."

"And where's that?"

"Just go back the way you came," Nick said. "Ride straight past that village without looking cross-eyed at it and you'll be fine."

"And what if they ride up on me again?"

Guiding Kazys away from the ridge and back toward the narrow trail, Nick replied, "Fall out of your saddle again. They seemed to think that was pretty funny."

"Hilarious. You damn near got my leg snapped in two."

"Better than your neck," Nick said in a tone that was colder than the bottom of a frozen lake.

Rather than try to bargain or plead any more, Lester stayed put and let Nick go. Although his mouth was still, his brain was chugging like the piston of a steam engine. He squeezed the reins tightly and shifted his feet in the stirrups. His eyes snapped back and forth quicker and quicker as Nick moved farther away.

Finally, Lester managed to spit out a few desperate words.

"I know where you're headed!"

Nick was just snapping his reins to get Kazys to jump a small pit where a piece of the trail had broken off. He landed on the other side, turned and said, "I know you do. I've mentioned it a few times."

"Not just which direction. I know the spot you're looking for. It's the spot where Barrett Cobb is buried."

Nick pulled back on his reins so quickly that Kazys shook his head to protest the bit pulling at the corners of his mouth. Nick sat in the saddle like a statue that had been chiseled out of ice. "What the hell do you know about Barrett?" he growled.

At first, Lester had felt relieved when Nick stopped. Now he wished the other man was safely moving away from him again. Doing his best to keep his chin up and the fear from his face, Lester said, "I heard he was buried not too far from here."

"Who told you?"

"Some friends of mine."

Nick was across the gap and within inches of Lester's face in the space of a heartbeat. "That's why you're here? To defile a grave?"

"Considering what's buried in there with him, Cobb himself shouldn't have been too surprised that there'd be folks coming after him."

"What do you know about it?"

"Just that him and his gang pulled off one hell of a job before he was killed, and none of the stolen jewels were ever found."

Nick furrowed his brow slightly and leaned forward less than half an inch. His movements were slow and didn't cover much space, but Lester pulled back as if he'd found himself in front of a rockslide.

"And how do you know so much about Barrett's last job?" Nick asked. "Are you a lawman?"

"Hell no." Lester gulped. "But I can read a newspaper. Anyone in this part of the country has either heard something about that job or something about the search for Cobb or his gang. When nobody found anything or anybody, word started to spread."

"Rumors," Nick grumbled, as if he'd just uttered a profanity.

"You should know all about that."

Nick nodded to himself and looked Lester up and down. Letting out a breath, he eased back in his saddle and took on a more relaxed posture. Nick let his eyes wander just until he could see Lester following his lead and relaxing as well. That way, when he snapped his hand out to grab Lester by the front of his shirt, Nick was sure to put a fresh scare into him.

"Don't lie to me again and don't take me for a fool," Nick snarled. "That is, unless you want me to shoot you full of holes and leave your carcass for the Indians."

Lester shook his head vigorously until his hat toppled off. "I wouldn't dream of it!"

"Either you were a friend of Barrett's or you were chasing after him, because no newspaper stories are that detailed."

"I wasn't after him . . . or you! I swear."

Nick asked, "Do you know who I am?"

Lester winced as he realized just how far ahead of his brain his mouth had been running. "Yeah, I know who you are. My cousins live not too far from here. There's been plenty of talk about you and Cobb after all the shootings and such over the last few years."

"So your cousins were after Barrett's grave?"

"No, I swear!"

Nick gave him a shake and pulled Lester forward as if he was about to pitch him off his horse.

Rather than struggle, Lester lost the will to fight and went limp.

"I've been on the run myself," Lester whined. "Sometimes my cousins would get some work from Cobb since he was always lookin' for steady gun hands. They would send me some money, since I couldn't risk getting honest work from someone who would pay me real wages. They would always send word about the hell they had to raise to earn it. They also said Cobb was a good man."

"He's been dead for years," Nick pointed out.

"He was still a good man. My cousins told me so. They told me all about how he would—"

"Oh, for Christ's sake, shut up," Nick said. "Just tell me what you know about where Barrett is buried."

Lester blinked a few times as hope began to show within his watering eyes. "My cousins found the spot."

"How?"

When Lester spoke, his words spilled out of him like water from a broken dam. "Two of them were supposed to meet up with Cobb after that last robbery with them jewels. They heard the shooting and went to see if they could help. One of them saw you two riding off, but couldn't keep up. They caught up with you a while later, but you were carrying a body across the back of your horse. They followed you until they figured you were probably about to bury the body and then waited for you to leave the area."

As he listened to Lester's account, Nick thought back to the way things had actually happened. Barrett had always been a fast talker and had almost convinced Nick to join him on that one final job. But Nick had known there would never be a final job where Barrett was concerned. Barrett wouldn't stop robbing, just as surely as a fish wouldn't stop swimming. When Nick had gone along with him, he'd done so just to make certain his friend didn't get himself killed.

Perhaps there had been other reasons at the time, but that was the only one that stuck out in Nick's mind anymore. When the job was done, Barrett's plan had proven to be as good as any of his others. They'd gotten the jewels and Barrett was ready for the next job. The only difference was that this time, Nick wasn't.

It wasn't the first time the friends had fought, but this would turn out to be the last. Nick's hand was forced and he fired a shot that still echoed within his nightmares to this very day. To make amends, Nick had buried his friend with his precious jewels. He'd gone over the incident a thousand times since he'd first set out from Ocean, and the absurdity of it was still enough to strike him squarely in the face.

Nick shook the ghosts from his head and realized that Lester was still talking.

"There wasn't anyone around when I buried him," Nick said. "I made sure of it."

"They never knew exactly where the spot was,"

Lester replied. "But they had a pretty good idea."

"So you or your cousins are some of the assholes looking to dig him up."

Lester thought long and hard about how he should answer that. Even though he knew his life could very well depend on what he said next, he couldn't come up with anything more profound than, "Not me. It was my cousins."

"You're here to meet up with them?"

Lester nodded.

Nick nodded as well. With a grin that sent a chill down Lester's spine, Nick said, "Then we'd best not disappoint them."

NINETEEN

—◆—

As Nick rode from one trail to another, he kept a close eye on his newfound partner. He didn't trust Lester any farther than he could throw him. Then again, Nick figured he might be able to throw Lester quite a distance. He might even be able to test that theory if the little rat proved to be even slimier than he seemed.

Lester didn't sit still for one second. During the entire ride, he was constantly squirming in the saddle, shifting from one side to another, nervously glancing at various points on the horizon. His jumpy reflexes were getting quite a test, since there was no shortage of things scurrying about on the edges of his field of sight. Critters scampered across the trail, going about their lives as the two horses ambled by.

The last time Nick had been to the Badlands was when Barrett was with him. He didn't remember things quite the way that Lester had described, but the two accounts were close enough to make Nick glad he'd jumped off that train when he did.

Otherwise, he might not have been able to cross paths with one of the grave robbers he'd been hoping to catch.

As Nick led the way deeper into the Badlands, each ridge and every rock seemed familiar. While all of these lands had already been claimed by one tribe or another, the rocky patch that Nick now rode through was too rough for any Indian in his right mind to live on.

For every flat stretch of trail, there were twice as many spots where a horse or man could slip and crack their skull against a rock.

For every spot that could make a nice little campsite, there were three patches of sand that were being watched by anything from a nest of poisonous spiders to wild coyotes. Like any other sort of prey, Lester could sense that he was in over his head. And, like any self-respecting predator, Nick strode confidently into the heart of the Badlands.

As he drew closer to the spot where he knew he would find Barrett's final resting place, Nick felt a calm settle over him. Even Lester felt it and he allowed the breath he'd been holding to finally seep out of his mouth.

"This is as far as you go," Nick said as he drew Kazys to a stop.

Snapping his eyes wide open, Lester asked, "We're not there yet?"

"We're close, but not quite there. What did you think? Just because you got as close as you did, I'd just lead you in the rest of the way?"

Judging by the expression on Lester's face, that was almost exactly what he'd thought. Now that he realized the error of his assumption, Lester suddenly felt more isolated than if he'd been stranded in the middle of a desert. Even the small animals that had been scurrying about seemed to have chosen this moment to run back into their holes.

"Just so you know," Nick announced, "the moment I see anyone riding toward me who I don't recognize, I'm shooting them first and you second." After letting that sink in for a second or two, he added, "Is there anything else you'd like to tell me?"

At first, Lester kept perfectly still.

Then, as the thoughts churned through his mind and his imagination wreaked its havoc, Lester started to twitch. Just the corners of his eyes twitched at the start, but then the tremors worked through his face until he was almost shaking.

"There's someone else coming," Lester spat out. "He made me swear not to tell you."

"Then why are you telling me?"

"Because I don't think he's gonna hold up his end of our deal. He was supposed to cut me in on a percentage of whatever we found in that grave, but then he saw you and wanted to cash you in for the price that's on your head."

Nick nodded and looked around as he said, "A bounty hunter."

"That's right." Dropping his voice to a harsh whisper, Lester added, "And he could be anywhere. He could be watching us right now."

"What was your plan?"

"I was supposed to get in close and keep you occupied until he could get a shot. For all I know, he's got us both in his sights right now."

"He doesn't," Nick said confidently.

"How the hell can you be so sure?"

"Because he would have killed you before you spilled so much about what was really going on. That either means he's not close enough to hear us, or you're making this up to save your skin."

Lester's eyes widened to the size of saucers as he shook his head violently. "I didn't make it up! I swear to God!"

Oddly enough, Nick believed him. He had taken enough twists and turns while riding to this spot that he would have noticed if anyone else had been following him. For all the ridges, gullies and trenches in the area, there were plenty of spots to hide in, but not a lot of ways to move silently from one spot to another. There were too many loose rocks and nervous critters around for a man to go unnoticed for long. Nick knew that much from firsthand experience.

Also, Lester was too scared to be lying well enough to pull the wool over Nick's eyes. Nick had lost count of how many chances he'd given Lester to trip up on his stories. So far, Lester hadn't tripped over much of anything other than his own tongue. Lester could be an exceptional liar, but Nick's eyes were telling him to go along with his gut reaction.

The surrounding landscape was jagged and made up of sharp lines. Even a man lying on his belly could be spotted if he was trying to spy on Nick and Lester from afar. If such a man was closer, he would have made noise, disturbed a rabbit, or done something else to tip his hand. If he was good enough to avoid doing all of those things, then there wasn't much Nick could do about him.

"Come on," Nick said as he turned Kazys toward a wide, rocky slope that led to the east.

Lester leaned back in his saddle as if that would put him out of harm's way. "Where are you taking me?"

"You came along this far, you might as well come along for the rest."

"Y . . . you're gonna shoot me and bury me with Cobb."

"I dragged Barrett a hell of a lot farther than this. If I'd wanted you dead, I would've done it a long time ago, just to keep from hearing you whine so much."

Lester glanced around, but found nothing to give him any solace. Reluctantly, he nodded and gave his reins a limp-wristed flick.

Waiting until Lester caught up with him, Nick got Kazys moving just fast enough to keep pace with the other man. "What did you say your name was?"

"Lester."

"I'd rather not kill you, Lester. In fact, I'd like you to get a good look at what I'm about to do and then go tell all your friends or cousins about it. In fact, tell everyone you know. I'll even give you some money so you can buy drinks at all the saloons from here to Texas, have a few beers, and tell the story some more."

"What do you want me to say?"

"I couldn't care less," Nick replied. "I'm not the sort who enjoys swapping stories with a bunch of drunks. In my youth, perhaps, but I did plenty of other stupid things back then that I've also given up."

"But . . . why would you want me telling folks about you? Don't you know there's a price on your head?"

"I know," Nick said.

Lester blinked and waited. When a hammer didn't fall for what he'd already said, he decided to keep going. "I heard you were a killer. I heard about some of the things you've done and if even half of them stories are true. . ." He couldn't even finish that sentiment as the conclusions ran through his mind.

Holding up his gun hand, Nick said, "Take a look at that."

When he caught a full look at the gnarled remains of Nick's fingers and the scars that were smeared across his flesh like so much tar, Lester winced.

Nick recognized that look, having seen it on plenty of other faces. "That's just a taste of what I've been through." He lowered his hand and let his eyes settle upon the trail that wound in front of him. "Whatever's out there . . . whoever's out there . . . it all gonna come to me whether I run from it or not. After a while, a man just gets sick of running."

"So why bother to come here?" Lester asked. "You need your money back?"

Nick shook his head. "You ever see one of your friends get killed?"

"No, but my brother was stabbed in Dodge City when I was nine."

"All right, then. How'd you like it if a bunch of assholes decided to dig up your brother, pull the rings off his fingers, rip the pins off his suit, or take whatever else you might have buried him with?"

"I don't suppose I'd like that too much."

"There you go."

Something caught Nick's eye. It wasn't much more than a small movement to his left, but it didn't blend in with the rest of the movement around him.

Nick had come too far to divert his path now. The grave was somewhere just ahead, and it was in a spot that would allow him to get a good look in all directions. His memories were of a pristine spot with nothing but open land for miles around. The land around him now seemed to rise up and close in on him like a set of giant hands getting ready to slowly crush him between them.

Kazys let out a few strained breaths as he negotiated a steep incline. Some loose rocks slipped from beneath his hooves, but the horse never lost his balance. Lester's mount was having a bit more trouble, but still managed to climb the incline and get to the level ground on top.

The first thing to hit Nick's senses was how perfectly the spot matched the memories he'd been sifting through moments ago. At the top of the incline, the land flattened out into a wide stretch covered by rust-colored soil. The dirt was hard and full of rocks, which made it heavy and reluctant to blow too far no matter how much the wind howled. A few trees sprouted here and there, but were outnumbered by tough, thorny bushes.

The spot was somewhat larger than Nick had recalled and since he hadn't marked the grave with so much as a simple cross, he'd wondered if he'd be able to find it.

As it turned out, Nick didn't have any trouble at all finding Barrett's grave. All he needed to do was look for the hole that had been torn into the ground and the broken wooden planks sticking up like crooked, petrified fingers.

TWENTY

Nick dropped from Kazys's back and ran to the desecrated grave. Stopping at the edge of the hole, he looked straight down at the mess of broken wood, which led down to a skeleton lying on its side. Nick dropped to his knees and began pulling the splintered boards up one at a time.

He cleared a spot toward one end of the hole, climbed down into it and reached toward the remains with both hands. Everything was there, right down to the bandanna Nick had tied around Barrett's head. Everything, that is, except for the jewels that Nick had given to his friend for safekeeping.

Nick didn't even realize he'd climbed back out of the hole. One moment he was standing more than waist-deep in dirt. The next moment, he was rushing over to grab Lester by his arm.

"Who did this?" Nick snarled as he pulled Lester closer to his level.

It was nothing but sheer panic that kept Lester from being pulled off of his horse altogether. His feet were wedged firmly in the stirrups and his hands were gripping the saddle horn so tightly that his knuckles had turned white. "Did what?" Lester asked.

Shifting so he could stretch out his other arm and point toward the grave, Nick snarled, "That! Tell me who did that or you'll be buried in there with what's left of Barrett!"

"I don't know!"

"All right." With that, Nick took hold of Lester with both hands and pulled him completely from his saddle.

Lester came along kicking and squirming. Although his hands were peeled from the saddle horn, one of his feet remained ensnared within the stirrup. After a few strong pulls, Nick got Lester's foot loose and dragged him toward the grave. Once he was certain there was no way he was about to break free of Nick's grasp, Lester began to talk.

"I told you I'm not the only one who knows about this!" Lester squealed. "It could've been anyone else who heard the rumors! Anyone else would've come looking for all that money!"

"But you seemed to know a hell of a lot," Nick said as he continued dragging Lester along. "You and your cousins had a good idea of where to look and what was here."

"Yeah, but—"

"And don't try to tell me that anyone would be stupid enough to spread around where this spot was when they were intending on getting those jewels for themselves!"

As Lester tried to come up with something to say that would get him out of this mess, he found himself being hauled up by his shirt. Nick's hands may have been wounded, but his gnarled fingers clamped around Lester's shirt with so much strength that they even got some skin clamped between them along with all that dirty cotton.

Lester felt his feet leave the ground. When he looked down, he could see the broken planks stretching up toward him as if they meant to grab his boots and pull him into the gaping, stinking hole.

"Jesus Christ!" Lester hollered.

"Unless that's the name of the man who did this, I don't wanna hear it," Nick growled.

"I don't know if my cousins did this or not! I been on the run for the better part of a year!"

"You stopped running long enough to check in with your cousins."

"They sent me letters, but I barely got a chance to answer them." The more he talked, the shakier Lester's voice became. Soon, it was difficult to tell if the streaks down his face had been put there by sweat or tears. "When I haven't been runnin', I've been getting my ass dragged here and there by someone or other trying to cash me in for the reward money."

"My heart's fucking aching."

Feeling himself slip out of Nick's grasp, Lester sucked in a desperate breath and spat out, "I know where they're at!"

"Yeah?"

"Yeah! I'll take you to them!"

"You want me to believe you'll double-cross your own blood?" Nick said. "My guess is that you're saying whatever you can just to keep from being buried alive in this hole."

Lester looked down again as he thought about those words. Somehow, Nick had struck a chord that hit harder than when Lester had been worried about dying. Seeing the body curled up on its side amid all that dirt and broken wood made something crack within Lester's brain.

"I don't got a choice!" Lester said. "I'd rather take my chances with you than with Kinman!"

Lester felt the grip holding him over the grave tighten for a moment. Then the bottom of his boots scraped against the ground and he was set down. Nick let him go just long enough for Lester to realize he was standing on his own again. When he started to make a move, Lester nearly slipped straight into the very pit he was trying to avoid. Nick's hand snapped out again to grab Lester by the collar. That was the only thing keeping Lester perched on the edge of the grave.

"So you're with Alan Kinman?" Nick asked.

Lester nodded slowly. "Yeah," he whispered. "He said he already crossed paths with you. He said he met up with you in—"

"In Rock Springs."

"Yeah," Nick replied in a tone that mocked Lester's frightened whisper. "I know. A man like that's not too hard to miss." After studying Lester's face, Nick asked, "Why do you look so surprised?"

"I . . . uh . . . didn't know you knew who he is."

"I know. Kinman's a well-known bounty hunter," Nick said. "He's tracked down a bunch of my friends and he's been after me for a while. I've managed to stay ahead of him because I make it my business to know which bounty hunters need to be watched."

"Well, Kinman's got his sights set on both of us."

"What interest does he have in you?"

Blinking at the turn in the conversation, Lester replied, "I stole a horse."

Nick shrugged. "It must have been a real good horse or it must have belonged to a real wealthy man for Kinman to step in."

"The horse is dead," Lester squeaked.

"And so are we, if Kinman has a say in the matter." With that, Nick pulled Lester forward just enough for him to be able to maintain his own footing at the edge of the grave. He didn't, however, allow Lester enough space to feel comfortable.

"I know . . ." As Lester started to talk, his heel slipped backward and down a bit into the grave. After wobbling and waving his arms, he managed to catch his balance just long enough for Nick to pull him forward again. "I know what Kinman is capable of. The man's crazy. He's a cold-blooded killer."

Although he didn't say anything to that, Nick pictured the faces on those dead Chinese piled outside of Hale's door. He also pictured the grim smile on Kinman's face when he'd had an opportunity to put down a few more Chinese just to put a few more dollars into his pocket.

"The only reason I'm still alive," Lester continued, "is because I told him about this place." Seeing the scowl that came onto Nick's face, Lester winced. "I didn't have no other choice."

"What do you think Kinman will do when he sees this hole instead of the treasure he was expecting?" Nick asked.

"Probably shoot me."

"Which is a damn fine alternative to what I have in mind."

"All I want is to get the hell away from here. All I did was steal a horse and that was over a year ago. I'd serve jail time like I was supposed to, rather than hand myself over to a monster like Kinman. Hell, that rancher down in Texas has probably got himself worked into such a lather that he'll gut me when he gets ahold of me."

"You stole that horse in Texas?"

Lester nodded.

Shaking his head, Nick said, "They would've strung you up no matter when they caught you. Even I knew better than to steal a horse from a Texan."

"Well, if they string me up in Texas or if I get buried in that hole, I'm dead either way."

"Now you're using your head. You forgot one thing, though."

Lester thought about that for a moment before asking, "What?"

"I'm the only one who has any use for you while you're alive." Seeing Lester's eyes dart back in the direction from which they'd come, Nick added, "Now that we're at this spot and there ain't nothing but an empty hole, I doubt Kinman will be too pleased. Even if you track down those jewels for him, what do you think your chances are of getting away alive?"

"Not . . . too . . . good?"

Nick squinted and then grinned. "I see. He offered you a piece of the reward if you two managed to bring me in, didn't he?"

Lester thought of plenty of ways to answer that question. Unfortunately, every one of them required him to appear much more collected than he could manage under current circumstances.

"It's all right," Nick, said. "I figured as much. Just ask yourself one thing, though. If Kinman is such a big, bad bounty hunter, why didn't he just come after me himself? After all, he did have plenty of time riding with me back in Rock Springs."

The dazed expression on Lester's face made it clear that he wasn't able to come up with very much. "I guess he wanted to be sure," he replied in a wavering tone that wasn't even enough to convince himself it was the truth.

"I'll bet he's plenty sure when he's shoving you around," Nick said. "He must still be sure that you'll do what you're told if he let you come all this way on your own."

"He's gotta be watching us."

"Probably, but . . ." Nick motioned toward the uprooted grave and said, ". . . there's not much left for him to see here. If we get moving now, though, we could get a head start. I know a few shortcuts through these parts that'll put him so far behind us he'll never catch up."

Lester's eyes widened as some of the color drained from his face. "You mean run away?"

"Why not? You'd rather take your chances with a bounty hunter? Those assholes aren't much better than the law. The only difference between them and the jackasses who wear badges are whether they take their bribes above or below the table."

"You really think we could make it?"

"I know a little something about staying ahead of bounty hunters and I've slipped out of Kinman's sights more than once."

"He doesn't even think you realize he's a bounty hunter."

Nick grinned proudly and said, "My point exactly."

Lester started to think some more. He also started to slide backward into the open grave, which seemed to influence him a lot more. "Fine, fine. I'll join up with you, but I want your word that I'll go free after it's over."

"I'm not a bounty hunter," Nick said, "so rewards don't mean much to me."

"And all I can do is take you to where my cousins might be. I don't know for certain whether they've got them jewels or not."

"I'll take my chances."

Reluctantly, Lester lowered his head. "It's a deal."

Nick felt something brush against his gun belt and he reflexively backed up a step. It was Lester, offering his hand across the few inches that separated them. Nick shook Lester's hand, thinking about how he could most effectively put the other man to work in the little time before Kinman caught up with them. As he started to weave a plot in his head, Nick couldn't help but think that Barrett would have been proud.

Suddenly, Lester's grip tightened around Nick's hand like a set of iron tongs and before Nick could pull his arm away, Lester was pulling him forward. Since Nick had shifted into a sideways stance to put his gun farther away from Lester, his shoulders were in line with one another. That made it even easier for Lester to sidestep while pulling Nick forward.

Nick felt as if he was falling through molasses. He could see Lester moving aside, but there wasn't anything he could do about it. Nick's other arm flapped behind him like a donkey's tail. His front boot skidded against the ground for an inch or two, which was just enough to carry Nick to the edge of the grave.

After another shove from Lester, Nick pitched around at an awkward angle and toppled into the hole. He landed solidly upon the lower half of Barrett's coffin. When he looked down at the body of his friend, he swore he could hear Barrett laughing at him.

Once he'd gotten his feet beneath him, Nick climbed out of the grave. His gun was already in his hand and his finger was touching the trigger on the off chance that Lester was waiting for him up top.

He wasn't.

Even though there wasn't anyone in sight, Nick had a pretty good idea where to look. He turned toward the spot where they'd left the horses just in time to see Lester snap his horse's reins and charge straight toward him. Nick took aim with his pistol, but his shoulder hit the ground, knocking his aim off center.

Lester twisted in his saddle to look back over his shoulder. Seeing the gun in Nick's hand, he ducked down low over his horse's neck and let out a sharp yell as he dug his heels into his horse's sides. The animal bolted forward and dragged Kazys by the reins along with him until Kazys finally managed to pull free.

Nick got to his feet, straightened his arm and sighted along the top of his pistol. He wouldn't have had any trouble whatsoever in dropping Lester's horse, but the rifle shot that tore a piece out of his right ear was enough of a distraction to affect his aim.

"Son of a bitch!" Nick shouted under the blast of his own pistol.

Wheeling around to face the direction the rifle shot had come from, he dropped to one knee. He saw Kinman riding over the ridge that led back down along the path to the gravesite. The bounty hunter still held his rifle to his shoulder and was taking aim again as Nick fired.

Nick's round was less than an inch off its mark. It would have caught Kinman in the face, if the bounty hunter hadn't been sighting along the top of his rifle. Because of that, Nick's bullet ricocheted off the rifle and knocked the stock against Kinman's shoulder and head. The impact, harder than a punch, caused Kinman to wobble in his saddle. A few more shots went off, but none of them hit him. In fact, Kinman didn't even hear any lead flying past him. He saw Nick walking in the opposite direction and firing at something in the distance. Kinman took that opportunity to get his rifle back up to his shoulder and take a shot of his own.

Nick had figured that he had a few seconds to try and drop Lester while Kinman was shaking off the knock to the face. Once those seconds were up, Nick turned and found himself looking down the wrong end of Kinman's rifle.

Gritting his teeth, Kinman squeezed his trigger. All he got for his effort was the gut-wrenching *clack* of metal slapping down on metal.

Nick had taken his shot as well, but had done so on the assumption that he was about to be killed.

Aiming quickly, he fired and sent his bullet to the larger target of Kinman's torso.

The bullet slammed into Kinman's body like a kick from a mule. It sent him rolling backward from his saddle as the rifle flew from his hand. Sliding down his horse's flank, Kinman threw his arms out and braced himself for the landing. When he opened his eyes again, Nick was standing over him.

Glaring down as the blood rushed through his veins, Nick pointed the modified Schofield directly between Kinman's eyes.

Kinman let out a hacking, grunting laugh that shook his whole body. That, combined with the fresh bullet wound and the fall from the horse, was enough to send him straight into unconsciousness.

TWENTY-ONE

———— •◦• ————

Kinman didn't expect to wake up. Part of him had thought he might have a chance if Lester had a loyal bone in his body, but that hope lasted about as long as the proverbial candle in the wind. When he did wake up, Kinman was able to move, but that only brought him a torrent of pain that hit him hard enough to drop him flat onto his back.

"I was just about to check on you," said a voice nearby.

Sucking in a breath, Kinman pressed a hand to his wounded side and sat up. He was still in the same spot where he'd landed and his pistol was lying nearby. Another quick check told him that his backup pistol and knife had been taken from him.

"I figured you'd be long gone." Kinman grunted. "Actually, I figured you would have killed me while I was out."

Nick's coat was off and his shirtsleeves were rolled up. He took off his hat, swiped some of the long, graying hairs from his face and cleared away the sweat from his brow. "Seems like you've got an angel on your shoulder today. With that kind of luck on your side, my gun might have blown up in my hand if I tried to kill you."

Kinman squinted and choked back another wave of pain. "A killer talking about angels, huh? I guess I have heard it all."

Nick was quiet for a few seconds before he shrugged and rolled his sleeves back down.

"Where's Lester?" Kinman asked.

"He got away."

"Oh yeah. I recall that much. He also got your horse. Seems like one of us is stranded here." Just as he said that, Kinman spotted Kazys doing his best to graze on some dry brush not too far away. "I thought I saw him take your horse."

"He did," Nick said with a chuckle. "At least, he tried. He got about twenty yards before I let out a whistle and the old boy came running right back to me. I guess Lester's priorities have changed if he actually let this horse go rather than steal it."

Kinman's eyes darted toward the grave. Rather than the gaping hole and splintered planks that had been there before, there was now a neat pile of dirt. One of the planks was leaning against Nick's leg. "You stayed here to fill in that hole?"

Nodding, Nick said, "I just got finished. It was a little rough without a proper shovel, but I made do. I am a professional, you know."

Kinman struggled to his feet and winced as more pain shot through him. Grabbing his side, he found some blood, but not nearly as much as he'd expected. A quick look down there was enough to show him that torn scraps from his own shirt had been used to wrap up the wound.

"It was messy, but nothing serious," Nick said. "The bullet passed through and might have cracked a rib or two. Nothing too bad."

"Speak for yourself. You're not the one who feels like his damn ribs are on fire."

"No," Nick said as he turned his head and pointed to the bloody pulp hanging from his ear. "I'm the one who's missing a piece of my head that won't grow back."

Squinting to observe the damage he'd caused, Kinman grunted. "Yeah. I guess we're even. So that's where your friend's buried?"

"Yep."

"And were the stories true? I mean, was there some kind of treasure buried in there with him? The Reaper's Fee?"

Nick nodded solemnly as he looked back to the newly repaired grave. "Those stories were true, all right."

Kinman flinched and took a few steps toward the grave. "I suppose you reclaimed it?"

"No," Nick said as his hand drifted toward the gun at his side.

Snarling through clenched teeth, Kinman said, "Fucking Lester. Who the hell would have thought that little prick had it in him to get those damn jewels and actually get away from the both of us?"

His head turned as he glanced around the area. When he turned back around to find Nick calmly sipping from his canteen, he added, "You're pretty calm for a man who lost all that money."

"It wasn't my money."

"I know. You and Cobb stole it. At least, that's how the story goes."

Nodding slowly, Nick admitted, "That story's right."

"And you're just willing to let it go after coming all this way to claim it?"

"I didn't come to claim the money. I came to make certain my friend's grave wasn't dug up so his body could be torn apart by a bunch of wolves. I've seen that happen before, and it ain't pretty."

Kinman stared at Nick as if he didn't know what to make of him. He looked at the grave and saw how the ground had been piled up and leveled off to an almost perfect slope. He then looked back to Nick, whose face was calm and wearing a subtle smile. Then, Kinman reached for his gun.

"You pick up that pistol and I'll finish the job I started," Nick said simply. "Since I know you're out to claim the price on my head, I don't have any problem with leaving you out here for the wolves. Like I said, that ain't pretty."

Freezing with his pistol inches from his grasp, Kinman asked, "Why'd you keep me alive?"

"Would you rather I didn't?"

"No, it's just peculiar. You're no fool, Graves. I know that much simply because a fool couldn't have walked through as much hell as you have and still live to see another sunrise. We were shooting at each other a little while ago and now we're sitting and talking like neighbors. At the very least, I would have figured you'd keep my weapon from me."

"You can have them all back if you like," Nick said. "The rifle's bent to hell, so it won't do you much good."

As he got to his feet, Kinman gritted his teeth and used the pain in his side to spur him on. Once standing, he pressed his hand against his wound to find it was pretty much as Nick had described it.

Kinman picked up his gun smoothly and quickly enough to get it in his hand before Nick could react. He wasn't quick enough to take aim, however, before Nick had drawn his modified Schofield and pointed it directly at him.

"Damn," Kinman said. "That's a hell of a draw for a man with no fingers."

"Years of practice. Would you like to test my aim as well?"

"No," Kinman replied as he opened his hand and let his gun drop into its holster. "Not just yet."

"I did what I came to do, but you're right about one thing. I don't like the thought of Lester or his cousins running around with what belongs in that grave with Barrett. The reason I kept you alive and moving is because I'm pretty sure you can track Lester down without too much trouble. You'd get to a weapon sooner or later, so I figured I'd cut out that dance so we can get down to business."

"I would've had a much better time if you hadn't stayed here to fill in that hole."

"Then maybe you're not as useful as I thought."

There wasn't the first hint of panic on Kinman's face as he held up a hand and motioned for Nick to stay put. In fact, the bounty hunter seemed a bit weary as he nodded and said, "I can track him down. That won't be a problem. But why should I?"

"And you said I was the one wasting time?"

"Unless I'm getting something out of it, I'd be wasting time in tracking that asshole down when I could save the effort and drop you right here and now."

Nick squared off with Kinman to make sure the bounty hunter could see the holster that had been repositioned across his belly. "You could sure as hell try."

The two men stared at each other for a few seconds as the tension in the air shifted from cold to hot. Finally, Nick was the one to break the silence.

"You were after Lester at the start, right?"

Kinman nodded. "Yeah."

"Then you can have him. The price on his head must have been worth the trouble of coming after him and dragging him all the way back to Texas."

Although Kinman didn't try to deny that, he wasn't about to give Nick any encouragement, either.

"His cousins must be wanted, too," Nick continued. "At the very least, there's got to be one or two of them that have prices on their heads. Any group of thieves who are good enough to stay out of jail must have worked up some sort of bounty between them."

"True."

"When we find them, they're all yours."

"What about the Reaper's Fee?" Kinman asked. "I'd be earning a cut of that, too."

"I'll pay you five hundred dollars on top of whatever bounty you collect."

"Make it a thousand."

Nick narrowed his eyes and finally nodded. Before he could agree to it, Kinman spoke again.

"Two thousand," the bounty hunter snapped. "A shitload of jewels has gotta be worth plenty more than that."

"Sure," Nick said slyly. "If you can find a jeweler to buy them who doesn't already know they're stolen. After all this time, there's a list of those jewels posted in every shop that's carrying enough money to pay you off. Anyone else might just turn in whoever's trying to sell that many stolen jewels to collect the reward being offered for their return." Raising his eyebrows, Nick added, "It's not always fun to be on the other end of those rewards, now, is it?"

Kinman nodded and let out a sigh. "You're a sly one, Graves. No wonder I could never catch up to you all these years."

"How's fifteen hundred?" Nick asked.

"Sixteen."

"Deal."

Kinman offered his hand, but Nick didn't make a move to shake it.

"I'll take your word for it," Nick said.

"Come on, now. After all the fun we had in Rock Springs, you can't trust me enough to shake my hand?"

"That was before you shot at me."

"That was also before you were told what I do for a living."

"I knew about that back in Wyoming," Nick said. "I wouldn't have made it this long if I couldn't pick out a bounty hunter on sight."

"All right," Kinman replied, his hand still extended. "But shake it anyway. I can't have you going back on our deal due to some outlaw's loophole."

Nick stepped forward so that his right hand could reach out and grasp Kinman's. His body remained in a sideways stance as his left hand stayed within a few inches of his pistol. When he shook Kinman's hand, Nick kept his eyes locked on the bounty hunter. Although every muscle in his arm was ready to draw the modified Schofield, Nick wasn't given an excuse to follow through. The handshake was made and the deal was sealed.

"You're not planning on double-crossing me, now, are you?" Kinman asked.

Nick shrugged and stepped back. "I don't know. Are you planning to drag me in no matter how things turn out with Lester?"

Both men glared at each other uneasily, but neither gave an answer. Both of them already had all the answers they needed.

TWENTY-TWO

———— •◆• ————

Despite all his cursing and fuming when Lester had gotten away, Kinman would have been lying if he'd said that the escape came as a surprise. He'd dragged more than his share of prisoners from one place to another to know that every last one of them, no matter what they said or did, would always try to escape. It was human nature. It was the impulse that had put the prices on their heads in the first place.

Kinman had his tricks to keep prisoners in line, the least of which were the knots that kept their hands and feet bound to their saddles. One of the simplest and most effective of his tricks was to mark the horse being used by the prisoner when they were asleep or otherwise indisposed.

In Lester's case, Kinman had spent a bit of time on the first night they'd made camp chipping various patterns into two of the shoes worn by Lester's horse. All it took was a good knife and some quiet time, and Kinman carved a few marks that would show up just fine in the horse's tracks. One thing that always surprised Kinman was just how many times this trick had worked over the years. Then again, it was an outlaw's nature to charge forward without ever bothering to look back.

After putting on a bit of a show working to pick up Lester's trail, Kinman followed it down a steep ridge that could very well have broken the necks of both horse and rider with one misstep. After what appeared to be a lot of slipping and sliding, Lester's tracks took off in one direction.

"He's headed south," Kinman said.

Nick rode behind and to Kinman's left. "That's the only way he could have gone."

"You want to do the tracking, you be my guest."

Nick responded by dramatically waving Kinman along.

They didn't hit a snag until Lester's prints met up with some others that looked to have been set down within the last few days. Although the other tracks were older, there were enough of them crossing back and forth across Lester's to make Kinman stop and climb down from his saddle so he could take a closer look.

"Looks like the Sioux pass through here quite a bit," Nick said from his saddle.

Kinman didn't take his eyes off the ground as he grumbled, "No shit."

"What was that?"

"What else do you know about the Sioux around here?" Kinman asked as a way to steer the conversation into more fruitful territory. "You seemed to know all about their villages and burial grounds."

"I only know what I needed to know to keep from getting killed."

"You spoke their language."

"Not too much," Nick admitted, "but just enough. Where'd you catch up with Lester?"

"I roped him in Oregon."

"He ran that far after stealing a horse in Texas?"

Kinman nodded. "Never steal a horse from a Texan. They tend to take it a bit more personal than most. I think I found Lester's tracks," Kinman said, even though he'd spotted the specially marked prints some time ago. "He's still heading south and it looks as if he's picking up speed."

"Makes sense. He's got a lot to run from."

Kinman climbed back into his saddle and snapped the reins. His horse was accustomed to the speed that suited Kinman's tracking. Kinman himself rode slouched and hanging a bit to one side. Even though he looked as if he might be drunk or wounded, the bounty hunter was merely putting his eyes as close to the ground as possible. When he pulled himself upright again, he winced and pressed a hand to his side.

"How's the wound?" Nick asked.

"Stings like a bastard, but I can keep riding. I'll need to stop later on to tend to it."

"Shouldn't be a problem. Lester's gonna need to stop before we do."

"Yeah, but he won't," Kinman said. "I know that for a fact. He's a little fucking weasel who's been running for a good, long time. No matter how good I track him, he'll beat us to his cousin's place."

"We'll just have to take our chances."

Once Lester rode clear of the Badlands, he felt as if he'd been shot from a cannon. Suddenly, there weren't dozens of obstacles threatening to trip his horse or send it skidding down into a ravine. The land flattened out a bit and the ground was covered with less gravel and more packed dirt. Those things were mighty fine sights for Lester's weary eyes and he couldn't hold back a smile once he felt the wind flowing past his face as his horse picked up speed.

Lester didn't know if the other two had killed each other or if they were hot on his heels. Assuming the latter, he kept his horse racing down the narrow trail, which cut straight through Sioux territory.

Every now and then, Lester caught sight of an Indian rider or a few figures perched upon higher ground. Making sure to steer away from them, he got away without an arrow lodged in his back. After riding for a while longer, he guessed that he couldn't have been too far from the Nebraska border. He pulled back on his reins so he could take a moment to breathe and get his bearings.

As the sound of beating hooves faded from his

ears, Lester filled his lungs and spat out some of the dirt that had collected in his mouth. Thinking back to how he'd gotten away from Nick, Lester cursed himself for not being able to get his hands on a gun or a knife during the struggle. As he thought about it some more, Lester was amazed that he'd managed to get away from the grave without being buried in it.

Craning his neck as he turned around in his saddle, Lester was shocked to find the jagged, multicolored landscape of the Badlands far behind him. The sun was lower in the sky than he'd originally thought, and the darkness was almost complete. Lester had only stopped for a minute, and he already wanted to climb down from his saddle and stretch his legs properly.

In fact, if he was climbing down anyway, he thought he might even find a spot where he could rest his eyes.

If he was resting his eyes, he might as well—"

Suddenly, Lester shook his head and slapped himself in the face. He hadn't allowed himself to leave the saddle just yet and he knew if he did, he'd give in to the rest of his weary thoughts as well. Wesley's place wasn't far from the Badlands. Maybe a day's ride, but Lester couldn't rest until he got there.

Feeling a dry pinch in his throat, Lester realized he couldn't remember the last time he'd had a drink of water. He checked his saddlebags for a canteen, and then realized he didn't have any saddlebags.

Lester snapped the reins and got moving again. He only hoped the old horse he was riding was up for a hell of a long run.

The sun crawled back into the sky sometime later. He'd ridden through the entire day and most of the night without stopping for any longer than his horse needed to stay alive. He'd found a stream along the way, but had only sucked down a few mouthfuls of dirty water before saddling up and moving on.

Lester could feel the other two closing in on him. Sometimes, he swore he saw Kinman charging toward him with that devil's smile that was always plastered on his face. Other times, Lester nearly jumped out of his skin when he thought he'd seen Nick Graves lurking in some shadow like the ghoulish gravedigger he was.

All of those things nipped at the back of Lester's mind just as surely as the two men were nipping at his heels. Lester didn't allow himself to look away from the trail long enough to take a breath. He didn't look away long enough to try and guess the time of day. He barely allowed himself to think of anything apart from where he was headed and who was after him.

When he spotted the town, Lester didn't allow himself to feel relieved. Thanks to the pounding he'd taken from riding so hard for so long, he couldn't feel much of anything. He rode up to the first saloon he could find and climbed down from his saddle. His legs were so tired that they were barely able to carry him through the door.

The saloon was just over half full. A few of the customers turned to look at Lester, but turned right back around again when they didn't recognize his face. Lester headed for the bar and used both hands to prop himself up against it.

"Looks like you've already had your fill, mister," the barkeep said. "Did Bob already kick you outta his place?"

"Been riding a long time, is all," Lester rasped. Having remained silent since the last time he'd talked to Nick, Lester didn't realize how scratchy his voice would be. Those last few words felt as bad as they sounded and scraped against his throat like nails. After clearing his throat, Lester asked, "Can I have some water?"

"Beer's the closest we've got."

"You can't find any water?"

The barkeep let out a beleaguered sigh and told him, "I'll charge you for beer."

Before he agreed, Lester patted his pockets to confirm what he already knew. "I don't have any money."

"Then you won't be drinking." Taking a moment to look at the wretched sight in front of him, the barkeep leaned forward and said, "I can give you a loan, but you'll have to pay the interest or work it off here. That's the best I can do."

"I. . .won't be here long enough."

"Then stop taking up the space at my goddamn bar."

Lester turned and left the saloon. On his way out, he heard a few jokes being made at his expense but was too tired to care much about that. In fact, he didn't even care what folks thought when he walked over to the same trough his horse was using and stuck his head into the warm water. It tasted bitter and more than a little salty, but it was still water and it went down just fine. When he pulled his head back up again, Lester smacked his lips as some of the grit in his throat was replaced by other, somewhat less scratchy, grit.

Walking over to his horse, Lester reached up to his saddle horn but didn't have the strength to pull himself up. Instead, he let out a breath and rested his head for a moment upon the battered leather. That's when he heard the saloon door swing open and someone step outside.

"Hey," the man who'd walked out of the saloon said. "What are you doing here?"

Lester savored the few moments of rest without removing his forehead from the saddle. "I'm leaving right now," he groaned. "Just give me a minute."

"Is that you, Lester?"

Lester's eyes snapped open, but he still kept his head in place. He thought of who would know his name and the first two possibilities made his stomach clench. Then he remembered where he was and where he was headed. He also realized that the voice didn't sound like either Nick or Kinman.

Slowly turning his head, Lester saw a young man with a thick head of dark blond hair staring back at him. His face was clean shaven, exposing its familiar curves. "Pat?" Lester croaked.

"Sure enough, Cousin. What brings you all the way out here? Still runnin' from that Texan whose horse you stole?"

Lester didn't smile until he'd reached out to place both hands upon his cousin's shoulders. "That really is you, Pat."

"Sure it is. Who else would it be?"

"I'll tell you about it later. Is Wesley's place a few miles south of here?"

Pat looked at him and shook his head. "It's a few miles west, just like it's always been."

Now, Lester gave his cousin a heartfelt hug. "Thank God I found you."

TWENTY-THREE

———◆———

Lester and Pat rode to a small homestead that consisted of a two-floor house with a porch that wrapped all the way around it and a barn that looked to be brand new. In fact, considering how clean and well maintained the barn was, it seemed as though Lester's cousins preferred horses to people.

A man and two women sat on the porch in front of the house. The man was obviously Wesley, but he'd cut his dark blond hair down to coarse stubble and let his beard grow down to well over a foot in length. His face was a little more weather-beaten and his teeth were a bit more yellow, but it was still the same old Wesley. Lester remembered his older cousin as a burly, rough-looking man with a voice that boomed like a cannon whenever he opened his mouth. Although Wesley's appearance had changed a bit since the last time, his mannerisms sure hadn't.

"I'll be pickled in rat piss!" Wesley shouted as he hobbled forward. "What the hell are you doin' here?"

"That's the same thing I asked him," Pat said as he climbed down from his saddle.

"And what'd he say?" Wesley asked.

"Nothin' yet."

"Then shut your hole and let the man speak. Maybe he'd like somethin' to drink first."

Lester's eyes widened and he practically flew down off of his horse. "That would be fine!"

Holding his arms out like a magician who'd just performed a trick, Wesley said, "You see, Pat? The man needs to wet his whistle. Go inside and fetch him something to drink."

"I'm taking the horses to the barn first," Pat declared.

Wesley patted the horses on their noses and scratched them lovingly behind the ears. Turning to glance at the women behind him, he grunted. "Fetch us somethin' to drink!"

The older of the two women got up and straightened out her faded yellow skirt. She was probably somewhere in her forties, but wore her years as if every last one of them had been a trial. "I just made some lemonade."

"Then go get it! Damn! How many times do I need to ask?"

She nodded and put on a thin smile. Looking to the men, she said, "It's good to see you again, Lester."

Wesley's voice thundered loud enough to rattle the dirty glass in the windowpanes. "Just get it, bitch!"

Neither of the women reacted to the tone in Wesley's voice. The older one headed into the house, while the younger one remained on the porch to continue the knitting that had held her attention since before Lester's arrival.

"Last I heard, you were runnin' from some Mexican about a stolen horse," Wesley said.

Lester's eyes were focused upon the front door of the house as he replied, "It was a Texan."

"Oh," Wesley said with a wince. "I wouldn't have done that."

"I know, I know." When he saw the door swing open again, Lester stepped onto the porch and took the glass from the woman's hand. "Thanks, Ann."

Before she could finish saying, "You're welcome," the older woman was refilling the glass Lester had already drained. She tipped a pitcher she carried in her other hand and smiled as Lester drank that helping just as quickly as he had the first one.

Refreshed, Lester blinked and looked around as if he'd just woken up. "Did you find that grave?" he asked.

"What grave?" Wesley asked.

Lester shook his head wearily. "You know the one I mean."

Shooing his wife back into the house, Wesley replied, "Yeah, we found it. So what?"

"Was the money in there? What about the jewels?"

Narrowing his eyes, Wesley leaned forward like a dog guarding its territory. "You ain't in line for one cent of that money, family or not. Me and Pat found it. Me and Pat dug it up. Me and Pat pried it out of that dead man's hands."

"Good Lord," the younger woman whispered as she set down her knitting needles and crossed herself.

By this time, Pat had returned from the barn and was close enough to listen in. "Keep quiet, Stephanie. You don't seem so picky when you're wearing that new necklace I gave you."

The younger woman was thin and had a narrow, somewhat angular face. Her skin was obviously accustomed to being pale, but had recently been burned after too much sun. Wisps of hair flew from the rest that was tied behind her head. Upon hearing her husband's voice, one of her hands reflexively drifted up to her neck.

Lester's eyes fixed upon the glittering necklace resting against her smooth skin. Lunging forward to reach for the necklace with both hands, he asked, "Where'd you get that?"

Pat's hand snapped down to clamp around Lester's wrist before Lester even realized his cousin had gotten so close. The grip tightened painfully as Pat shoved Lester's arm to one side.

"You know damn well where it came from," Pat hissed.

"You two really dug up that grave in the Badlands," Lester whispered.

Wesley rocked on his heels and smiled proudly. "We sure as hell did. I told you all about how we were supposed to be working for Cobb, didn't I?"

"Λ bit."

"When was that, Pat? A year ago?"

"Closer to three years," Pat replied.

"Whichever, it was one of the times that Barrett Cobb called on us to back him up on one of his schemes. Usually we just pick off anyone trying to follow him and his men on their way out of some town or another and this time wasn't supposed to be any different. Well, Barrett never showed. We went to meet him and found one of his men carrying ol' Barrett away. Cobb was dead as a doornail."

The door swung open again and Ann came out with two more glasses. Wesley and Pat each took one and then Ann walked back into the house. Stephanie was reluctant to follow her, but moved quickly once Pat nodded for her to get going.

Once his wife was inside, Pat said, "We thought Cobb was being brought to us, since the man carrying him was headed this way. But we followed him into the Badlands instead and he planted Cobb up there. We never got our cut and nobody ever found the jewels, so we thought they were probably buried there, too."

"And you let them set there for three years?" Lester asked.

"We didn't know for sure where them jewels were. Besides, you wouldn't be so quick to dig up a grave," Wesley snapped. "Not if you saw the man who dug it. He looked like death warmed over and he was one of Barrett's gunmen. Those fellas ain't to be trifled with."

"I've been hearing about those jewels for a while now," Lester said. Lowering his voice and looking around, he added, "Were you spreading them rumors?"

Pat shrugged. "We may have done some talking after things settled from that robbery. It ain't as if anyone can know we was really there."

Wesley sipped his lemonade and wiped away what he'd splashed onto his beard. He looked as if he would bust if he didn't spit out what he wanted to say next. "It was my idea to head back up there. I figured if nobody went to claim them jewels, they were rightfully ours, since we never got our share."

Pat corrected him. "You started talking about that a few months after the robbery. Just like you kept talking about it every couple of months after that. Just like clockwork."

Glaring at the younger man, Wesley said, "You could'a gone up there any time you wanted. Hell, I bet Stephanie would've gone up there on her own if she knew where to dig."

"Shut your damn mouth, Wes. I swear I'll—"

"You'll what?"

Pat took a swing at Wesley that clipped him on the chin. The older man's beard seemed to have absorbed most of the blow, since Wesley wasted no time in lunging at his cousin and knocking him off the porch. Both men, covered in spilled lemonade, landed on the ground, a pile of thrashing arms and legs. In no time at all, they were kicking up enough dirt to form a small cloud.

Setting down his glass, Lester jumped off the porch and waded into the brawl between his two cousins. He caught a few glancing blows for his trouble, but managed to get between the two men and pull them apart.

"You were right to stay out of there," Lester said just before Wesley's elbow buried itself in his gut. Doubling over, Lester lashed out with one foot and caught Wesley in the shin.

Although both cousins still had plenty of fight left in them, they pulled themselves back simply because Lester was in their way.

Hacking painfully, Lester said, "You were right. You hear me? You were right to keep your distance from there."

"See?" Wesley sneered. "I told you so!"

Before he could stop himself, Lester turned and smacked his older cousin across the face. Wesley looked more shocked than hurt by the blow and stared at him with his mouth hanging open. It was the only time that Lester had ever seen the man speechless.

"And you were wrong for going after it at all," Lester said. "I don't know about the rest of the men Cobb worked with, but one of them is a killer like I've never seen. You heard of Nick Graves?"

Pat nodded. "Yeah. Cobb used to mention him."

"Well I've heard plenty about Graves and I think all of it's true. I've seen Graves and he'd gun you down just as soon as he'd look at you."

Shoving Lester back as a way to regain his posture, Wesley asked, "When have you ever seen Nick Graves?"

"Maybe a day ago and he was in the Badlands at Cobb's grave."

Now, both of Lester's cousins were speechless. Pat turned white as a sheet and then squatted with his hands on his knees. Wesley ran his fingers over his head and then sifted through the tangled mess of his beard.

"Nick Graves is here?" Pat asked breathlessly.

"He was in the Badlands," Lester repeated. "At Cobb's grave. He's the one who buried him there."

"And you were there, too?"

Wesley's eyes snapped toward Lester. He lunged toward his cousin and grabbed him by the front of his shirt with both hands. "Are you working with Graves? You stupid son of a bitch, he'll kill all of us to get them jewels!"

To his credit, Lester tried his best to smack Wesley's hands away. Unfortunately, his best wasn't quite strong enough to do the job. After a few more attempts, Lester wound up simply grabbing Wesley's wrists. "I wasn't working with him," he said while tugging at his cousin's wrists. "He . . . he forced me to take him to the grave."

"But he already knew where it was."

"Not Graves. I mean another man forced me to take him there. A bounty hunter named Alan Kinman."

"So Kinman's here and not Graves?" Pat asked.

Lester squirmed at the end of Wesley's fists like a worm on a fishing line. "Actually, they're both here."

Wesley nodded slowly and ran his tongue over cracked lips. "You sure about that?"

"Yeah. I barely got away."

"Did they follow you here?"

"I don't . . . think so."

Wesley's fist slammed into Lester's chin hard enough to snap his head back like a rag doll. The impact wasn't enough to knock Lester out, but it sure took away plenty of his steam.

"You don't think so?" Wesley growled. "What kind of damned fool's answer is that? What the hell were you thinking, coming here with a couple of killers on your tail? And one of 'em's a bounty hunter? I should kill you right now, God dammit!"

Although Lester's jaw wasn't broken, he wasn't anxious to move it any more than he had to. "You're my family," he blubbered. "I thought I could . . . I thought . . ."

"You *didn't* think," Wesley interrupted. "That's the damn problem."

Suddenly, Lester's eyes cleared and the fear vanished from his face. "I thought I could warn you," he said calmly. "I heard all the talk you've been spreading all the way out in Oregon."

"We're not the only ones that have been talking about them jewels. It's been in the newspaper, for Christ's sake."

"You're the one that called it the Reaper's Fee," Pat pointed out."

Wesley grinned proudly and puffed out his chest. "I might've had something to do with that."

"Exactly," Lester said. "And now that folks have had enough time to spread their rumors, tell their own stories, Graves caught wind of it. Kinman's heard about it, too, and both of them are after that Reaper's Fee." Lester wasn't about to tell his cousins that he'd offered to bring Kinman this far to save his own neck and was relieved when neither of the other men asked about it.

Reluctantly, Wesley let Lester go.

"Is it still here?" Lester asked.

Both cousins looked at each other. Wesley spat onto the ground as Pat nodded.

"Yeah," Pat told him. "Most of it is."

"Let's see it."

"Why?"

"Because I came all this way," Lester said. "I'm your kin and I would have helped you go after it if you would have given me the chance. The least you can do is let me get a look at what all this fuss is about."

Pat looked over to Wesley, who eventually nodded.

"Go on and show him," the oldest cousin said. "Don't let Stephanie see what you're up to or she'll make you hand over another portion of your share."

"Kiss my ass," Pat muttered as he walked back to the barn.

Wesley grabbed hold of Lester once more, but not like the last time. Instead, he took hold of the back of Lester's neck and pulled him in under his arm. "You all right, cousin?"

"Yeah. I could use something to eat."

"The women will fix you up just fine. Is that true what you said before? About those men coming after you and all?"

"Yeah," Lester said. "I'm afraid it is. Are you gonna kick me out of here?"

"Nah. I may want to, but you're right. You're kin. Besides, you've got a bigger price on your head than me and Pat combined. I checked. That Mexican must really have it in for you."

"Texan."

"Whatever."

After another minute or two, Pat returned from the barn carrying a bundle in one arm as if it was his firstborn. Made up of battered leather tied up by a few lengths of twine, the bundle wasn't any bigger than a small loaf of bread. Pat kept his eyes on the house at all times. When he made it back to where Wesley and Lester were standing, he turned his back to the house and held the bundle out in one hand.

Pat peeled back the top layer of leather, and Lester could see the treasure that everyone had talked about. It wasn't as much as some had claimed, but seeing all those glittering diamonds, gold nuggets and bundles of cash was enough to take Lester's breath away.

"That's the Reaper's Fee?" Lester gasped. "It was really in that grave?"

Wesley nodded, admiring the bundle in Pat's hand. "Sure was. It was stuffed in Cobb's pockets."

"You . . . sifted through a dead man's pockets?"

"Sure. How else was I gonna get it out of there?"

Closing up the bundle, Pat carefully wound the twine back around it and said, "We already dug up a grave. The rest didn't seem like too much more to ask."

For the first time since he'd started in on all of this, Lester got a real good impression of the rage seething behind Nick's eyes when he'd been talking about someone disturbing his friend's grave. In a frightened voice, Lester said, "We might want to pack up and get the hell away from here."

Brimming with confidence over the fruits of his labor, Wesley said, "If those men want to come after my kin, they'll have a fight on their hands. Besides, there's three of us and only two of them, right?"

"But one of them's a known killer," Pat said. "I heard Graves killed his first man before he even fucked his first woman."

"I've heard plenty of bad stories about Graves, too," Wesley said. "That don't make 'em all true. "Just the same, though, maybe we should put the odds more in our favor. You still got them shot-guns from when Uncle Mike visited us last spring to do some hunting?"

"Yeah, but one of them's broken and we don't have any shells."

"Go back into town and buy some shells. Buy a new gun while you're at it. We make sure the wives are armed along with us and it'll be five against two. That should work out better all around."

"I just got back from town," Pat told him. "Stores are closed. I'm not heading straight back there."

"Then I'll go in the morning. Jesus Christ, you're a whining cuss."

"I'll go with you," Lester offered.

"You see there? Little cousin knows how to lend a hand when all of our asses are on the line." Wesley booted Pat in the backside as the younger cousin went back to put the bundle in its hiding spot. "We'll take turns keeping watch, and Lester and I'll head into town come first light. Odds are that them two won't even find us out here."

Lester nodded, doing his best to mirror Wesley's confidence.

He was given a room and allowed to sleep while the other two cousins kept watch. The more he thought about Nick's reputation with a gun and Kinman's reputation for tracking, the harder it was for Lester to get any rest.

TWENTY-FOUR

By the time he and Kinman had broken camp and ridden out the next morning, Nick knew how the bounty hunter was tracking Lester. It wasn't easy to spot at first, but Nick had managed to pick out the pattern that kept showing up among the tracks in the dirt. Kinman seemed to enjoy doing his job and was damn good at it, so Nick let him keep the lead. For the moment, their end goal was the same.

"You ever hear of Pat or Wesley Harbor?" Kinman asked after he'd gotten his bearings and was preparing his horse for the day's ride.

Nick cinched up the last buckle on Kazys's saddlebags and shrugged. "I've been to Boston Harbor."

"They ain't places. They're people. Ever hear of 'em?"

After thinking about it once more, Nick came up with even less than before. "No. I guess I haven't."

"They're Lester's cousins. By the looks of it, he may be heading out to meet them."

"If you know where to find them, we should be able to work out a shortcut. That should shave off some time."

"If I knew where to find them, I would've found them already. They're wanted men, mostly for working with your friend Barrett Cobb."

Nick recognized the way Kinman was staring at him. It was the look that was in a man's eye when he asked a question that he figured you already knew the answer to. It reminded Nick of the smug distrust that poured from a lawman's eyes. "Barrett worked with plenty of men. He used them for a lot of jobs so none of them would know too much."

"You worked with him, too."

"Me and Barrett also worked with a lot of other fellas. If you want to know where they are, I can take you to their graves. Some of them are still somewhere in Montana, but I'm sure you'd be more than welcome to have a look around. Those vigilantes just love bounty hunters."

"And they also love outlaws," Kinman said without missing a beat. Making sure to stare at Nick's mangled hand, he added, "I hear they take extra special time with the outlaws they like more'n anyone else."

Nick nodded and climbed into his saddle. Once there, he made a particularly nasty gesture with the hand that was still in Kinman's sights. "You want to lead the way or would you prefer to give Lester even more of a head start?"

"Don't you worry about Lester. I've been tracking him long enough to know how his little pea brain works. His kin lives somewhere around a town named Hackett. He'll run there just as surely as I'm sitting here."

"Then what are you waiting for?" Nick asked while waving grandly toward the trail. "Lead the way."

Kinman stared at Nick for a few seconds. In that short amount of time, Nick felt as if he could hear exactly what was running through the bounty hunter's mind. The smugness in Kinman's eyes, combined with the way he turned his back to Nick was proof that the bounty hunter thought he could take Nick down whenever he saw fit to do so.

As he watched Kinman snap his reins and get moving, Nick shifted his hand toward his pistol. He could put a bullet through that arrogant fool before Kinman even heard the shot that killed him. Nick could even dig a hole and plant Kinman in it without losing much time in his pursuit of Lester Peterson.

But of all the things Kinman was, he sure as hell wasn't a fool.

Nick thought about that as his fingers brushed against the specially tooled leather of his holster. It was strapped across his belly, as it was whenever he was expecting a fight. Nick could draw a fraction of a second quicker that way.

Kinman may or may not have known that Nick had caught on to the trick he'd pulled with the shoe of Lester's horse. Letting the name of that town drop, on the other hand, was something the bounty hunter had done on purpose. Any man would know that the name of the town closest to the spot they were after was a valuable piece of information. To a tracker, it would have been twice as valuable.

Perhaps Kinman was seeing if Nick would try to attack him and go on alone now that he had something to work with.

Then again, there was always the chance that Kinman was tired and had made a slip of the tongue.

No, Nick thought. That wasn't a possibility.

"We've wasted enough time already," Kinman shouted over his shoulder. "Stop lagging behind and let's get moving."

"No need to worry," Nick shouted back. "I know where Hackett is and we should be able to get there around noon or so if we keep a good pace."

Watching for Kinman's reaction, Nick kept his hand over his holstered pistol. The tips of his fingers might have been mostly numb, but he could feel the smooth, curved iron well enough.

Kinman stopped.

For the next few seconds, he sat upon his horse while slowly cocking his head to one side. Finally, he turned and looked back at Nick and Kazys. "The best pace in the world won't help us if we don't leave this spot. Is something wrong with your horse, or are you content to let that asshole and his cousins live like kings off of them jewels?"

"I'm just making sure I didn't leave anything behind," Nick said, still keeping his hand on his gun.

Kinman started riding, but slowly enough so he could hear what was going on behind him. Nick recognized the cautious way Kinman flicked his reins as well as the way the bounty hunter kept his ears pricked for any sound he could pick up. When Nick began to follow, he saw Kinman's posture relax a bit as both horses fell into a quick step.

There had to be something that Kinman was holding back. The more Nick thought about it, the more certain he became. A man didn't get a reputation like Kinman's by making slips of the tongue to men he clearly didn't trust. Then again, Kinman had made the mistake of showing himself back in Rock Springs.

Or had that been a test as well?

Nick had batted that thought around more than once, but it had been pushed aside in favor of everything else that had happened since then. Showing himself in Rock Springs could have been a fatal mistake or it could have been a piece of some other plan. Nick didn't like to bet on mistakes. Instead, he kept his thoughts churning as he and Kinman gathered up speed and rode toward Hackett.

Kinman only allowed himself half a smirk at Nick's expense. Even though he was pretty sure the other man couldn't see his face from behind him, Kinman didn't want to muck up whatever knots were being tied within Nick's brain.

Crossing Nick's path in Rock Springs had been a mistake. If he'd had his say in the matter, Kinman would have preferred to go after Graves the way he went after all of his targets: after some careful scouting and preparation. But sometimes a man had to play the cards he was dealt and Kinman was pretty happy with the way this game was going.

So far, Kinman had gotten Nick to change his mind half a dozen times on whether he should trust him or not. Considering the confusion that had surrounded their first run-in, Kinman figured that maintaining that confusion was his best bet.

Nick was going to take his shot and was simply waiting for his chance to come. Kinman knew well enough that any move he made toward his own gun would be met by a storm of lead from that Schofield Nick carried. It was only a question of timing. One fraction of a second either way would decide whether Nick or Kinman would wind up dead.

Kinman took a look behind him to find Nick right where he should be. The deck was stacked in Kinman's favor and all was right with the world. There was even more money waiting for him once he caught up with Lester and his no-good cousins. Hopefully, those boys had a wagon on that spread of theirs, because Kinman would need one to haul all of those bodies in to claim the rewards.

To make matters even better, Kinman had seen Nick in action back in Rock Springs. For that, alone, running into Graves was worth tipping his hand a little early. The gunman Kinman had heard so much about would have given him a run for his money in shooting those Chinamen for such an easy payoff. After seeing the way Nick had faltered when it came time to earning some of Hale's money, Kinman was more inclined to believe the stories he'd heard about how badly those Montana vigilantes had torn Graves apart.

Kinman rode ahead of Nick without much concern. Nick may have been a threat in his younger days, but he wasn't anything that Kinman couldn't handle now. In fact, Lester and his cousins might just do Kinman's job for him once they got to Hackett. Either way, Kinman figured this might be the last job he would need to complete before retiring to a nice little spread of his own.

TWENTY-FIVE

Someone knocked on the door and Lester didn't make a move to answer it. He was still half asleep and in a strange room, so he didn't think someone could be trying to summon him. When the knock came again, it snapped him out of his daze and got him to his feet. Lester walked across the small, cozy room and pulled open the door.

"You still in there?" Pat grunted. "Wesley's getting ready to head into town. You're still going with him, right?"

Lester nodded. "Yeah. I'm still going. I was just trying to . . . just freshening up a bit."

Pat's eyes moved down and up to take stock of the man in front of him. "You're barely even dressed."

"It's been a long couple of days. I suppose it's all just catching up to me."

"Well I can bring you some fresh water to splash on your face. Maybe you can get a bath when you're in town." Leaning forward and sniffing the air surrounding Lester, Pat added, "Definitely get a bath in town. There's a good spot where a friendly redhead will wash your back real thorough, like. Know what I mean?"

A blind man would have known what Pat meant, but Lester nodded as if to play along with the other man's attempt at subtlety.

"I'll let Wesley know you're pulling yourself together," Pat said. "I'll bet some coffee will help speed things along."

"That would be fine."

"All right, Cousin. I'm just going to get some things situated in the barn. Know what I mean?"

"Yeah I know what you mean."

After a quick nod, Pat turned and walked away from the door. Lester closed it and sat down on the edge of the little bed. The room was decorated sparsely and had nothing to cover the warped wooden slats of the floor. A small table stood in one corner next to the creaky bed. Actually, it leaned in that corner, since one of the table's legs was an inch shorter than the others.

Lester placed his head in his hands and closed his eyes. The room wasn't on the side of the house that caught much sunlight, so pressing his face against his palms brought complete darkness. It wasn't much of a comfort, however, since Lester's thoughts were still rushing through his mind like whitewater flowing over jagged rocks.

One of the things that bothered him the most was the set of rumors that had nothing at all to do with outlaws or the Reaper's Fee. They'd circulated among Lester's own family regarding another cousin of his that had gone missing shortly after Pat and Wesley had taken up their guns and stepped onto the wrong side of the law.

Lester hadn't known his cousin Matt too well. What he did know was the kid had always been a hell-raiser since the day he could walk. Word had it that Matt was in on the first job that Wesley and Pat ever pulled. Supposedly Matt got greedy and was killed for it. Matt was then buried quietly and nobody in the family talked about him much anymore.

Lester really hadn't thought about Matt until now. Something in Wesley's eyes had bothered him ever since Wesley had shown him those jewels, though. Now Lester wondered if that had been the same look Matt had seen when his time on earth was drawing to an end.

Thoughts like that were just another set of teeth gnawing at the inside of Lester's gut. With all the other worries he had, Lester was surprised he still had any guts left. Suddenly, one of his thoughts popped to the surface and made him snap his head up with his eyes wide open. Instead of another problem, Lester had actually come up with a solution. In fact, the more he thought about it, his solution might actually clear up some of the other problems that had been nagging at him.

"Oh my God," Lester whispered to himself.

Unlike some of his other ideas, this one actually stood up to a second glance. It even stood up to a third and fourth glance.

Lester hopped to his feet with renewed vigor. He

looked around his room, but only found the same
sparse furnishings that had been there before. As
he turned toward the door and reached for the
handle, someone knocked on it. Lester nearly
cleared the floor, but managed to control his shock
so he could open the door.

"Pat, do you have . . ."

Lester stopped when he saw who was out there.
Instead of Pat, it was Pat's wife, Stephanie. She
was a pretty young thing with short dark brown
hair. Her face was a little plumper than it had
looked the night before, but that could simply have
been because she was looking straight at him now
rather than down at the knitting upon her lap.

Stephanie smiled warmly at him and held up a
basin brimming with water. "Pat said you'd need
some water," she said. "Mind if I come in?"

"Oh sure," Lester said as he opened the door all
the way.

Moving with smooth, easy steps, Stephanie
walked past him to the small table in the corner.
Her hips swayed beneath her loose-fitting skirt,
which was just thin enough for Lester to be fairly
certain she wasn't wearing much of anything else
beneath.

Setting the basin on the table, Stephanie bent at
the waist so she could fuss with it for a few extra
seconds. Under normal circumstances, Lester
would think she was taking too much time. However, considering the disrepair of that table, he was
amazed she got it to support the basin at all.

When she turned around to face him, Stephanie dried her hands on the sides of her skirt. After the first few rubs, it seemed more as if she was caressing her hips rather than simply getting rid of excess water.

"Would you like some coffee?" she asked.

Lester's response was as quick as it was enthusiastic. "Yes. That would be perfect."

Stephanie lowered her head a bit as she walked past him. Her hand eased out just enough to brush along his stomach as she went.

Although he enjoyed watching her leave, Lester was even gladder once she was gone. He had to keep reminding himself that Stephanie was Pat's wife. No matter what she was doing to him or how much she seemed to enjoy doing it, Lester simply couldn't allow himself to give in.

Lester shook his head and dipped his hands in the water. While splashing his face, he did his level best to force those thoughts from his mind. Before he'd even put a dent in them, his door swung open once more.

He felt a gentle touch upon his shoulder at the same time the smell of coffee reached his nose.

"I would have brought you a whole pot, but there's nowhere to put it," Stephanie whispered to him.

Lester turned around so quickly that he almost knocked the cup of hot coffee from her hands. Now that he was closer to her, Lester found her face to be even softer and kinder than before. Her eyes were as clear as the water in the basin and the warmth he felt inside of him had nothing to do with the steaming cup being offered to him.

"Thanks," he said. "That looks real fine."

"Why don't you try some?"

Lester reached for the cup of coffee but bypassed it altogether so he could slip his hand along the side of her body. Stephanie responded by holding the cup away from them so she could press herself against him without fear of spilling the coffee onto the floor. Her lips pressed against his and opened almost immediately.

Although Lester had been the one to move first, he quickly felt as if he'd taken one step onto a downward slope and was quickly stumbling toward a hell of a fall. Stephanie's leg slid up and down along his side.

"I need something, if it's not too much trouble," Lester squeaked.

"I need it too, Sugar."

It took a hell of an effort to keep his mind on track, but Lester forced himself through it because he knew that effort wasn't going to get any easier if he waited. "Could I get some paper . . . and . . . maybe a pencil? I need to write a letter."

Stephanie let out a slow breath that heated up the side of Lester's neck. "We'll have plenty to write about real soon," she promised.

Most of Lester's brain was still trying to cut through the haze that was thickening in his skull. As much as he wanted to make certain she'd heard him the first time, he simply couldn't get his tongue to go through the process of repeating itself. There were just too many things vying for his attention. Lester could feel the curves of Stephanie's body rubbing against him and just as he was about to stumble further, she quickly pulled away.

Lester was left with an ache in his trousers and the cup of coffee in his hand. He felt as if he'd just been pulled out of a deep sleep when he heard his cousin's voice thunder through the room.

"You comin' or not?" Wesley barked.

Looking around, Lester found Stephanie closer to the basin than she was to him. She fidgeted with the crooked table while shooting a quick, knowing glance over her shoulder. "I'll get you that paper and pencil," she said calmly.

"I . . . uh . . . was just having some coffee," Lester said, praying to the Lord above that Wesley bought it. "And I also wanted to write a letter to Uncle—"

"Just get your ass ready to go," Wesley snapped. "I'm leaving in two minutes with or without you."

Hackett hadn't been much of a town since the nearby vein of gold had been picked clean. Lester could see remnants of the town's former glory reflected in the dirty, broken signs that hung above most of the storefronts. Places like the Golden Saloon and Strike It Rich Gambling Hall lined the streets. Turning a corner allowed him to see mining supply stores and assayers' offices that were now either empty or boarded up altogether.

Like most towns that were past their prime, however, the saloon trade was still booming. Wesley rode past a place called the Nugget and craned his neck to get a look through the front window.

"They put on a hell of a show in there," Wesley said. "Watch the girls kick up their skirts and then watch them kick up their legs for ya in a back room. Hell of a place! Don't look like there's anyone on stage right now, though."

"It's not even noon," Lester pointed out.

"It's always a good time for that kind of show."

Hearing that, Lester couldn't help but think about Stephanie. As if to distract himself from those thoughts, he patted his shirt pocket to find the letter he'd hastily written before saddling up. "Is that the sheriff's office?" he asked, nodding toward a small building with a shattered front window.

"Yeah," Wesley replied with a snorting laugh. "He's a marshal and he knows folks around here don't like him much."

"What about a post office?"

Wesley shifted in his saddle to show Lester an open-mouthed sneer. "You looking to settle here, or are you just flapping your lips some more?"

In response to that, Lester took the letter from his pocket and held it up.

It took Wesley a moment, but he finally nodded and turned back around. "Post office is that way," he said, jabbing a stubby finger toward a row of broken storefronts that looked like gaps in a filthy mouth. "In the back of the dry goods store."

"I'm going there to mail my letter."

"What made you want to start writing letters?"

Lester shrugged and smiled sheepishly. "With all that's happened, I haven't been talking to the family very much. I don't know when I'll be able to write again."

"You ask me, our family talks too much," Wesley said. "All them rumors and stories going back and forth."

Before he could catch himself, Lester spat out, "Like what happened to Matt?"

Wesley looked over at him with an expression that might have come from eating a piece of rotten meat. "Sure."

Lester nodded and pointed his horse toward the dry goods store down the street. "Well, it's only a letter. I'll catch up with you."

"I'll be down on Second Street at Smith's Firearms. Don't take too long. I'll be needing the rest of that money Pat gave to ya."

Lester watched Wesley ride away, and kept watching until his cousin rounded the corner. When he rushed into the dry goods store, he was already out of breath. "This the post office?" he asked the old man behind the counter.

"Yep."

"Where's the sack for the mail to be sorted?"

"Just give her here," the old-timer said as he stretched out a thin, liver-spotted arm. When he didn't feel anything placed in his hand, the old man stared at Lester and asked, "Do you have something to mail or not?"

"I do, but . . ."

Staring at the envelope in Lester's hand, the old man said, "There ain't no address on that."

Lester slapped the envelope onto the counter where the old man was sitting. Taking a pencil from his pocket, he quickly scribbled a word onto the envelope and then looked up. "What's the marshal's name?"

"Marshal Eaves?"

Nodding, Lester wrote another word on the envelope and handed it over. "I want this delivered to Marshal Eaves, but—"

"You can hand it over yourself. His office isn't far from here."

"I know, but I want it delivered. He shouldn't read it until later."

"You could have something to eat while you wait."

Resisting the urge to jump across the counter and throttle the old man, Lester said, "I'm not going to wait. I've got things to do. I need this delivered to the marshal a bit later."

The old man looked at Lester as if he smelled dung stuck to the bottom of his boot. "I was just trying to save you the postage."

"Here," Lester said as he took out some of the money Pat had given him to help buy the shotgun and rifle ammunition. "Take this as your fee. Just deliver the letter to the marshal and say it came in today's mail. Do whatever you need to make the envelope look genuine."

The old man snatched the money away with a speed that would have been impressive for a fellow half his age. "When do you want the marshal to get it?"

Lester pulled in a breath to steel himself. "Tonight should be fine. Say around five o'clock. No . . . better make it four."

"Four it is." Taking the letter, the old man tossed it onto an empty burlap sack folded on the floor behind him. He then placed both hands flat upon the counter and showed Lester a friendly smile.

Already on his way out the door, Lester shook his head. "That's all I need. At least, I sure hope it is. It damn well better be." He was still muttering as he left the store and headed for Smith's Firearms.

TWENTY-SIX

———— ◆ ————

The tracks took a few meandering turns, but led them toward Hackett. More than once, Nick played with the idea of breaking away from Kinman to do the rest of the tracking on his own, but that would have meant leaving the bounty hunter to his own devices. There were ways to make sure Kinman stayed put, but Nick didn't want to waste time on following those through. Besides, there was still a bit of time for Kinman to prove himself useful.

Nick could see a good portion of the town as Kinman reined his horse to a stop. They'd been riding a bit quicker than the day before, but not quite up to full speed. Kazys was breathing somewhat heavily, but Kinman's horse stood by without even shifting its hooves.

"You want to check the town?" Kinman asked.

"Do the tracks lead there?"

"Not as such, but Lester would've had to get some supplies and he might not be able to get everything from his cousins."

"We're here for Lester, so we'll follow his tracks," Nick said. "We've come too far to be thrown off the scent now."

"All right, then." Kinman shifted so he could look directly at Nick. He crossed one hand over the other as he let out a smooth breath. "Let's get something straight. If those jewels are there, we're splitting them right down the middle."

"We already negotiated this."

"That's when I wasn't sure if we'd be able to find Lester or not. Now that we're here I want to get all of this out of the way before there's any commotion."

Nick's voice was smooth and even as ice on a freshly frozen pond. "There's going to be a commotion right here and now if you push this too far."

"Then let's get it out of the way," Kinman declared, while shifting his coat aside so he could better reach his pistol.

"Or I could just follow the marked tracks that lead past that town and head straight to wherever Lester's holed up."

Kinman was taken aback, but it didn't last long. He regained his composure in a heartbeat and actually smiled good-naturedly. "You saw those, huh?"

"Yeah. I saw 'em."

"Then our original deal stands."

Nick nodded without moving more than the few muscles required to perform the action. Although the rest of him was still, the muscles were tensed like bowstrings beneath his skin.

Kinman kept still as well.

The next few seconds felt as if the world around them was holding its breath.

"How about we finish up one matter before moving on to the next?" Nick finally said.

"Fine with me."

To show he was the better man, Nick took his hand away from his holster and placed it casually upon his saddle horn. Kinman did the same.

"If Lester's still with his cousins, he'll probably be waiting for us," Kinman said.

"They're probably all waiting for us. That is, if they haven't already moved along by now."

Kinman craned his neck to look in the direction that the marked tracks led. "Lester's tired. He's been running for a while and has been hiding out for over a year. Once he gets around family, he'll settle in for a bit."

But Nick was thinking of a bit more than Lester wanting to rest up and get a hot meal in his belly. Nick knew a thing or two about being on the run and he also knew about what it was like to be hunted. There was a time when the prey wanted nothing more than to turn the tables and take a bite at its pursuers. It seemed like a foregone conclusion that now would be that time for Lester. Nick could feel it just as surely as he could feel the impulse to take a shot at Kinman.

Since there was still an outside chance that there was a bit of tracking to be done, Nick nodded and said, "I think you're right. Lester probably spent his first couple hours eating or sleeping. By that time, he's got to know that we'd be after him."

"He knows, all right," Kinman said with a grin. "The only question now is what he intends to do about it."

Glancing overhead to take note of the crisp, blue sky, Nick said, "It'll be dark in a while. Lester's probably not going to move until after the sun goes down."

"You really think he'll wait that long?"

Nick was nodding as if he'd only heard that question in the back of his mind. "He's dug in, so there's no reason to do anything when he can still be sighted. Riding at night will make it easier for him to slip away and try to regain his lead on us. That is, unless he's already long gone."

"Riding at night will also make it easier for him to trip up or stumble somewhere along the way," Kinman offered.

Nick shook his head. "He knows this land better than we do. The dark will only work to his advantage."

"Lester's been hiding out in Oregon for half a year or more. Before that, he was working his way up from Texas."

"He still knows this area. Even if he's been here once before, that's once more than me. What about you?"

Kinman shrugged and shifted his gaze forward. "I see your point. How do you want to approach him?"

"Let's find him first and work out the rest once we get there."

Both men snapped their reins and rode in a path that skirted Hackett's limits.

It didn't take long for them to ride close enough to catch sight of the run-down spread inhabited by Lester's cousins. Of course, finding it was doubly easy, since there were four sets of marked tracks that all led to the same spot. Two sets were headed toward the spread and two headed away, each like individual strands of a web that were all connected to the same central point.

"Jesus Christ," Kinman muttered from his spot in the grass well away from the house. "No wonder Lester came here."

Nick lay stretched out on his belly directly beside Kinman. Both of them squinted through spyglasses as various members of the household in front of them went about their business. Every cousin was armed.

"You see Lester yet?" Nick asked.

Kinman kept the spyglass to his eyes and said, "Nope, but his horse is in the barn."

Since he could only see a few noses inside that barn from this vantage point, Nick was about to question the validity of Kinman's statement. Then Nick took a look for himself and spotted one horse's nose that was splotched in a pattern of white, black and brown that seemed very familiar.

"That's Lester's horse all right," Nick admitted. "Good eye."

"It's what I do." When Kinman looked over at Nick, he saw the other man setting his spyglass down and taking off his coat.

"Stay here and give me a few minutes to get in closer."

"Oh, no you don't. We're going in together. If they see you, they'll start shooting and it'll be that much harder for me to get in to do anything but catch some lead."

"They won't see me," Nick assured him.

"And how can you be sure of that?"

"Because it's what I do."

Seeing Kinman's aggravation put a warm feeling in Nick's heart. He pulled his sleeves all the way down and buttoned them so they remained tight against his wrists. His holster was repositioned on his side and tied to his leg to keep it out of his way. By the time anyone knew he was there, Nick would have plenty of time to get the Schofield in hand. If not, he would have a lot bigger problems than shaving half a second off of his drawing speed.

Nick kept his belly in the grass and half-crawled, half-slithered toward the house. Whenever he reached a patch of higher weeds or bushes, Nick allowed himself to get his feet beneath him and scramble forward. It wasn't the quickest way to travel, but he got to the house without drawing a glance or making more than a subtle rustle to announce he was there. He circled around to the side of the property opposite the barn.

Just then, a door slammed and Nick froze in his spot. His belly pressed against the dirt and his legs stretched out behind him. The sun was on its way down, but it would be a while before dark. As steps knocked against the front porch, Nick eased his arm down to his holster and kept it there. He was ready to draw, but didn't want to tip his hand unless it was absolutely necessary.

The man who'd opened the door was a big fellow with a long, unkempt beard. He had a rifle in one hand and a shotgun in the other. Holding both guns over his shoulders, the bearded man strutted out and cleared his throat noisily.

"Take this shotgun, Ann."

When he heard the woman respond, Nick twitched. She'd been so quiet that he hadn't even heard her come outside.

"Keep it," she replied.

"We been through this already. There's some men that might be comin' and we'll need all the help we can get when they arrive. You don't have to hit anything. Just fire and keep them off their balance."

"I ain't taking no shotgun, Wesley, and that's that."

Nick heard a few more heavy steps, followed by the creak of a rocking chair. He pushed himself up a bit, but couldn't see much more than the back of the chair and the big man leaning down to it. The post at the corner of the porch was blocking Nick's view of the woman Wesley was talking to.

"You're taking this shotgun and you're helping to defend this house, God dammit," Wesley snarled.

"Defend this house or defend those goddamn jewels? I'd be more than happy to do one, but not the other."

"If you want to keep living off that money, you'd best do both."

"Then talk to Stephanie," Ann said. "I'm sure she'll fight to the death if it means she can gussy herself up with some more diamonds."

Nick could feel the tension building as if it was heat rolling in on a summer day. Although he'd never met the man or his wife, he knew what was coming.

"Take it!" Wesley snapped. He extended his arm and shoved the shotgun at her.

That was followed by the sounds of a wheezing breath and creaking wood. As soon as Nick heard that, his stomach began to clench. His instinct was to do something before things went any further. Then again, he was also desperately looking around for a sign of Lester or the other cousin Kinman had mentioned. He could hear movement coming from somewhere, but couldn't narrow it down since Wesley was creating such a ruckus.

"I won't take it!" Ann insisted. "What if the law comes? You want me to shoot them too?"

"You'll take it because I say so, bitch. Otherwise, I'll knock you through the goddamn window."

Nick gritted his teeth and waited another couple of seconds. It became quiet, but that ended with the sound of flesh slapping against flesh.

"You gonna do what I say?" Wesley asked. "Or do I need to smack some more sense through that fuc—"

"That's enough!" Nick said as he straightened up and drew his pistol.

Wesley towered over Ann as both of them turned to look at Nick.

"Leave her be," Nick said.

Wesley and Ann responded at the same time by taking their weapons and aiming them at Nick.

Nick's eyes widened as he reflexively dove for cover. He'd been expecting Wesley to make a move like that, but hadn't counted on Ann doing the same. Since he wasn't sure which to shoot first, Nick opted to try and live through the next few seconds to see if he could come up with a better plan.

Wesley's rifle went off and sent a round through the air fairly close to where Nick had been standing. By the time Nick hit the dirt, he heard the roar of the shotgun. The buckshot spread out as it left the barrel and some of it scraped along the backs of Nick's legs. He gritted his teeth against the pain, more surprised than hurt that Ann had been the one to draw first blood.

"Serves me right, I guess," Nick muttered.

As soon as he heard steps thumping against the porch, Nick rolled to one side and prayed he could reach some of the taller grass nearby.

Another shot from the rifle punched into the soil not far from where Nick had been lying. Nick fired one round toward the porch, but knew he wouldn't hit anything but a wall if he was lucky, since he was still in the process of rolling. When he came to a stop, he popped onto one knee and found himself looking at the woman who'd been sitting in the rocker.

Ann looked right back at him over the top of her shotgun as her finger tightened around its trigger.

TWENTY SEVEN

———◆———

Nick was running toward her even as the hammers of Ann's shotgun dropped. He bolted straight past Wesley so he could grab hold of the shotgun and twist it out of Ann's grasp. Only when he was holding the shotgun himself did Nick realize what he'd done. Ann stared at him with eyes as big as dinner plates and her mouth hanging open.

"You already emptied both barrels," Nick told her.

But that didn't do much to soften the blow. She still stared at Nick as if he had dodged a hail of gunfire without breaking a sweat.

The truth of the matter was that Nick wasn't sure whether she'd emptied both barrels or not. He'd already been in her sights and she was already pulling her trigger. If she'd saved a barrel for him, he would have been dead either way.

Ann's jaw began to move as she regained the power of speech. Less than two seconds had ticked by, which was more than enough time for Wesley to turn and see what was going on. Nick looked at

Wesley just as the man was swinging his arm around to take a shot. The next thing Nick did was extend his arm and throw himself back against the house. The shotgun Nick had taken caught Ann across the chest and knocked her back into her rocker, just as Wesley's rifle spat out a plume of smoke.

Nick's back hit the house as a bullet hissed past him. Since Wesley didn't seem like the sort of man to get flustered under fire, Nick turned away from him and ran for the corner. It was a bit farther than he would have liked, so he raised his modified Schofield and squeezed off a round to cover his escape.

"Jesus!" Wesley yelped as Nick's bullet took a small piece out of his shoulder. He rolled with the momentum of the passing bullet and dove away from the porch. When he brought up his rifle again, the only one in his sights was his wife.

"Where the hell'd he go?" Wesley asked.

Ann's eyes were still wide and she turned as if in a daze.

"Answer me, woman! Where'd he go?"

Ann looked at the corner where Nick had gone and then looked back at her husband. She opened her mouth to speak, but only a few strained grunts came out.

Wesley was back on his feet and stomping onto the porch. As he passed his wife, he slapped the palm of his hand against her face and shoved her back down onto the rocking chair. "Just stay put and keep out of the way, you useless pig."

Stepping around the corner, Wesley was propping his rifle against his shoulder when he saw Nick standing calmly with his back against the side of the house. Snapping his head back, Wesley nearly tripped over his own boots before Nick took a shot at him. The Schofield's bullet whipped through the air past Wesley's face like an angry hornet as the scent of burnt powder filled his nostrils.

"Dammit, Pat, what the hell are you doin' in there?" Wesley shouted.

When he heard that, Nick saw some movement through the window beside his face. Glancing that way, Nick saw a younger man with a gun in his hand. The instant he saw that gun raised up to fire, Nick pushed away from the wall and sent a pair of shots into the house.

Glass shattered loudly as the shots blasted through the air. Inside the house, Pat fell to the floor as he fired blindly at Nick. One of Pat's shots took out the remains of the windowpane, while the other punched straight through the wall.

Nick moved away from the house as he tried to decide if he should waste his remaining bullets by trading blind fire for more blind fire. Deciding to make better use of the next few seconds, he pulled some fresh bullets from his gun belt and began dumping the empty shells.

"You ain't taking them jewels from me, you son of a bitch!" Wesley shouted as he rounded the corner.

Snapping the Schofield shut, Nick was about to fire when he heard another shot crack through the open air. This one didn't come from inside the house or even from the porch. It had come from behind Wesley and opened a messy hole through the bearded man's chest.

Stumbling forward, Wesley twisted around to try and return fire, but was hit a second time. The next bullet caught Wesley in the side of the neck and took a good portion of meat along with it. Not knowing which way to turn, Wesley looked back at Nick as he coughed up a mouthful of blood.

Nick closed the Schofield with a snap of his wrist, kept the pistol at waist level and fired a round through Wesley's forehead. Once Wesley finally dropped and fell face-first to the ground, Nick was able to see Kinman standing behind him.

Still holding his smoking pistol in hand, Kinman said, "You were supposed to wait for me."

"Let's clear this house out before we haggle over details."

Shifting his eyes toward the shattered window, Kinman said, "Best watch yourself."

Judging by the tone in the bounty hunter's voice, Nick might have expected Kinman to be warning him about getting cut from the broken glass. When he took a look for himself, Nick saw Pat charging toward the window with a crazed look in his eyes. It was all Nick could do to jump clear of the window before catching the hell that was about to be thrown through it.

Not only did Pat fire through the window, but someone else was firing as well. Nick gritted his teeth as the hailstorm of lead rushed outward. Kinman stood his ground and waited for Nick to look his way before pointing calmly toward the front porch. Nick nodded to acknowledge Kinman's signal and then pointed toward the back of the house. Both men headed off in the directions they'd chosen as the gunfire from within the house subsided.

Nick treated the next window he was approaching as if it were a bear trap. Rather than walk straight past it, he stopped with his back against the wall and his gun held at the ready. Considering how flimsy the walls of the house were, Nick wasn't about to stand and wait for a bullet to punch through the wood. Instead, he took a quick glimpse through the window, saw an empty room, and then moved along.

The back of the house opened out to a wide couple of acres that were overgrown with more weeds than shrubs. The back porch wasn't much more than a platform with a few steps leading to the ground. There were no windows between him and those stairs, so Nick rushed the back door.

Slamming his heel against the door, Nick sent an explosion of splinters into the house as the door's frame gave way. Inside, he found a small kitchen and pantry leading to the sitting room at the front of the house.

"Who's there?" Pat shouted from another room. "Is that you, Wesley?"

Nick held his gun in front of him as he moved through the house. With all the noise coming from the other rooms, he didn't have any trouble keeping his steps from being heard. To his left and away from the kitchen, Nick saw a short hall leading to a closed door. He knew that had to be the room with the broken window and he prepared himself for anything to come through that door.

When the door opened, a younger woman stood there with tears streaming down her cheeks. "Are you the law?" she asked.

Nick didn't have time to say a word before a man's hand took Stephanie by the shoulder and pushed her out of Nick's sight. Pat then filled up the doorway. Firing from the hip, Pat pulled his trigger again and again as a visceral scream rolled up from the bottom of his lungs.

All Nick had to do was take a step back into the kitchen and every last one of Pat's rounds burrowed into the wall or flew into the next room. Once the firing was over, Nick took a cautious peek around the corner to find Pat closing the door again.

Gunfire came from the sitting room, announcing Kinman's entrance into the house. Within seconds, someone raced out of the front room like a quail that had been flushed from a bush. Nick pressed his back to a wall and listened for those steps to draw closer. Lester raced straight for the back door, without so much as glancing in Nick's direction as he passed.

Nick took a few lunging steps and grabbed hold of the back of Lester's collar. Squirming reflexively, Lester pulled himself out of his loose-fitting shirt like a snake shedding its skin. His arms flailed in front of him and he finally managed to get hold of the door. Pulling it open, Lester used every bit of his strength to sprint outside.

As Nick ran after Lester, he could hear more yelling and shooting behind him. A woman screamed. Something heavy hit the floor. The last thing Nick heard as he followed Lester to the barn was a man's voice roaring over everything else.

"Shut your damn mouth and put the gun down!" Kinman shouted.

There was a moment of silence followed by another pair of shots.

Nick didn't have time to figure out what had happened, since Lester had made it into the barn. He knew better than to rush in there after Lester, so he shouted, "Come on out of there or I'll drag your dead body out myself!"

Hearing the creak of hinges, Nick stepped back and got ready for whatever was about to come through that door. Hearing the rustle of hooves through loose hay, Nick swore under his breath and ran to pull open the door himself.

Nick got a real good look at the immaculate interior of the barn, mostly because of the light flooding through the wide-open rear door. Lester was in the saddle and riding through the rear door on the back of a sleek black mare. Nick was just able to see the bundle tucked under Lester's arm before the black mare broke into a run and turned sharply out of Nick's sight.

While Nick might have thought his luck was running dry, he quickly changed his reasoning when he saw two more horses already saddled and ready to go in the stalls to his left. Seeing that one of those horses was the run-down old-timer Lester had ridden before, Nick kicked open the gate of the other one's stall. Moments later, he was racing out of the barn and thundering after Lester.

It seemed that Lester knew his horseflesh, since he'd already pulled into a bigger lead than Nick had expected. Digging his heels into his own horse's sides, Nick snapped his reins against the animal's flanks and hoped for the best. Sure enough, the horse bolted forward. The speck that had been Lester's silhouette grew larger by the second as Nick chewed up the ground between them.

As he rode, Lester swung his arm behind him and fired off a few quick shots from a pistol his cousins had given to him. The bullets sailed away without getting close enough for Nick to even hear their passing. Even while squeezing off another shot, Lester wasn't looking behind him. Instead, his eyes were facing front and searching the horizon.

"Come on," Lester grumbled as he focused on the trail that led into Hackett. "It's almost six-thirty. Where the hell are you?"

When Lester crested a gentle rise, he spotted a group of four horses galloping toward Wesley's house. Lester smirked and snapped his reins again. "There you are!"

Closing the gap between himself and Lester, Nick spotted the approaching riders as well. The way they were moving toward that house, Nick had to assume they were racing to back up Lester and his cousins. Nick turned around to see if he could spot any trace of Kinman.

From this distance, the house actually looked peaceful.

Nick figured the bounty hunter could handle himself, so he turned back around to set his sights on Lester. When he did, Nick saw that the group of riders had split up so two of them could intercept Lester and the other two could move along to the house. Considering how fast they were all going, Nick guessed it would be only a minute or so before everyone got to meet on a more personal level.

The uneasy feeling in Nick's gut didn't get any better when he saw Lester turn to meet the other two riders head-on. It got even worse when he saw Lester wave his arms wildly over his head like some kind of crazed bird.

The two riders slowed down to meet up with Lester and started looking in Nick's direction as Lester flapped and waved back at him.

Nick pulled back on his reins and held his gun at the ready. It was too late to try and approach from another angle and it sure as hell was too late to turn back.

Pulling his horse to a stop, Nick swung down from the saddle so all that flesh and bone was between him and the other men.

"Toss that weapon and be quick about it, mister," one of the other two riders shouted. "Don't force us to kill you."

There was something odd about the way that rider tossed his threat at Nick. He didn't talk like someone out to get their hands on a load of stolen jewels. When Nick glanced around his horse to get a better look, he found Lester and both other riders pointing their guns at him.

Sure enough, those two were wearing badges.

TWENTY-EIGHT

———◆———

Only lawmen made threats as if their words alone were enough to make another man quake in his boots. Nick was fairly certain that neither of them would pull their triggers right away. The two lawmen were younger and didn't carry themselves as if they had any business holding a gun.

Typical deputies.

"Where's the marshal?" Lester asked, as if purposely verifying Nick's assessment of the other two.

"Never mind about the marshal," the first deputy said. "Is this the man who came to raid this place?"

Lester looked at Nick, smirked and then nodded. "It sure is."

Since he now knew who he was dealing with, Nick changed his entire demeanor. Wearing a shocked and somewhat fearful expression, he asked, "What's the meaning of this? That man stole my property!"

As Nick had expected, those words put both deputies' heads into a spin.

Seeing the confusion growing upon the lawmen's faces, Lester climbed down from his horse and shook his head wildly. "No, no! Don't listen to him! He was the one shooting at me! He's Nick Graves!"

"Did anyone see me fire a shot?" Nick asked innocently. As he spoke, Nick held up his hands to sheepishly display his gnarled fingers.

"I'm the one who told you about the raid!" Lester said. "I'm the one who wrote that letter. I paid to have it delivered to you." Hearing the crackle of gunshots coming from the house, Lester jabbed his finger in that direction and said, "See? There's the raid I warned you about. The marshal's in the thick of it right now!"

Both deputies looked back and forth between Nick and Lester. Then they looked at each other. The confusion was still on their faces. In fact, it had even gotten a little worse.

Suddenly, a voice drifted through the air from the direction of the house. It was a man's voice, but was a bit too far away for specific words to be heard. Just because they couldn't understand what was being said, both deputies were still instantly put onto the edges of their saddles.

"Did you hear that, Jim? I think that was the marshal," the older of the two deputies said. "He may need help."

As if to drive that point home, more gunshots crackled around the house.

"You go on ahead, Stan," Jim said. "I'll stay here with these two."

Stan nodded and steered his horse toward the house. He moved slowly at first, but snapped the reins once he'd made it a few steps without Nick or Lester trying to take a shot at him.

The deputy who was left behind had a strong build and a very youthful face. His chin looked as if it couldn't sprout whiskers if his life depended on it and his eyes flashed with the intensity and uncertainty that came with inexperience. His gun was in a steady hand, but the way he held it didn't inspire confidence.

Nick kept his movements slight and his voice calm so as not to elicit any hair-trigger responses from the young lawman. "No need to get jumpy. We can straighten this out easily enough."

"I ain't jumpy," Jim said.

"There's nothing to straighten out," Lester snapped. "Why the hell would I have brought the law here if I was the one doing anything wrong?"

"I think I know the answer to that," Nick replied. "And it doesn't have anything to do with fulfilling your civic duties."

Lester looked at Nick with more ferocity than he'd ever shown. "You're an outlaw," he said. "A killer. You don't know a damn thing."

"Seems to me like this whole fight is a great way to cover your escape," Nick pointed out. "You might be on your way across the state line by now if you didn't have me to worry about. Did you pick one of your cousins to help you inform the law or was it one of the wives?"

Jim straightened his arm and pointed his gun at Nick. "Shut up, both of you!"

Lester didn't even take notice of the deputy's gun. His eyes were locked upon Nick until the gunfire at the house flared up again. The moment he saw Jim look toward the house, Lester swore under his breath and brought up his gun to take a shot at the only one of the two men who wasn't ready to shoot back.

The bullet didn't draw blood, but whipped a few inches from Jim's stomach and through the coarse hair along the back of the neck of the lawman's horse. Feeling the lead nip its neck like that brought the horse up onto its rear legs as it let out a loud, surprised whinny.

Lester's shot surprised Nick almost as much as it did the horse. Nick regained his composure quickly, however, and returned fire as Lester took his second shot.

Nick's bullet caught Lester in the ribs, but didn't do much more than scratch him. Lester's next bullet raked along the deputy's back, burrowing deeply enough to twist the lawman in his saddle. With his horse still kicking and fretting, Jim toppled from the saddle, just managing to swing his legs down before risking a broken neck.

As soon as Lester saw the deputy disappear over the side of his horse, he pulled his reins and started to ride away. He fired a shot or two behind him, but that wasn't nearly enough to buy him a ticket away from there. Before his horse could build up a head of steam, a shot ripped through the air and slapped solidly into flesh and bone. Lester didn't feel any pain, so he snapped his reins again. His horse's only response was a pained groan as it dropped to its front knees and started to fall onto its side. Lester was just quick enough to hop from the saddle before the horse flopped over.

"You shot my horse!" Lester said as he wheeled around.

Nick rode up to him and swung down from his own saddle. "If you'd rather I shoot you, I'd be happy to oblige."

Lester reflexively grabbed for the fresh wound across his ribs. It was barely even bleeding, but he kept his hand there as if to keep his innards from spilling out. "A man doesn't just shoot another man's horse."

"He's not supposed to steal another man's horse, either. Sometimes bad things happen don't they, Lester? Like the law stumbling upon this place at just the right time. How'd they manage that?"

"He wrote them a letter," Kinman said as he rode up to them on the horse that Nick had passed up back at the barn.

Both Lester and Nick turned toward the bounty hunter. Kinman nodded to Nick and then shifted his eyes toward Lester as he lifted his arm and sent a bullet through Lester's eye.

The shot snapped Lester's head back and spun him around on one foot. The bundle he'd been clutching flew from his grasp and his pistol dangled from his other hand by one finger through the trigger guard.

"That prick's more trouble than he's worth," Kinman said, climbing down from his saddle. "He ain't worth as much dead, but that Reaper's Fee will more than make up for it."

Nick wasn't surprised by much anymore, but seeing Lester's head explode in such a cold-blooded manner was enough to send a chill through anyone. Keeping his thoughts to himself, Nick said, "I suppose all the shooting from a little while ago was you dealing with those lawmen the same way you just dealt with Lester."

Kinman actually managed to look surprised by that. "What? You think I'd shoot those fine lawmen? Me and Marshal Eaves are on friendly terms. He's even got enough to pay up on the bounty being offered for those two shit stains Lester called his cousins. I did take care of the others in that house, though."

"And the women?"

Kinman nodded slowly. "Can't be too careful. Them bitches had guns."

"So where are those lawmen now?"

"I sent them off in the other direction, but I suppose they'll be back before too long." Kinman kept his gun aimed at Nick as he walked to Lester's body. "At least I hope they will," he added. "I could sure use the backup."

Nick had no trouble picking up on the shift in Kinman's voice. He didn't have an explanation for it, however, until he saw Jim moving his horse up alongside Kinman's.

"Marshal Eaves sends his regards," Kinman said to the young lawman.

"Who are you?" the deputy asked.

"Ask Eaves. He'll vouch for me. The name's Alan Kinman."

The deputy nodded and relaxed a bit. "I heard of you."

Feeling what little advantage he'd gained slipping away, Nick stepped between Kinman and the bundle Lester had dropped. The moment he took that step, Nick saw the deputy snap his gun up and aim it at him in a shaky grip.

"You don't want to do that, boy," Nick said. Before he could say anything else, Kinman interrupted.

"You hear that?" the bounty hunter asked. "Sounds to me like this outlaw's threatening you."

"That dead man there said he was Nick Graves," the deputy replied. "Is that true?"

Kinman holstered his gun as he walked over and scooped up the leather bundle. He opened it, took a look inside and smiled. "It's true, all right. Don't you know a wanted man when you see one?"

Wincing and pressing his free hand against the deep scratch along his back, the deputy said, "No."

"Well, why don't we go and fetch the marshal? It'd be wise to have all the help we can get in bringing this animal to justice. They should be just east of that house back there."

The deputy was hesitant to take his eyes off of Nick. "What do we do with him? I heard tell that he rode with Barrett Cobb."

"That was a while ago," Kinman said. "He don't have as much fight in him these days. Ain't that right, Nick?"

Nick let out a slow breath as he weighed his options. For all he knew, the kid might have his price, like most other lawmen, or he could be a straight shooter just trying to do his job and earn his wages.

"You're finished, Graves," Kinman said. "You can talk as tough as you want right now, but we both know you ain't fast enough to shoot us both before we put you down. Lord knows you're too old to run."

Nick's gun weighed heavily in his hand as he looked at the other two men. The longer he waited, the smaller his window of opportunity became. He was down to two choices. One of those choices simply couldn't be allowed to pass.

Kinman nodded with a confident smile still embedded in his face. "You got a rope, Deputy?"

"Yeah."

"Bring it over here and let's get this mad-dog killer ready to be delivered to a cage, where he belongs."

Jim took the coiled rope hanging from his saddle and climbed down from his horse.

Lowering his head, Nick allowed his gun arm to drop. "Maybe you're right, Kinman. I've done some things that no man should be proud of. I've robbed more money than I can count and I've killed more men than I care to think about. Perhaps I do belong in a cage."

"Cobb's paid his fee," Kinman said. "Time for you to pay yours."

Nick nodded as his face shifted into an expression that was the coldest thing the bounty hunter had ever seen. "Maybe it is," Nick said. "But I'll be damned if a bastard like you will be the one to collect."

Kinman's instincts were good enough to know what was coming. He just wasn't fast enough to do anything about it.

Nick brought up his gun, aimed, and fired from the hip in less time than it took to blink an eye. His modified Schofield barked once to send a round up into Kinman's chin that dug a tunnel that opened at the top of his skull.

The bounty hunter's arm was bent midway up to take a shot of his own, his finger clenching around the trigger, and that shot went into the soil near Nick's left boot. When his back slammed against the dirt, Kinman dropped the bundle and spilled several rough diamonds to the ground.

The deputy was so startled by Nick's lightning-quick shot that he nearly dropped the rope and his pistol. To his credit, he did manage to lift his gun and point it more or less in Nick's direction.

Ignoring the sound of approaching horses, Nick kept perfectly still . . . perfectly quiet . . . and watched until he finally saw the deputy's eyes flicker toward the jewels scattered upon the ground.

"I don't want to shoot you, boy," Nick warned.

"But . . . but I saw what you did."

"Kinman was the murderer. He killed those women in that house. Ask your marshal what he found in there. Or, better yet, go see for yourself."

The deputy shook his head. "I know who you are. I saw what you did."

The other horses were getting closer. It had taken them a while to pinpoint the location of Nick and the deputy, but they seemed to have narrowed down the general direction.

"Well, now," Nick said with a sly grin. "Looks like we're going to have to work something out."

Less than a minute later, Marshal Eaves and his other two deputies rode up with their guns drawn. They surrounded Nick in a matter of seconds and took aim the moment they saw him standing amid the two bodies.

Eaves was a tall man in his early sixties who wore a battered felt hat that might have been older than his other two deputies put together. The gun he carried was a newer-model Colt, however, showing that the marshal at least had his priorities straight.

"Don't you move a muscle," Eaves said. "Where's my other deputy?"

"He's gone," Nick replied.

Eaves couldn't take his eyes off of Lester's body, which lay facedown in the dirt. Nodding to one of his deputies, he said, "Go check that one there. That other body looks like Alan Kinman."

The deputy climbed down from his horse without once taking his aim away from Nick. He circled his target cautiously until his boots nearly tapped the side of Lester's head. Kneeling down and taking a closer look at Lester's face, the deputy stood upright and got away from the corpse. "It ain't Jim."

"You know who it is?" Eaves asked.

After thinking for a moment, the deputy shook his head. "Don't think I've ever seen him."

Eaves looked to Nick. "Is that one of the boys who lived with Wesley and Pat?"

Nick nodded. "He was their cousin."

"Well, he's dead now. So's Kinman and everyone who lived in that house. Even the ladies were gunned down like dogs. What've you got to say about that?"

"Me and Kinman were after the bounty being offered for Wesley and his cousins," Nick replied with a shrug. "One of the men tried to kill me, so I shot him. Kinman shot up the rest of that house."

The marshal showed Nick a humorless grin. "That's mighty handy. What about that dead man lying there?"

"Kinman shot him, too." Looking up so his eyes met the marshal's, Nick added, "That bounty hunter was one hell of a shot."

So far, both deputies had been content to keep their mouths shut and watch the marshal. When Eaves seemed to be at a loss, the deputy still on his horse said, "He's carrying a gun, Marshal."

"Go on and get it from him, Chuck."

Chuck climbed down to walk past the first deputy. Unlike the other deputies, Chuck held his gun in a steadier hand. His eyes didn't have the unchecked energy in them that made him look like he would act without thinking first. He stopped well out of Nick's reach and kept his gun trained on him.

Nick held up his hands, palms out, so everyone could get a good look at the mangled remains of his fingers. The deputies winced slightly, but the marshal didn't flinch. When Chuck snatched the pistol away from Nick, he looked as if he'd been forced to pick up a cow pie.

"This thing's barely even a gun," Chuck said.

The marshal was quick to reply, "Take it from him anyway, and step back so we can tie his hands." Looking at Nick, he said, "You're coming with us, mister. What's your name?"

"Nicolai Petkus."

The marshal took the Schofield that was handed over to him, and the two deputies tied ropes around Nick's wrists and ankles. "I ain't never heard of a Nicolai Petkus."

"I suppose that's a good thing," Nick said.

"Yeah, well you're still gonna hang for killing these folks, Nicolai."

"Don't I get a trial?"

"Sure do."

Nick held his chin up and said, "Then I shouldn't hang. There's not one witness here who saw me kill anyone who wasn't shooting at me first."

The fact of the matter was that Nick would have staked every bit of that Reaper's Fee on the fact that there weren't any witnesses who could attest to his shooting anyone at all.

At least, he would have wagered those jewels if they were anywhere to be found.

The Reaper's Fee was gone. Every last bit of it had disappeared, along with the sole witness to Lester and Kinman's final seconds on this earth. In return for the Reaper's Fee, that deputy simply had to ride far away and forget what he'd seen. Jim had been just frightened enough and just greedy enough to take Nick's offer and start running. Nick's faith in lawmen was sent right back down to the cellar, but at least those jewels had done some good.

Somewhere, Nick was certain Barrett was laughing his ass off at how that loot had been put to use.

Once Nick was bound tightly within those ropes, Marshal Eaves looked him in the eye and said, "I've got some bad news for you, Nicolai. I spoke to Kinman before and he never mentioned working with anyone. He did mention rounding up more than just Wesley and Pat, though. He must have had his sights set on someone real good, because the two dipshits who lived here weren't even worth enough for me to come get 'em myself."

"He must have meant him," Nick replied, nodding toward Lester's body. "I hear he stole a horse from a man down in Texas."

Eaves winced at that and shook his head. "That could be. It ain't wise to take a Texan's horse." Raising his voice as he looked at his deputies, Eaves announced, "All right, boys. Let's take our prisoner to his cell."

"He's a damn killer," Chuck said. "We should string him up for what he done to them ladies back there."

"We don't know who the hell he shot," Eaves replied. "Wesley was a crazy asshole, so he could have done it. This ain't ours to decide. That's what judges are for. This man'll get what's coming to him once he's on trial."

With that, Eaves snapped his reins and rode toward the trail that led back into Hackett.

Nick didn't put up much of a fuss as he was lifted up onto the horse that Kinman had been using. In fact, he did his best to make the deputies' job easier by going where he was pointed, sitting where he was supposed to sit and keeping his mouth shut. Part of his brain still raced with ways to get away from the lawmen, get out of his ropes or possibly get a weapon, but Nick set all of that to the side.

Once he was tied to the saddle and bound up like a prize calf in a rodeo, Nick's options had dwindled down far enough to put that unquiet part of his brain to rest.

The quiet did him some good.

TWENTY-NINE

———◆———

Ocean, California
Three weeks later

Mail was delivered to the Tin Pan Restaurant same as always. It arrived at the usual time, dropped off by the owner of the cigar shop across the street.

"Here you go," the cigar shop owner said. "Looks like there's some excitement for ya."

Catherine smiled and took the small bunch of letters. The man from the cigar shop always expected excitement when Catherine got a letter that wasn't from someone in her family or a notice from a distributor. When Catherine spotted the familiar, florid handwriting on the envelope, she nearly dropped over.

Since he wrote out most of his own burial notices and funeral invitations, Nick's handwriting was very distinct. She'd been sick with worry over the last few weeks, and she hadn't expected to hear from him in this manner. After pouring herself a glass of water, she sat at a table in the back of her place and carefully opened the envelope. She read the letter slowly, savoring each word, but also dreading the next.

My Dearest Catherine,

First and foremost, I must insist that you do not worry about my safety or well-being. I have done what I set out to do and made certain that my friend can rest easy once again. I have, however, run into some trouble which finds me in a jail cell in a town called Hackett until I can be transferred to a larger prison. I am to be tried, although I do not know when. If you must know the particulars, you may request them from the Shannon County courthouse. I do not know my docket number, but it should be filed under P for Nicolai Petkus.

Catherine felt a coldness in her face. When she reached up to pat her cheek, her hand came away sweaty. A few drinks of water helped and she felt the liquid run through her system to chill her all the way down to her core. The name in the letter had struck her as odd, but only for a moment. Catherine recalled Nick telling her about someone in his family by the name of Petkus. Although there was some comfort to be had in that, it wasn't enough to keep her hands from shaking as she held the letter and read on.

I know you are upset, but please do not cry. You know how much I hate it when you cry. Unfortunately, this has been a long time coming. Honestly, I am glad it is finally here. In all my years, I have never spent more than four nights in a jail cell. My father would tell me that I deserve to serve my time. He would tell me that I have earned it. Perhaps he is right.

I have tried to put a great many things behind me, but that doesn't mean I have paid what is due. Plenty of folks who mourn for someone they have lost just need to do something, some little thing, to set things straight in their own heads. For me, this is it. I deserve to cool my heels in a jail cell and let the cards fall where they may. The only reason I have taken the shortcut that you know I have taken is because I wish to see you again.

Catherine took a few more sips of water. Her nerves had calmed down a bit, but they still threatened to overwhelm her. Despite that, she couldn't help but smile at Nick's way of putting things in his letter. His little shortcut was most definitely giving the law that false name. He was right about one thing, though. If they knew who was truly in their custody, those lawmen would have dumped Nick into a cell and thrown away the key.

Either that, or they would have taken him out and . . .

Her next breath caught in her throat as Catherine knocked that thought straight out of her mind. Whatever Nick had done in his youth, she knew he'd been paying for it in his own way for plenty of years. Considering what he'd done to step in for her or plenty of other folks, she figured he'd already paid his debt. In Nick's mind, however, she knew that probably wasn't enough.

He never talked about it too much, but she could always see the haunted distraction in his eyes when he thought she wasn't looking at him. Catherine knew he still thought back to his wilder days as if the sting of gunpowder was still in his nose and all that blood was still on his hands.

To comfort herself, she continued reading. Every curve of every letter on that page put the sound of Nick's voice firmly in her thoughts.

I will try to write you as much as I can, but I don't know how reliable these deputies will be in mailing my letters. Just know I love you more than I ever thought I could love someone and I will do whatever is necessary to see you again. For now, though, please do not try to find me. I am putting my younger self to rest and that is not a man you would care to meet. Also, seeing you on the other side of these bars would only make me want to tear them from the ground before it is truly time for me to leave.

I told you not to cry and I mean it. You are a strong woman, Catherine, and will only grow stronger in my absence. When I return, we can start a new life together. I only apologize for not being able to start it sooner. Do not worry about me. I have been in much worse places than a cage.

Just so you know, I am content to stay here. They are transferring me to another jail, where I believe some old acquaintances of mine are residing. There are some things I'd like to straighten out with them as well.

If I do not return, do not be angry or sorrowful. I will have lived on my own terms and done my best to square away all of my debts. You will find some money stashed in my workshop. There isn't much, but it should be enough to get you anywhere you want to go. In the event such unfortunate events come to pass, keep that smile on your face because that is what I will want to see when I look in on you again.

This had to happen sooner or later, Catherine. Better now and on my own terms than later, when I wasn't prepared for it. Once this debt is paid, I can live the rest of my years content in the knowledge that I owe nothing to anybody.

Catherine smirked at that. She could practically hear Nick telling her that he could walk away from any jail cell as if the door were unlocked. In the past, it might have made her uneasy to know that it could be true. Now, it brought her some comfort. Not a lot, but some was better than none.

My trial is impending, but nobody seems to be in much of a rush. Things got messy here, leaving nobody but myself and the law to straighten things out. This is a first for me, so I have no predictions as to the outcome. I do not trust the law that has imprisoned me, but I owe a debt that is being paid in their currency. Things could have been a lot worse, but Barrett kept that noose from tightening around my neck. When I return, I will explain what that means to you over coffee and a big breakfast. Right now, I need to finish writing before the deputy leaves to send the day's mail.

I love you Catherine. I always have and I always will.

Yours,
Nicolai

PS—I told you not to cry

Catherine wiped the tears from her face and looked around as if someone nearby was actually going to scold her. She folded the letter and tucked it away in her skirt pocket.

"Was that from Nick?" one of the girls who waited tables asked.

"Yes."

Wiping off the table next to Catherine's, the server nodded. "I could spot that fancy handwriting anywhere. Is he coming home soon?"

"No," Catherine replied. "Not for a while."

Nick stretched out on his cot, which required him to dangle one leg over the side. The ceiling of his cell wasn't much higher than the top of his head when he was standing, and it was built at a slope toward a window that wasn't much larger than a slice of toast.

The cot made his back ache. The food sat in a warm lump at the bottom of his belly. He desperately missed Catherine and would kill to ride Kazys for miles at a full gallop. But all of that would have to wait.

For now, Nick was home.